Ruth A.
Casie

The Highlander's English Woman

The Stelton Legacy

Timeless Scribes
Publishing

Timeless Scribes Publishing LLC

Print
ISBN-10: 1-945679-04-2
ISBN-13: 978-1-945679-04-9

Digital
ISBN-10: 1-945679-03-4
ISBN-13: 9781-945679-03-2

This edition published by arrangement with Timeless Scribes Publishing LLC.

www.TimelessScribes.com

Dedication

To Paul – for his encouragement, support, and understanding of what it takes to get a book written.

To Eliza Knight – for her support and encouragement.

To DM Comfort – who makes my words sing – I really miss our coffee time together on the east coast.

To Emma Kaye – I wish I had her eagle eyes! She's the best copy editor EVER.

RUTH A. CASIE is *USA Today* Best Selling author of swashbuckling action-adventure, some are time-travel, all her stories are romances about strong empowered women and the men who deserve them, endearing flaws and all. Her Druid Knight novels have finaled in the NJRW Golden Leaf contest. The Guardian's Witch, part of the Stelton Legacy series was a Reader's Crown Finalist. Ruth also writes contemporary romance with enough action to keep you turning pages. She lives in New Jersey with her husband, three empty bedrooms and a growing number of incomplete counted cross-stitch projects. Before she found her voice, she was a speech therapist (pun intended), client liaison for a corrugated manufacturer, and international bank vice president in product and marketing management, but her favorite job is the one she's doing now—writing romance.

***

Ruth loves to hear from readers, too, so drop her a line at Ruth@RuthACasie.com or visit her on Facebook: facebook.com/RuthACasie. She's also on Twitter: @RuthACasie. If you'd like to receive her newsletter and receive a free book, please sign up at www.RuthACasie.com. Thanks!

The Highlander's English Woman

Chapter One

A dour faced James Maxwell Collins, in full regalia, rode atop his destrier, sixteen of his best men with him. They cantered through the forest, the metal tack on their mounts' harnesses tapped out a rhythmic beat. Jamie breathed in the heady aroma of damp leather, musty moss, and fallen leaves. The rain drenched landscape turned the rutted trail into mud and forced his column onto higher ground. Just as well. While he preferred to take his time and walk the woods between his home at Cumgour and his Reynold cousin's at Glen Kirk Castle at the edge of the Northumberland Forest, today he chose a more dangerous and faster route. His men would suffer bad weather no matter which track they took, and speed was of the essence.

Richard Reynolds was dead, killed on a Welsh battlefield serving his English king. The idea of him gone was still unreal. Richard was too young, too brave, too good to leave this world. His loss came in waves of awareness. Jamie would never see his friend again.

For eighteen months Jamie and his men served The Maxwell, Lord Herbert, his father's older brother at Caerlaverock Castle.

Everyone was stunned when the news of Richard's death arrived. His small group left immediately, and after three days of hard riding, reached Cumgour and stopped long enough to change horses.

Lord Wesley and Lady Darla buried their only son before news had reached Caerlaverock. No time for Jamie to say a final good-bye to the man he knew from childhood, a distant relative and closer friend.

"No other person could represent me better," The Maxwell said.

"Why? Because I'm fourth in line to lead the clan?"

His uncle's laugh was low and throaty. "You're not only a distant relative like me. You fostered with Wesley and are close to the family. I would go, however, with my obligations to the Parliament in Scone, the uproar here concerning spoiled grain and this… this ghost, I can't possibly leave now. People and their superstitions drive me senseless, but I must stay. Instead of going with me, you'll go for me. I can't send a better man."

"I completed my year of service six months ago. After delivering your message, I'd like to return to my Cumgour and farm my land." Jamie was tired of asking. It had gotten him nowhere. He was still here. But he kept asking.

"The harvest is over. There's no pressing need for you to return." No pressing need. His family. His life. He was a farmer, not a warrior. He let out a deep breath. He would keep reminding The Maxwell his service duty was completed until he released him.

"I don't blame you for wanting to return home, but not now. Not with our problems with the grain and now this damned ghost. Go to Wesley and Darla while I go to Parliament. You'll have to return to me in a week." The Maxwell held up his hand to ward off Jamie's objections. "That will give you one day with family and I'm sorry you can't stay longer. Once this problem is

solved, you can return home and be a farmer, although it is a waste of a good fighting man." The Maxwell relaxed, an affectionate smile spread across his face. *"You've served me well and earned your farm."*

The Maxwell let out a long breath. *"Too bad you can't bring Darla to us when you return. With her special gifts, she would put this ghost to rest."*

Magic. He didn't believe in spells and charms, but he would believe in the devil himself if that would help make things right at Caerlaverock so he could go home.

He and his men came through the forest onto the Marsh, a few yards from the English border. He slowed his horse to a walk.

"Sean, I'll take four men and go on. You and the others wait here. We'll be back by morning." His captain inclined his head and signaled his troop to move on.

Twelve of Jamie's men peeled away and rode toward the cliff where a dry cave would provide shelter while they waited. Jamie was sensitive to Wesley and the situation. Tensions at the border were high and he was a Scotsman on English soil. A larger traveling party could be... misinterpreted.

Jamie and his remaining four men navigated across Bells Burn, the stream separating Scotland and England, then headed up a rocky pass through the dense Northumberland Forest.

Richard had been one of the best soldiers he knew. Intuitive, resourceful, and loyal. No one could stop him. Jamie gave a bitter laugh. He understood his friend's capability better than most, as many times as they sparred when boys. Neither one held anything back. Every bout ended the same, no matter the winner, with laughter and a draft of Wesley's fine ale.

What did that matter now? Richard lay cold in the ground. Jamie blew out a strangled breath around the knot in his chest. At least Richard hadn't been left to rot on some forgotten battlefield as so many others. For all the man's faults, Bryce Mitchell did the decent thing and brought Richard home.

He snapped a low hanging branch as he passed, wishing he held the neck of the man who killed Richard. Over and over again, Jamie berated himself. He should have been with Richard, protected his back. Except his allegiance lay with Scotland, not the English or their king. Jamie pulled his wool around him to ward off the building breeze, and adjusted the Maxwell crest. At least the light drizzle that added to his misery had ended. His small party trudged on.

He stopped at the forest's edge. Glen Kirk Castle beckoned tall and welcoming across the broad meadow. He stole a glance to his right. The stone wall of Glen Kirk's cemetery was a few yards away.

A numbness blanketed him. He was no stranger to death. He let out a deep breath. The reality of this final good-bye tore at him. He pulled the reins to the right and nudged his horse forward.

At the cemetery wall, he dismounted, his back to the gate. He steeled himself, turned on his heel, and walked into the sacred ground. Richard's newly dug grave overshadowed the others, demanded his attention. A small smile played on his lips. Just like Richard to be in control.

Jamie weaved through old gravestones and finally stopped at Richard's side. Silence. The rustling of dried leaves caught in a sudden gust skidded across hard stones. Silent and still, he looked down at the grave. His chest heaved as he worked to ease the knot in his throat. One deep breath, then another.

"I'm angry at you for even going to Wales. I'm angry at you for not taking care." His chin quivered, his eyes dampened. After a few moments of silence, he blew out a painful hot breath and knelt next to his friend. "But more than that, I'm angry at you for dying," he said, his voice fading to a whisper.

He laid his hand on the damp flower petals that covered the grave. "Rest in peace, my friend. Know that I will care for your family as I would my own." He pulled the Maxwell crest he wore with pride from his wool and buried the amulet with Richard, next to a charm Lisbeth must have added to his grave. "On my honor as a Maxwell, so do I swear."

Forged by grief and tempered with love, Jamie rose with a new sense of purpose. He walked to his men and mounted his horse. The five turned and rode in silence toward Glen Kirk.

Jamie gave a signal to the tower guard, then trotted across the field and through the gate. The hollow clop of their horses' hooves on wet cobblestones echoed through an empty bailey. No rousing greetings. A somber mood permeated the grounds. Even the castle dogs that ran to greet him stayed in the barn. If not for three horses equipped for a long journey tied nearby, he would have thought Glen Kirk was deserted. Jamie dismounted. The stable boy took his horse's reins.

"Jamie. The guard told me you arrived." Lord Wesley's captain came out of the gatehouse.

"Gareth." His somber mood lightened at the sight of his old mentor.

Weathered with thinning salt and pepper hair, he remained tall and straight, his eyes clear and wise. This was the old warrior who instructed young squires in soldiering. Five aspiring knights trained together. Richard, Jamie, Bryce Mitchell and his cousins, Reeve and Harmon Gaulter. They practiced and battled while Richard's sisters, Laura and Lisbeth, cheered them on. That was before Bryce's taunting created a rift between the two of them that became intolerable.

Jamie gave Gareth his hand. The old soldier threw his other arm around him and pulled him close.

"You've been away too long. I must be getting old. I actually miss you and your rowdy ways." Gareth shook his head. "I sent a message warning the village women that you're back. Now that I think of it, I may have done you a favor."

A flush rushed up Jamie's neck. "It's a burden I have to bear. They seem to be drawn to my... many attributes and who am I to disagree?" The fact he and Richard listened attentively, especially to women who always appeared to be around them, left them both with reputations. Jamie had the advantage of not being the Lord's son and well, perhaps he did more than listen on occasion, but not as indiscriminately as everyone would believe.

"I swear you're taller than a tree. And here I worried you would be the runt of the litter. There must be Viking blood in your family line." Gareth eyed him from his toes to his head. "You're bigger than the others." He placed his hands on either shoulder as if measuring the expanse. "And you're definitely the broadest of the three. Yes, you turned out well, for the runt." Months of absence melted away as they renewed their easy camaraderie.

"You think I'm brawn, you should see my wee sister," Jamie teased slipping into a burr that sent Gareth into peals of laughter.

"You forget I know your wee sister. She may be five feet and a slip of a thing, but she certainly knows how to keep you in your place. It amazes me to watch how she tames you."

Gareth glanced toward the Keep and the smile faded from his face. "In truth, I'm glad you are here. They can use your company."

"I wish I returned for happier reasons rather than

this untimely duty." Jamie started for the Keep. "You coming along?"

"Not right now. I'm here to see Alex Stelton and his men off. You go on. I'll settle your men at the barracks." Jamie nodded and made his way across the bailey.

"Good day, Ann." The housekeeper held the door wide when he reached the top step. "Still as beautiful as ever."

"You save your sweet talk for those ninnies who don't know any better." Ann's severe expression didn't fool him. Her attitude was the same one she used when as boys he and Richard filched freshly baked tarts off her cooling rack.

"Sweet Ann, you're the only one for me." He raised his eyebrows in an over exaggerated ardent expression and clutched a hand to his heart.

The housekeeper swatted his arm and chuckled. He bent and kissed her forehead.

"How are they?" Jamie took on a somber tone and glanced toward the hall as he removed his cloak and gloves, then gave both to her.

"As good as one can expect. The family will be glad you're here. You go on. You know the way." Ann padded off.

He stepped to the entrance of the great hall, a place as familiar and comfortable as his own. Servants on the far side of the room busily prepared the raised dais table for the afternoon meal. Trestle tables and benches were pulled away from walls and ready for others in the castle. The family sat at the hearth, their favorite gathering place.

Large silk tapestries hung on whitewashed stone walls. A few depicted battles and others portrayed gardens. The familiar wall hangings added color and warmth to the room. The sideboard, dressed with linens, displayed silver plate. Family banners dangled from the rafters. A fire roared behind the grate, and above the fireplace hung the family crest. The hall was warm, comfortable, and filled with the aroma of lavender and spice, but none of that dispelled the melancholy.

Darla's head turned toward him. She sprang from her chair, ran to Jamie and hugged him close. A handsome woman, her hair had turned a glistening snow white since last they saw each other. Her face lit up in a smile, although it didn't hide the stress of the last few days.

"Jamie, I'm glad you are here."

"I was with Herbert when news arrived or I would have been here sooner. He's sorry for your loss. We all are."

She gave him a weak smile and patted his arm. Darla's tear-swollen eyes said it all and he grieved even more. He offered her his arm and escorted her back to Lord Wesley, their daughter, Laura, and a gentleman who sat with them. Stelton, he assumed.

"Do you know Alex Stelton?" Darla sat next to Wesley and laid her hand on his. "His mother and I are friends at court."

Alex put down his tankard and rose.

Jamie nodded. Yes, he knew Stelton. He had only seen him from afar, but he was one you didn't forget. Richard told him Stelton was one of the English king's favorite knights. Shorter than Jamie, which was nothing out of the ordinary. Stelton had dark, wavy hair with a lock that fell over his forehead. His eyes, a silver-blue held vast knowledge and understanding. The words just and honorable came to mind.

"You're not leaving?" Darla asked Alex.

"I must be on my way. I've overstayed my welcome and have drunk too much of Wesley's ale."

Wesley let out a rusty laugh. Alex inclined his head

to Darla and her daughter and approached Jamie. "We meet at last. I'm sorry it's under these circumstances. Richard spoke of you often and with great respect. Many will miss him. My family and I included." Alex said.

"Richard told me much about you and your six brothers, how, as boys you terrorized Edward's court with your games and antics. There was a time I resented not being English." Yes, he could see what Richard admired in this man.

"Someday we will have to sit, drink Wesley's ale, and talk of Richard. I'm sure we both have stories to keep us up until morning," Alex said.

"Any excuse to drink Wesley's ale. Have you been able to get his recipe?" Jamie tilted his head toward Alex and whispered in a conspiratorial tone. Alex's eyes lit with laughter.

"No, but that doesn't mean I didn't try while I was here." Alex took his great coat off a bench and put it on. "It was good to meet you."

"Keep the wind at your back," Jamie said.

With a respectful nod goodbye, Alex left the hall.

Jamie turned to the family sitting around the hearth. Wesley slouched in his chair staring at the fire, grief still raw on his face. He had aged over the year. His gray hair thinned, his eyes rimmed red and dulled with pain.

"He's been like this since we buried... the burial." Laura, Richard's sister, was next to him. "Father tires easily and stays locked up inside himself. Mother is the sole person who can reach him, although I have hope. Alex did make him laugh."

Jamie's focus turned to Laura, the younger of the two sisters. Laura and Lisbeth were alike from their slender, petite size bodies, long auburn hair, and large green eyes with a fan of thick lashes. The sisters may be similar in appearance, however, not in temperament. Lisbeth was the deep thinker. Laura was head strong and outspoken, the feistier defiant sister.

"How are you and Lisbeth faring?" He gazed back at Wesley.

"It's a challenge keeping everyone's spirits up. At times, I succeed." She shrugged. "Other times, I fail miserably. Lisbeth stayed at the Keep for a while then left for the hunting lodge to be alone."

Jamie turned to her. Her drawn ashen face disturbed him.

"The rain has stopped. Would you care to take some fresh air in the garden?" Jamie presented his arm. Laura answered by looping her arm through his and drew him out the door.

He went willingly. Her warmth chased away any lingering chill from his journey. *She's Richard's little sister*, a warning voice whispered in his head. He took a breath and led her to the garden door.

"I understand you're skeptical of Lisbeth's gift, but she told me she saw Richard's death before Bryce carried... brought Richard home. Now, she blames herself for not taking action." Laura sighed heavily. "Everyone blames themselves. Father shouldn't have let him go, not that he could stop Richard. Mother should have seen this coming, not that she could. And Lisbeth..."

"I understand all too well. I berated myself for not being with him, protecting his back." They reached the stone porch.

Formal gardens sprawled before them with raised flower beds, neat hedges, and bare trellises waiting for next year's roses. He waited with her in silence, willing her his strength.

"Is it wise for Lisbeth to be alone?" Jamie finally asked, and gazed past the lawn to the well-worn path on the other side of the garden gate.

"She's not unaccompanied. John escorted her to the hunting lodge at Ann's request, over Lisbeth's heated protest." She turned to him. "I haven't thanked you for coming to us. I know The Maxwell has his demands and travel is a hardship."

He stilled her trembling hand. Her brows creased in pain over eyes that stared off without seeing. He waited.

"I find it difficult to comprehend we'll not see Richard again." Laura's voice choked and she shrugged with resignation despite tears that threatened at the edges of her eye.

"Me as well," Jamie said. He had the same thoughts.

"How long are you staying with us?" Her question was reasonable but he dreaded answering.

"I return to Caerlaverock tomorrow." He took a deep breath and saw a momentary flash of disappointment in her eyes.

"Then we best return to the others. They'll want to spend time with you, too." They moved on toward the hall.

"I have no words, nothing to say to comfort you." He could barely get the words out.

"Your presence is enough."

He held back a nervous smile. He visited to give the family comfort. Instead, she comforted him.

"How are my Maxwell cousins?" Laura asked. Jamie guided her toward the great hall.

"They are well when I last saw them."

"You'll let me know your decision, Wesley."

Jamie brought Laura to a halt. An exasperated male voice drifted out of the great hall.

"I want to make the announcement as soon as possible. With Richard gone and Glen Kirk so close to the Scottish border, you need someone strong to hold back the devils." Lord Bryce Mitchell of Ravencroft, the manse next to Glen Kirk, stood with Wesley and Darla.

Standing at the great hall entrance, Jamie stiffened when Laura's pulse skittered into a panic beneath his fingertips. Jamie's free hand covered hers until the beat settled into a normal rhythm. If Bryce couldn't feel sympathetic toward the family, couldn't he at least curb his speech?

"You didn't waste any time getting here." The rude remark directed toward Jamie raised his temper even more. Bryce's baiting tactics hadn't changed since they served Wesley as squires. Bryce wasn't foolish to pick a fight with him, at least not here.

When they trained, Bryce took aim at him whenever possible, most often urged on by Reeve. Richard and the girls rallied to his defense, but Bryce's intolerance of Jamie's Scottish background stayed near the surface.

Bryce gasped for air, seething after having lost a foot race to him.

"You're nothing. A filthy Scot beggar. Go back to your tribe of mongrels. You're not fit to be here." Bryce pushed him hard.

Jamie didn't go down. Not satisfied, Bryce rushed at him again, this time with fists. Jamie ducked and backed off. Bryce kept up the assault.

Jamie didn't care for bullies or being baited by them. He wouldn't fight.

"Here, here Bryce. That's enough." Richard grabbed his friend's arm but Bryce shook him off. Reeve pulled Richard back.

"Enjoy the spectacle. It's time he learned his place," Reeve said.

"Stay out of this," Bryce screamed at Richard, then turned to Jamie. "Fight, or are you a puny coward, too?"

Jamie said nothing. He held his fists at his side and stepped back again.

The fight started in the yard, progressed to the field, and finished near the pond. A small group of people followed and urged Jamie to defend himself.

The next punch caught the Scotsman in the chest. He didn't flinch.

"You should be lying on the ground by now. Don't say I didn't warn you." Jamie pulled up his arms to protect his face as best he could against the onslaught of punches. He didn't retaliate.

His face cut and bloodied, he still didn't strike back.

"Fight, damn you," Bryce shouted and followed with a quick barrage of solid body punches.

He held his position and didn't fight back.

In a close clinch, Bryce muttered for Jamie's ear only. Jamie pushed his tormentor away. Years of restraint from insults and attacks disappeared with the maliciously whispered words.

Bryce threw his punch. Jamie caught the left jab in his palm mid-strike. Alarm and panic flashed in Bryce's eyes. The bully stared at Jamie's hand holding his fist.

Jamie almost tore Bryce's arm out of its socket as he pushed it aside and set his stance, one foot in front of the other.

For a moment Jamie thought to stop the madness, but the idea quickly died. Bryce had no idea what he let loose.

Before Bryce threw his next punch, Jamie exploded with a rapid cannon volley of left jabs at Bryce's jaw. Stunned, Bryce dropped his defenses.

Jamie's right cross burst from his shoulder as he shifted from his back leg to his front, throwing all his weight into the swing. He caught Bryce squarely in the face. Blood exploded in an arc of fine spray as Bryce's head snapped back. Droplets flew, the warm blood spattered across Jamie's face.

Bryce's head came forward. Jamie followed with a left uppercut and caught him under his chin. The solid strike lifted Bryce into the air, then sent him to the ground. To everyone's amazement, Bryce laid unconscious at Jamie's feet. No one said a word as he stood panting over the prone figure. Every ounce of him wanted to drag Bryce on his feet for another round. Instead, he marched away.

"If you'll excuse me. I look forward to calling on you soon, Laura. Tomorrow?" Bryce looked down his nose at Jamie. "For now, I'm sure the family would like to be alone. Come, Collins." Bryce sounded as if he ordered his dog to heel.

"How considerate to understand our family's need for time together. All our family." Laura stressed the word all and tightened her hold on Jamie. "As for tomorrow? I regret I'm not seeing callers. I'm sure you understand."

Bryce's eyes widened at Laura's cut. The man gave a curt nod, slapped his riding gloves against his thigh and marched out. His footsteps thundered down the hall.

Jamie ignored the retreating figure. "I can speak for myself."

"I'm well aware you can take care of yourself. I had no intention of addressing your leaving as much as responding to his request for an audience."

He smiled and inclined his head. Definitely the feistier sister, but he did enjoy Bryce's discomfort at her cut.

"What was Bryce doing here? I passed him in the hall. He didn't appear pleased," Lisbeth asked as she entered. "Jamie. Ann told me you arrived." She smiled and pecked him on his cheek.

"Bryce came to extend condolences from his family to your father and me." Darla fussed over Wesley.

"The nerve of the man—"

"Now, now, Wesley. This is not the first time Bryce made the request. Let's not dwell on that. We'll find a solution." Darla gestured to the table. "Ann laid out our meal. I'm sure Jamie is hungry after a long ride. Besides, I'm eager for news from Caerlaverock."

Chapter Two

It had been two years since Laura saw her Cousin Herbert, his wife, and three sons. Herbert worked on constructing his new Caerlaverock Castle for years, the old one prone to flooding. With work nearing completion, her family held off travel to Scotland.

"Is Cousin Herbert well?" Laura asked, sitting next to Lisbeth at the table. The enjoyment of visiting her mother's Maxwell family would be well worth the torture of a four-day carriage ride.

"Cousin Herbert regrets he couldn't be here, pressing obligations at Scone Parliament. Besides completion of Caerlaverock Castle, these are hard times. The late season crops did poorly. Grain is rationed and with winter coming it will only get worse. As a result, tempers are short and easy to ignite. People look somewhere to put the blame." Jamie took a pull on his ale. "Excellent, Sir. Excellent."

Everyone enjoyed Glen Kirk's ale. Only her father and his brewer knew the ingredients and their proportions. Her father enjoyed that his friends and sometimes his adversaries tried to loosen the recipe from him. That often entailed drinking a lot of ale. Her father always had the last laugh. He walked away, not always steady, but he left them no wiser to sleep on, or under the table.

"I'm glad you're enjoying the ale. To her surprise, her father dipped bread in his soup and ate the morsel. "Now what is this about blame? Everyone understands no one is responsible for a poor yield." He took the last of the bread from the plate and continued to eat. For days her father had no appetite. Laura passed him more bread happy to see his renewed interest in food.

Her mother glanced at Jamie and gave him an appreciative smile.

"The crops did poorly. Of course, you're right. Poor crops are no one's fault. But, people want to blame someone. They think they found their suspect. The ghost." Jamie savored his ale, smacked his lips, then drank some more.

It didn't appear he was in any rush to continue the tale. Laura wagged her dangling foot under her chair. Irked by his cool, teasing manner, she tore a piece of bread from the loaf with a bit more force than planned.

"Ghost? What ghost? There aren't any ghosts in Caerlaverock. The stones are barely completed," her mother said as if ghosts were an everyday occurrence.

The kitchen door opened. A waft of rich smelling spiced meats preceded Ann who carried in a platter. After days of no appetite, Laura's mouth watered.

"Our ghost is a new addition to our castle family. Several people witnessed the apparition, including Herbert and his wife." Jamie closed his eyes.

"Are you going to inhale the meat pie or put one on your trencher and eat it?" Laura asked. She glared at Lisbeth who daintily took a meat pie from the platter and didn't try to hide her smirk.

"Cousin, you have no idea how wonderful Ann's meat pie smells. For weeks, we've had nothing cooked with grain, but I won't bore you with my misfortunes." He bit into a pie.

"Tell me more about this ghost." Her mother's eagerness wasn't surprising. After days of worrying about her parents, Laura was glad to see both engaged in a conversation about something other than Richard.

She bit her lip and held back the blast of threatening tears. A groan built in her chest and she struggled to keep it at bay. She didn't want to ignore Richard. Never that. But discussions about him left everyone in tears. She preferred to retire to her room and scream into her pillow. No, a conversation about something other than Richard was good.

"It's a thorny issue. Appears to be a love story gone wrong," Jamie said between bites. "Evan, a footman, was betrothed to Angel, a housemaid. You may remember them, Darla."

"Yes, a pretty and lively young woman. She helped me several times when I visited," Mother said, a wine goblet in her hand. "Angel's mother is a cook. Evan must be the young man she talked about. She was proud of him. Ah, I remember, Herbert planned to elevate Evan to the castle Marshal."

"You're correct. He gave Evan the position when they moved into the new castle. He made a big show of it. Lots of ale." He turned to Wesley. "Not nearly as good as yours, Sir."

Her father raised his tankard in a silent salute and they both drank.

"Evan and Angel had been part of the castle staff since they were children, and grew to be very much in love, so Angel said when she attended me. She always made me smile with her enthusiasm," her mother said.

"With recent concerns and difficulties, their

wedding was to be a welcome distraction." Jamie stabbed a piece of meat on the platter one of the servants brought. He devoured the venison.

"Go on, don't stop telling the story now," Laura demanded. "What does that have to do with the ghost?"

He gave a heavy sigh, put the meat on his trencher, and turned to her. He cocked his head to the side, raised an eyebrow and gave her a glassy stare. "After a rather loud argument, a castle servant found Evan dead, stabbed in the chest." He returned to his meal, picked up the venison, and took another bite.

"And?"

He ignored Laura's outburst.

"And," she said, a warning in her voice.

He drained his tankard dry, then faced her.

"They found Angel's dead body under his. Apparently he killed her." He glanced past her and smiled. "Would you please pass the ale?"

"Jamie, please. No more teasing," her mother said.

He sat back in his chair and wiped his hands on a linen. "The rumor is Angel learned Evan tainted the castle grain. She approached Evan to get his confession. Their ensuing argument turned into an all-out fight. In a fit of anger, he killed her. Distraught over what he did, he killed himself."

Her mother dropped her knife. The speared venison flew off and fell to the floor. Duke, her father's hunting dog, snapped it up. Laura glanced at her mother.

"Totally absurd if you ask me," her mother said, sputtering in disbelief.

"Not long afterward, a ghost appeared. Those who have seen the apparition believe the ghost is Evan. No one knows how to put the spirit to rest. Personally, I think they all had bad ale. Nothing compares to yours, Sir." He lifted his re-filled tankard to his host.

Her father smiled and let out a small chuckle. He raised his tankard, then continued to eat.

"I don't believe the story." Her mother shooed Duke away from the table. "Evan would never hurt Angel. I remember them both clearly. She was sensible and reliable. And Evan was devoted to Herbert. He would never be unfaithful to the family. Something here is amiss. When did the deaths occur?" Along with her mother, she and Lisbeth lost interest in their meal.

"Three weeks ago. I know your next question. If the ghost's appearance is so recent, why is he blamed for the hardship?"

"Precisely," Laura, Lisbeth, and Mother said in unison.

"There is nothing or no one else to blame." Jamie's gaze went from her mother, to Lisbeth, and to her. Gone was his playful manner. "After his death and the ghost's appearance, the idea he was responsible for the troubles arose. To be honest, better to blame someone already dead than some living person they all trust."

The sobering thought lingered.

"Pass me the venison," her father said. Everyone at the table let out a breath and returned to their meal.

"Mother, too bad you can't go to Caerlaverock and help poor Evan," Lisbeth said.

"No, I can't leave now, but it is a pity." Her mother hesitated, her food almost to her mouth. "I wonder what he's trying to tell you." She shrugged and continued with her meal.

"Tell me? I hardly knew Evan in life. What could he possibly want to tell me in death?" Jamie looked as if he were weighing the question. "Although Cousin Herbert agrees with Lisbeth, he said you had a way with ghosts and it was unfortunate you weren't available."

"So does Laura." Her mother put her linen on the table, sat up, and elbowed her husband.

"Me?" Laura dropped what was left of her meat pie.

"You have a special skill of getting to the bottom of issues. If anyone can find out the truth of these deaths and how to put Evan's poor soul to rest, you can," her mother said, a smug look on her face. "The more I think of it, the more the idea pleases me. Yes. You'll go to Herbert in my place."

Laura stared at her mother. Of course she wanted to help her cousin, but she couldn't leave now. Surely her father would bring Mother to her senses.

"You're right, Darla. Besides, a trip would be good for Laura and the sooner the better."

Laura stared at her father. What was going on?

"No, no, that's not necessary." Jamie put down his knife and almost bolted out of his seat. His gaze bounced from her father to her mother and back again. If he didn't stop scrubbing the back of his neck, he'd rub the spot raw. Wait, why didn't he want to take her to the castle?

"Jamie, you know I can't leave Glen Kirk now. Nor can I stand by and watch my cousin suffer when help is easily at hand. Take Laura to Caerlaverock with you. If she cannot put the ghost to rest, at least she will enjoy a long overdue visit with the family." Her mother's tone and convincing words didn't fool her. What was her parents' hidden plan?

"Of course, Darla. I'm sure Herbert will be happy for Laura's visit and accept any help she is able to provide," Jamie said.

Annoyed, Laura scrutinized Jamie's reaction more carefully. The fact that he didn't want to take her to Caerlaverock was evident in the death grip he had on his tankard. She lightly touched the top of his wrist and hoped he relaxed his hand before he crushed the cup.

His muscles jolted under her fingertips. He put down the tankard and tucked his hand under the table.

"I'm glad that's decided," Mother said.

Ann put a platter in front of her father.

"Ah, roast duck." Wesley rubbed his hands together like a child at the holidays. "Has Herbert's design solved his flooding problem? I was quite taken with his plans when I visited with him last. Unique, very unique."

Lisbeth leaned toward her.

"Do you think Mother's eagerness to get you away may have anything to do with Bryce being here?"

Laura chewed on her fruit fritter. She had conveniently forgotten about Bryce's visit.

"You don't think he had the audacity to come here and offer for me now, while we mourn Richard?" She knew the answer as soon as the words left her lips and disliked Bryce even more.

"Yes, I do. And I think the sooner you're safely away from Glen Kirk, the better." Lisbeth straightened.

"Why me and not you? You're the oldest," Laura said.

Lisbeth's mouth curved into an unconscious smile. "He's afraid of me." She turned to Laura. "Bryce and his cousins didn't tease me. They think I'm a witch."

"Fair enough. But that doesn't explain why Mother and Father won't tell me about Bryce's proposals? This isn't the first time he's offered. Why do they keep Bryce's proposal from me?"

"I can think of several reasons. One, they don't like or trust him. Two, they don't want you to think you're obligated to marry him. And three, these are tenuous times and they don't want you in the middle of politics."

"Those are still not reasons to keep his proposals from me. I'm not a child." She leaned toward Lisbeth, her eyes cold. "Everyone thinks I'm a child."

"My dear sister, you are not a child. No one thinks you are. Not even Jamie." Lisbeth glanced past her at the man named, and inclined her head.

"Jamie," she blurted, scarcely aware of her own voice.

"Yes," he answered.

She closed her eyes hoping he'd shrug it off.

"Laura, did you say something?" he called.

She twisted toward him. "No, I was speaking to Lisbeth. I said, plainly, something had to be done about poor Evan." She spun back and faced her sister. "Don't you dare laugh or I'll tell—"

"Hush. You adore Jamie. Don't deny it. That secret is safe with me. Ann is here with spiced wine. Supper will be over soon." Laura turned away, but Lisbeth touched her arm. "Don't fret. Mother is aware of what she's doing. Enjoy your wine."

Laura listened to Jamie paint a picture of Caerlaverock and how the stones glowed with the colors of the sunset. He went on and on and made the castle sound magical. By the time he finished, the platters were cleared away and spiced wine almost gone.

"Come, Wesley. No more discussions about the castle. You'll forgive us." Her mother rose from her chair. "We've had a long day."

Laura watched her parents leave, their heads together in deep conversation. Jamie's company and talk about the castle had brightened them both.

"That leaves the three of us," Jamie said.

"No, the two of you," Lisbeth replied. "I'm glad you're here, Jamie. I thought they would never smile or laugh again. If you'll forgive me, the stress of the last few days has taken its toll on me as well. I'll see you before you leave." She kissed her sister and left the hall.

She should excuse herself, too, but it wasn't

hospitable to leave guests alone. The tumult of the day quieted. She focused on the fire and allowed herself to relax.

"Do you have any idea why Darla wants you away from Glen Kirk?"

She stiffened.

"I see that she wants me to visit Caerlaverock to help Cousin Herbert in her place." She spun in her seat and faced him. "The bigger question is why you are against taking me? Because if you are, James Maxwell Collins, I'm sure Gareth or one of the men will gladly escort me."

"Wait, lass. I've not said I wouldn't take you with me. I'm simply inquiring as to why Darla is so anxious for you to be away." His soft tone and softer eyes quieted her. Lisbeth was right. It had to be Bryce. She cringed at the idea of marrying that man. She wasn't interested in him.

"Has Bryce said anything?" He moved forward in his chair. "Has he done anything to—" His fist pounded the table making her jump. Even he figured out the connection.

"No, never." Her hand instinctively covered his to ease his concern. "He makes me uncomfortable."

His muscles were hard, but his skin was surprisingly soft. Her hand lingered a bit longer.

"You said the ghost appeared after Evan died three weeks ago. You don't have much time." She removed her hand, got up, and sat by the dying fire. Jamie followed.

"What do you mean much time?" He stirred the embers to life.

Laura eyed the muscles under his shirt as he stretched and maneuvered the heavy log. Finished with tending the fire, he faced her. He looked powerful, his chest broad and muscular. Strong angular facial features were in perfect proportion. His deep-set green eyes and the way they changed colors to suit his mood had always fascinated her. Gold strands threaded through his dark ginger hair reflected in the fire's glow and gave a soft halo effect. A smirk touched her lips. Jamie was no saint. Gossip of his escapades was legendary with the village girls. There was a time when even she dreamt of the smart, playful, and sensitive man. She could hear Lisbeth's mocking laugh. Nervously she moistened her lips. A young girl's fascination, nothing more.

"Laura, you didn't answer the question. What do you mean not much time?" He sat next to her and handed her a glass of sweet wine. She cleared her mind of the local gossip and childish thoughts. There was more to the man. She let out a deep sigh. She was no more than a sister in his eyes. Still, he was a steadfast friend she could trust.

"Ghosts appear for a reason, most often to complete some mission. They must finish their task or suffer consequences." She took a sip of her wine.

"What are Evan's consequences?" His mocking tone irritated her. She tried to disguise her annoyance.

"If Evan doesn't complete his task within thirty days of his death, he will be doomed to be a tormented soul and haunt Caerlaverock Castle forever."

"I'm well aware that Darla, Lisbeth, and you believe in such things, that you even have a gift. Ghost? Trickery if you ask me. I'm not inclined to—"

"Believe us. You don't believe my mother is a great healer? You don't believe Lisbeth can see the future, and you don't believe I—"

"I meant no disrespect. I think all three of you are intelligent women. Your mother has a knack with herbs. Lisbeth is insightful and sees situations for what they are. And you, you're smart about dealing with people. Magic doesn't make things happen. What a childish idea." He sat at the edge of the chair. "I believe hard work and taking action bring results." He paused, staring at the floor with his hands clasped. "So did Richard. He had a hard time believing in your... magic. If it followed the family line as you were prone to tell him, he was proof magic didn't exist. He didn't have any."

Childish, she screamed in her head. Why the... the big... She counted to ten. Then counted to ten again. From the set of his jaw to the steely look in his eyes... no, his mind was made up and there was no way of making him think otherwise. Who was being childish? His attitude was no surprise. She had let it bother her more than usual.

"The magic in our family is from the Maxwell side. And, if it's any consolation, Mother doesn't acknowledge Lisbeth's gifts. Although she believes Lisbeth's ability to heal others is greater than her own. Even you have magic. It's buried deep, but you have it, but let's not spend what little time you have with us over these old arguments that we never resolve. Instead, let's talk about Evan and Angel."

"Yes, Evan and Angel." The strain in Jamie's face relaxed. Of course, anything to change the topic.

"Something is not right about their deaths," Laura said. "Mother is certain Angel didn't have a quick temper and Evan would never turn traitor to the family. You need to know the truth. If Evan didn't kill Angel, that means a murderer is in the castle. The Maxwell and the rest of the family are in great danger."

She studied his concentration, the wrinkle of his brow. If only she could read his mind.

"Who found them? Where were they found? What time of day? Who saw them last? If they argued, who heard them?" She let him chew on the questions.

Finally, he gave her a hint of a smile.

"You make sense. There is a lot that may have been overlooked. A closer inquiry to find facts should be done. According to you, we must resolve poor Evan's death in one week." He rose to his feet. "We best leave at first light and travel light. No carriage."

She rose to her feet as he gave her a sideways glance.

"Fine. I love to ride," she said, but groaned inside.

Chapter Three

"Do you need all of this?" Jamie ran his hand through his hair.

Laura crossed her arms in front of her and stood next to two large satchels, a travel bag, a basket of food provided by Ann, and a bedroll. The sound of her tapping shoe on the cobblestone could be heard from beneath her skirt.

"Wait," her mother called from the doorway. John followed her through the bailey carrying another bag. "I want you to take a package to the family."

"I'll find another horse." Jamie rolled his eyes and marched to the stable mumbling under his breath. Laura let out a heavy sigh.

"Here's a letter for Herbert from your father. Make sure you give it to him as soon as you arrive. Safe journey." Her mother hugged and kissed her.

"Smile and stop looking so pitiful. You may not settle the issue with poor Evan, but you'll visit with the family in the new castle. Besides, The Ancestors are with you." Lisbeth's cheery voice did nothing to dispel her anxiety.

"Lisbeth, the charms you sprinkle about are your talismans to The Ancestors, not mine. They bring you peace."

"As you wish. I find that if nothing else, the charms make me think and sometimes that's all you need." Lisbeth tucked a charm into Laura's pocket. Laura didn't bother to argue. It was pointless.

"Is that why Jamie wears one of your charms around his neck? To make him think. Let me tell you, it's not working."

Lisbeth muffled a laugh. "Here, take these with you." Lisbeth clipped a strand of deep purple agate beads around her neck.

Jamie marched out of the barn with a pack horse. After his men fastened the baggage to the animal, he tested the ropes and made sure everything was secure.

"But these are yours. You always wear them." Laura tried to take off the necklace. Lisbeth slapped her hands away.

"Take the beads. They'll help get to the truth of the matter. There are eight on the chain. Don't lose any. There are consequences."

"Consequences?" Laura asked as her fingers brushed over the smooth stones.

"Lose a bead, lose something precious to you. Don't give me that sour face. The clasp is tight." Lisbeth stepped back and admired them. The ancient agate beads and gold chain necklace had been handed down in the family. "The agates sparkle on your neck. That's a sign they are well-matched to you."

"Thank you. I'll take good care of them," she whispered.

"And smile. I don't know why you hate to ride. You're such a good horse woman." Lisbeth kissed her.

Gareth helped her mount up. Their goodbyes said, Jamie led the small column out through the gatehouse.

Three miles into their journey, Laura stopped at

the crest of the hill where the Glen Kirk road crossed the trail to Ravencroft.

"It's a beautiful sight." The morning sunlight bathed the Glen Kirk castle tower.

"Yes, it is, but we best continue on. We've a lot of ground to cover before we rest." Jamie prodded their horses ahead and veered off the trail.

"This isn't the way. Where are we going?" She glanced down the trail.

"To Caerlaverock by a different route." His exasperated tone didn't amuse her.

"Why not the usual route?" She halted her horse and brought the small column to a standstill. "This way is much more difficult."

Jamie turned in his saddle, his hand on his battle horse's rump. "If we don't stop to admire the flora, this route will take a day off our trip." He gave his men a nod and moved forward. The riders closed in around her. Her palfrey, shorter than the soldiers' warhorses, made it difficult for her to see around them. Minutes later she stopped trying.

After an hour's silent ride, they arrived at a small clearing. The Bells Burn was a few hundred yards ahead. Six riders emerged out of a thicket and blocked their way. Jamie's men closed rank in front of Laura and kept her hidden from view. She struggled to see past her protectors and caught glimpses of the riders. They were from Ravencroft, the Mitchell crest clear on their cloaks.

"You're on Mitchell land," the leader of Bryce's guards said. Her head dodged around until she saw who spoke. She recognized the man. He often accompanied Bryce to Glen Kirk. This confrontation was going to become messy fast unless she did something. Laura pulled her horse back, urged it around the others and caught Jamie's men by surprise.

"We are not," she insisted.

"Lady Laura," the man sputtered. "I didn't notice you with these men."

"Lord Bryce has you on patrol? You can't recognize a woman among five men?" Jamie's soft cough concealed his laugh. She wanted to swat him.

"And you have no idea of the Ravencroft boundary? Actually, you're deep on Reynolds' land. What, sir, are you and your bullies doing on Glen Kirk land?" She didn't have to pretend, her temper veered sharply to anger. Now she understood. Jamie's route, while difficult, kept them on her father's land to the border.

Bryce. She had no illusions about his interests. They were for Glen Kirk, not for her. Ever since Richard went off to Wales, he visited with father. To help keep Glen Kirk secure. He strutted around as if he was the heir apparent. Well, he was not, and if she had anything to do with it, he never would.

The beads around her neck warmed. A soft gasp of surprise escaped her lips. Encouraged, knowing she was right, Laura walked her horse closer to the Mitchell patrol. Out of the corner of her eye, Jamie's posture tensed, but his casual expression never altered.

"How. Dare. You. Stop. Me." She spat each word. The men remained silent, like reprimanded schoolboys. "I'll make sure to tell my father how Lord Bryce takes liberties with Glen Kirk property. Or should I tell him a Ravencroft patrol lost their way in the forest and I needed to provide them with directions?"

Scarlet stains appeared on the leader's cheeks. Laura was aware she made an enemy, but with good cause. The Mitchell men stared at each other, not knowing what to do.

Jamie pulled up beside her, relaxed, touches of humor around his mouth and eyes. His men on either side of them.

The Ravencroft leader gave Jamie a begging stare.

"Don't look to me for help. I don't envy your position." Jamie nodded to Laura. "I'm sorry for it, but I can't offer you any protection. You'll have to deal with Lady Laura yourself."

Bryce's man stared at her, a slack expression on his face.

"Forgive me, Lady Laura. We thought something improper—"

"Improper. How ridiculous." Laura's horse reacted to her shout. She took a strong hand and calmed him. "Lord James is my mother's cousin. Not that I need to give you an explanation. But," she said, pretending to be soothed, "I do thank you for your concern for my safety and assure you that your assistance is not needed. I can certainly handle one Scot and four of his men."

Jamie sat on his mount, his hand casually on his sword hilt.

"Leave us now. I'll tell my father what's happened here and let him decide what to mention to Lord Mitchell."

"Yes, m'lady." He dipped his head in a quick bow and signaled his men. They wheeled around and made a fast retreat.

Jamie's small company didn't move. They waited until they no longer saw or heard Mitchell's men.

With speed, he moved the group across the field to the shore of Bells Burn. Jamie's man, Sean, and the eleven Collins men waited for them on the other side.

Their small caravan didn't stop. Twelve riders pulled into line, the only acknowledgment being Jamie's brief nod. They rode on through the forest for an hour before anyone spoke.

She couldn't read his face, but she knew Jamie well enough to grasp the irritation boiling below his cool aloof façade. In his decision not to tell her the whole truth, why they took the more dangerous route, she was justified in not communicating her intended action.

"We'll rest the horses by the Liddel Water up ahead." Jamie's voice startled her after the long silence.

They rode on through the thinning forest, the end in sight, she and Jamie the last to ride out of the trees onto the narrow plain and meandering Liddel Water.

Jamie helped her down from her saddle. She held on to him until she was steady on her feet. Several hours in the saddle stiffened her joints, a painful reminder why she disliked long rides. He threaded her arm through his and walked with her.

"Next time we meet a group of soldiers—"

"Please, no lecture. I was aware what was at stake. I'm not a child. Those men were ready for a fight whether they knew I was with you or not. I came out fighting and put them in their place." Her breath came in spurts. His muscles tightened under her hand. She didn't care that she vexed him. She wasn't one of those senseless ninnies that gathered around him willing to jump and do as he commanded. She was more than capable of taking care of herself.

"I'm not your enemy. Perhaps you should let me finish my sentence, if not my thoughts."

She stopped walking, but he pulled her along.

"Mitchell is looking for a reason to come across the border and for a way to extend his holdings. Glen Kirk is in his sights." Laura pulled her arm away from his. He grabbed it, re-threaded it through his and pulled her along, again.

"It would be easy for you to have an unfortunate accident. Those men do not care. Once they grasped you rode with us, I imagine they thought to rescue you from the grips of the likes of me and tell everyone you didn't know any better. After all, you're only a girl."

"I can protect myself. Richard made sure of that."

Laura jerked her hand away from him and wound her arm, ready to let loose.

He caught her fist in his hand and pulled her close.

"Here, here. You know I speak the truth."

She didn't struggle. Her heart sank to her toes one minute then rushed to her throat the next. Any time now, it may settle back in her chest. She was sure after all these months apart her childish fascination for him had subsided. She was no better than the Glen Kirk women who fussed over him for attention. She didn't want a trifling relationship, certainly not another of his conquests.

But the closeness of him took her breath away. A deep breath to slow her hammering heart didn't work. Instead, her head filled with the aroma of leather and spice that was uniquely him. *Pull your hand away.* But instead she let it linger. His hand was smooth and soft. His grip gentle yet firm.

"You've been protected at Glen Kirk as a young girl should be, but these are dangerous times, for both of us. Don't argue with me on this. You're more than capable of taking care of yourself with words, but you still need me in a brawl. If I'm to fight, it will be on my terms, no one else's."

"Let me go." They stared into each other's eyes. She dropped her gaze. "Please," she added softly.

He released her and stepped back. A flash of red rushed up his neck.

"I understand," she said. Young girl. That galled her. She didn't rant like a petulant child. As if she didn't know these were dangerous times. Calling out Bryce's men was reckless. To keep the words on the tip of her tongue behind her teeth, she bit the side of her mouth and was rewarded with the salty taste of blood. Didn't he understand that she saved them all from a massacre?

"We best return to the men," he said. "I'm sure the horses are refreshed."

Laura turned with as much dignity as she could muster and walked ahead of him. To cool her temper, she dipped a small linen square into the river and washed her face and hands.

Young girl. That was still an insult. She was only a few years younger than him and he would bristle at being called a boy.

The heat of the argument over, clearer thinking prevailed. He was right. Tension was high between neighbors and confronting the Mitchell patrol had been a bold move. She didn't want him or his men at any disadvantage. Calmer, she mounted her palfrey.

The troop continued on. At dusk, they reached Cannonbie on the Esk River. Sean rode up beside Jamie.

"The coach house won't have enough room for everyone. Their surrounding grounds are too muddy," Sean said. "The men and I are better protected and drier here at the edge of the forest. I'll have everyone ready to move out at first light when you and Lady Laura return." Jamie agreed and signaled the men to make camp.

With Laura's bedroll and travel bag tied to her horse, she and Jamie came out of the woods and spotted a gray curl of smoke that smudged the dusky sky. The coach house was less than fifty yards away. She looked forward to getting off the horse and resting for the evening. The idea that she would be laying in a soft bed rather than on hard ground almost made her groan in anticipation.

They plodded down the trail and turned into the building's court yard. Mud. She couldn't locate one dry place to walk.

"Wait here." Jamie dismounted. Noise filtered out of the door as he disappeared inside. She scanned the yard. The ground was mucked up from one end to the other. Great glops of filth sprayed the walls. Chickens stood at the partially open barn door, smart not to venture out.

The inn door opened and Jamie came out. He lifted her off her horse and set her on the small entry while a stable boy appeared and gave him their bedrolls and travel bag before he took the horse to the barn.

"We're lucky. We got the last room." He opened the door for her.

"One room. Where do you plan to sleep?" He didn't plan to stay in the same room with her. The idea made her mind sputter. He ushered her into the public room.

"Look around. Do you think I'm going to leave you in a room by yourself even if they had two rooms?"

She stood by the public room door. Once white washed walls appeared dingy with smoke and spattered with food and ale. The hearth blazed hot and smoky. Scattered lanterns created small intimate circles around tankards. Men, many she wouldn't want to be near, filled the room. Now that she looked with care, other than a serving woman, she was the only female in the lot. The odor of foul air filtered into the space. She glanced at Jamie. He didn't appear much happier.

With her travel bag, two bed rolls and a blanket in hand, Jamie directed her upstairs. They passed through a door into an open-air gallery that ringed the coach house yard. At the far end, an open staircase led to the yard below. Jamie stopped at the last room and put a rusty key in an equally rusty lock. After a few strong shoves, the door sprung open. Hinges let loose with a clawing metallic screech sent chills up her back.

"At lease no one can sneak into the room at night. They would wake the dead." He walked in first, scanned the room, then stood aside for her to enter.

A window with a tattered cloth hanging from a pole across the top filled the wall across from them. The makeshift curtain didn't hide the damaged window or the bare oak tree that brushed against the building. On the wall next to the door, a chest with a broken piece of polished metal was against one wall.

She turned her focus to the massive bed to her right. Jamie pulled back the blanket and examined the linen. Laura shivered, not from the cold, but one look at what he expected her to sleep on made her ill. He laid the blanket over the mattress, then their bedrolls.

"You'll be comfortable enough in the bed. You stay here. After I check on Sean and the others, I'll speak to the men downstairs. Reivers roam this area. I want to know what we face tomorrow." Before she could say a word, he left.

"The audacity of the man." She stamped her foot. Did he expect her to sleep in the same bed with him? Like one of those… She stared at the door. Her fists so tight her fingernails left impressions. What was she supposed to do now? Laura shrugged out of her coat. Her temper didn't ease as she paced.

Her stomach rolled from hunger. She stood in front of the door, her anger at a boiling point. Her stomach rumbled again.

The men in the public room may smell bad, but they didn't scare her. She spent time in the public room by Glen Kirk, although she wasn't acquainted with anyone here. Ach, the innkeeper's wife would be nearby. Her decision made, she pulled on the door. It didn't move. Again, she tried to open the door, still it didn't budge. In frustration, she slammed the flat of her hand against the door by the lock and when she stepped back, it popped open without a sound.

"So much for waking the dead." With a swish of her skirt, she left and closed the door behind her.

The sun had slipped behind the ridge, taking with it what little heat it gave. Laura, her arms wrapped around her for warmth and her breath leaving a trail of white puffs of frost, hurried along the gallery toward the public room stairs.

"I asked for Joseph when I secured the room. He's run this inn since I was a boy." Jamie was with Sean a few yards into the forest. "The innkeeper told me his brother, Joseph, passed away after a long illness following a reiver's attack."

"I didn't know the man had a brother," Sean said.

"He didn't. There's nothing we can do now. I'm glad you suggested the men stay here."

"I suppose you want to make the castle by nightfall tomorrow?"

"Yes. The sooner we reach Caerlaverock, the better. Be ready to leave at first light. Assign one of the men to cover our tracks. At least they won't know where we're headed. That should give us some advantage. Safe night."

"Many thanks for the warm wine." Laura sat in a corner away from the other travelers and tried to smile though the tart, almost vinegary liquid forced her lips to purse. How anyone could drink this was beyond her, but she persevered.

"Where do you and your husband travel?" the innkeeper's wife asked as she set down a bowl of greasy stew. Some splashed over the side and made a small puddle on the table.

The woman picked up a badly stained rag from the floor and wiped up the spilled stew. The rag's sour fragrance was only a bit worse than her dinner.

"Jamie's not my husband. He's my mother's distant cousin. He's escorting me to Caerlaverock Castle. I have family there."

"Would you like some more wine or bread, perhaps?" The woman's tone was soft, but Laura was sure it held a slight bitterness.

She shook her head and dipped a slice of crusty bread into the stew. She should have stayed hungry. "No. This is quite enough."

The door opened, letting in a chill and Jamie. The meal was bad enough. She had hoped he'd be with his men until she went back to her room. She turned away from his penetrating stare, but not fast enough. The corner of his mouth twisted with exasperation as he moved toward her. They had spent hours together. He must be tired of her company. She was tired of his.

"What are you doing here? I thought I left you in the room," he said through clenched teeth.

Laura paused, her stew-soaked bread almost to her lips.

"Here, here. Don't you disturb this fine woman," the innkeeper's wife said shaking the filthy rag at him. "She told me you're not her husband. You have no rights here."

The room quieted and Laura's irritation turned to panic.

Jamie, his feet solidly planted and his hands on his hips, exploded into peals of laughter and caught everyone off guard.

Laura thought he was a crazy man. She was sure everyone else had a similar impression.

"And you believed her. I've been burdened with this woman for years. I would gladly give her up, however I just spent weeks searching for her. You see," he said and turned to the rest of the room as if he was giving some great speech. "She ran away from me and our four babes. Left us just like that." He snapped his fingers. "The wee one is so small, not even walking."

That got her to her feet.

"Off to see the world, she said. And fancy things she wanted. She stole what little money I saved and spent it all on fineries. Look at her clothes." His outstretched hand pointed from her toes to the top of her gown. A vicious rumble went through the room.

How dare he say she would leave her babies? If she had any, she certainly wouldn't leave them with him.

Her chest heaved and her hands crushed her skirt, she grabbed it so hard. Unable to listen to another word, she took her bowl of stew and threw it at him. He ducked. The plate sailed past him and hit the innkeeper's wife behind him.

The room went silent, the only noise from a patron who snored in his seat by the window. Mortified, Laura remained rooted to the spot. The woman slowly wiped limp pieces of onion and flecks of beef off her face with the dirty rag. The room burst into an uproar.

In two steps, Jamie hoisted her over his shoulder. Shouts told him to punish the ungrateful woman. She could only guess at the meaning of some of the words they threw at her. Jamie took the steps two at a time. He entered their room, kicked the door closed, then dumped her on the bed. He stepped over to the small table and lit the candle. The flame flickered from the breeze let in by the broken window.

"I'll give you ten minutes to undress and be under the covers before I come back."

"But—"

"Not a word from you. You could have gotten us both killed. What were you thinking? Ten minutes." He left the room.

The sound of the tumbler falling into place echoed. She gaped at the door in disbelief. His high-handed actions were too much for her to tolerate. She had no intention of spending one night in the same room with him.

A quick glance at what was at hand and she took action. Laura found a rag in the chest and stuffed it in the window to stop the breeze. It took some time, but she pushed the heavy chest in front of the door, then stepped back and admired her work. Satisfied with the results, she dusted off her hands. Let him try to break through that. She pulled her night clothes out of her travel bag. Eager to be ready when he returned and found his way barred, she hurried and changed. In bed with the candle out, she yawned and waited. He could spend the night in the forest with Sean and the others. She pulled her bedroll close and made herself comfortable. He could...

Her eyelids drifted close.

Sitting in the tavern near a window with an ale, he celebrated his first accomplishment, removing Laura from Glen Kirk. She may have protested Bryce wasn't a cause for concern, but Wesley and Darla's insistence he take her to Caerlaverock spoke otherwise. The reason had to be severe for her to leave now, while mourning for Richard.

Jamie sipped his drink and moved on to a more pressing issue, avoiding the thieves that traveled the roads. He observed other men in the room. He struck up conversations with some of them, most were farmers, although he was sure the men at a nearby table were reivers. Reivers raided farms and stole from travelers that had no protector or connection to the raiders' own kin. This time of year, late fall, was best for raids, nights were long, and cattle and horses were fat from grazing.

An hour later, having gathered as much information as possible, Jamie climbed the stairs. They had a long way to go tomorrow if they wanted to reach Caerlaverock before nightfall.

He hoped giving Laura more time alone would ease her temper. Never in his life had he wanted to strike a woman, but she tried his patience. Another reason he needed to reach the castle at once. The faster he got her into Herbert's care, the better.

A thin layer of ice glazed the gallery walk. His breath turned to frost as he hurried to their room and turned the key. The door opened an inch. He pushed on it, but the door wouldn't budge. Something substantial blocked the other side. He peaked through the opening, but all he made out was wood. He straightened. The chest. She pushed the chest across the door. He started to slam his hand into the door jamb then stopped.

Annoyed, to say nothing of tired and cold, he had no plans to remain outside in this weather, nor did he intend to sleep downstairs for his coin to be lifted.

Spying the staircase to the yard, Jamie went down the ice rimmed steps and around the building to the oak tree. A sizeable branch was close to their bedroom window. He gave the tree a shake and was rewarded with a shower of water-soaked slush. Satisfied it would hold his weight he scaled the oak, opened the window and climbed inside. He tripped on a rag on the floor nearly turning over the small side table.

He froze.

A moonbeam gave off enough light for him to see her wrapped in her bedroll. Her soft, even breath told him she slept soundly. He let out a deep sigh, took off his boots and coat, and settled on the bed.

He glanced over and adjusted her blanket. Satisfied, he wrapped himself in his bedroll, showed her his back, and went to sleep.

Hours later, Laura pulled the blanket around her and shuddered. Ripples of shivers ran up her back until her teeth chattered. The rag must've fallen out of the window, but she didn't want to venture from under the covers and lose what little heat she had. She rearranged the blanket and again searched for a comfortable warmer spot.

"Shush, you sound like a buck plodding in the forest." Jamie moved next to her and touched her hand that held the blanket to her throat.

"Faith, woman. You're as cold as ice." He cuddled her against his chest, then pulled his blanket around them both.

"How did you—"

"Did you really think you could keep me out? Now hush." She stiffened with apprehension. She sighed as her body thawed, and moved closer, greedy for more of his heat.

Jamie's rhythmic breathing soon turned to soft snores.

A moan escaped her lips as she fell asleep.

The woman would drive him to drink. He continued to "snore."

What had he gotten himself into? His chest burst with pride and a bit of fear when she faced off against Bryce's men. Smart. She read that situation well. Her swift actions surprised him and put Bryce's men on the defensive from the start. She was as fearless as a lioness protecting her cubs. Even downstairs she held her own.

He took a deep breath. Lavender and spice. She'd make a fine warrior's wife.

Good thing he planned to be a farmer.

Chapter Four

"Time is with us. We should be at the castle by nightfall."
Jamie rode in the front of the column with Sean.
Traveling since first light, it was well past noon and they
had only stopped for necessities and to rest their mounts.

"Did Lady Darla give you any spells or powders to
help rid us of the ghost?" Sean's tone dripped with
sarcasm. Jamie held back a smirk. Of all his men, Sean
was the least to believe in spells and magic. They both
believed hard work and action affected an outcome,
not luck or unearthly beings. He couldn't say that about
some of the others.

"No, she sent along Lady Laura to help us figure
out what needs to be done to... appease him."

Sean gave him a sideways glance. "I did wonder
why we were saddled with the lady."

"Lady Laura will be with us for a week doing
whatever it is she does. When it doesn't work, we'll
thank her for her kind efforts and take her back to
Glen Kirk all sweet and nice." He neglected to mention
his biggest reason for removing Laura from Glen Kirk.

She needed to be protected from Bryce. The issue had been in the back of his mind since they left Glen Kirk. Keeping her at Caerlaverock was a temporary solution. She'd have to go home eventually.

These were difficult times. He watched how English sympathizers suffered at the hands of politically motivated thieves. Keeping an Englishwoman in Scotland was dangerous for her as well as The Maxwell. He hoped his uncle could find another way to protect her.

"Lady Darla is sure Evan didn't kill Angel."

"Lady Darla is perceptive," Sean said with admiration. "I don't think Evan killed Angel either. Where were the wounds? Do we know the condition of the room when they found the bodies? Was there a fight? Who overheard the argument?" Unsurprising, Sean's endless questions were similar to Laura's.

"Yes, exactly. Everyone happily accepted the explanation and didn't search any further. Not even me. In a small way, we should thank Evan." How could he be so accepting of the explanation? He knew Evan and Angel well enough to question the conclusion he was given.

"Evan? What for?"

"Once his ghost appeared, Lord Herbert locked the pantry. The supplies are either in the corridor or in the storage room underneath the castle, a bit of an inconvenience, but it prevents the room from being disturbed. It will be difficult to find answers, but not impossible. I suppose the staff is our best source, and perhaps, the two families," Jamie said.

"Both families had been close. Intertwined would be a better word. Trying to figure out who belongs to which family is a challenge. They did everything together. Now, each blames the other and everyone else takes sides." Sean shook his head. "You even have to be cautious at the tavern. A misspoken word starts an argument and sends tempers flying."

"If Lady Darla is right, and Evan and Angel were murdered by someone else, it would resolve the family problems, although, it leaves us with a bigger one. Who murdered them? Perhaps that's what our ghost wants." Jamie let out a small chuckle and cast a glance at his captain. "Our ghost wants justice."

"How will Lady Laura help?" Sean asked.

Jamie ran his hand through his hair. "I'm not sure. I have no idea how she does what she does, and, truth be told, I don't want to know as long as she stays out of our way. Our job is done once we present her to Herbert."

Jamie glanced over his shoulder at Laura. She squirmed in her seat. Yet she made no complaints and maintained the pace. His men were used to being driven hard. He thought her more delicate, but he was wrong. She was a warrior.

"Tell the others we'll be making a short stop at the Annan River."

"I'll speak to the men and see if they have any information about the murders," Sean said and Jamie nodded. The captain wheeled away and fell in with the men.

Jamie slowed to let Laura draw up next to him.

"We'll stop up ahead at the river for a brief rest."

"Not on my account. I can go on." She lifted her chin and stared ahead.

"Not on your account at all. I'm concerned about the horses. I pushed them hard. They need to rest before we go the last ten miles. I want to reach Caerlaverock before the gate closes for the night. I'll not sleep on the ground when I can have a cozy, warm bed."

"Of course. The horses," she said. Her knuckles were white from strangling the reins.

She argued at every turn. At times he wanted to throttle her. Except last night. The memory of her warm body cuddled next to him, the fragrance of lavender and spice, the sound of her soft breath sent spasms through his body. She still slept when he woke before dawn. He didn't move her head off his chest or her arm from across his torso. It was as if they were an old couple who slept together every night. When he did move, she cuddled closer, but only for warmth. Last night she was warm and in his arms as he had dreamt a hundred times. He shook his shoulders. But she was Richard's sister and not for him.

He came out of his reverie and straightened in his saddle as if dowsed by a bucket of cold water. His building manhood quickly collapsed along with his pride.

"I've been thinking about Evan's ghost. If we—"

"Laura, when we arrive at Caerlaverock, I'll bring you to Herbert. You can tell him what you need for your spells and incantations. I suspect, since you mentioned the ritual must be completed within the next five days, that I'll be returning you to Glen Kirk whether you put Evan to rest or not." Her blood boiled at his dismissive attitude. Spells and incantations. Was that what he thought? That she didn't have a brain in her head?

Arguing with the stubborn Scotsman never got her anywhere. Besides, she didn't need his help. *Look at him sitting on his warhorse, so sure that his way was the only one.*

All along he'd treated her as a child. No, that was wrong. He treated her with indifference. He pacified her then sent her on her way. He didn't take what she said into account. He didn't see how she'd always come to his support. Even on that day when he unleashed his fury on Bryce.

Is he all right?" she asked Gareth as he marched out of the barracks.

"Stubborn and more stubborn. Won't even let me help him.

Here, see if you can." He handed her clean linens. "Except for a few cuts and bruises, he'll be fine. I've never witnessed Jamie hit someone. I didn't know he knew how."

Gareth stalked away shaking his head.

Laura entered the barracks. Jamie sat at the table, staring at nothing. His bedroll near his feet, tied and ready to go. His face was a mess: a large cut on his lip, his cheeks rough and bloody, his nose caked with blood.

She dipped one of Gareth's linens into a basin of fresh warm water and dabbed it on his forehead. He didn't swat her hand away. She took that as a good sign. At the end of the day, she took care of his bumps and bruises. He relived every moment with her. Today was different. Silent support was all she could offer him now.

Laura progressed and cleaned the rest of his wounds. Finally, she put the stained linens in the basin and sat across from him. She didn't say a word.

"Thank you," he finally said. He picked up his bedroll and started to leave. A wave of panic rolled through her. She grabbed his arm.

"Where are you going?" She was afraid if he left she'd never see him again.

"I need to go." He sounded cold and distant. Her heart raced until she feared it would burst. She held him tighter.

"What do you mean you need to go? You're family. If anyone is to leave, it should be Bryce."

He gently removed her hand from his arm and turned toward the door.

"Why are you doing this? Because a foolish boy who is half the man you are called you out?"

"No," he said with a hurt look in his eyes.

Gareth stepped into the room.

"Not at all. I'm leaving because I wanted to kill him. If he hadn't fallen, I would have kept at it. I was a berserker. Not in control. If I stay here, near Bryce, I don't know that it won't happen again."

"You've made a powerful enemy," Gareth said. "It doesn't

matter who was right or that he taunted you. You bested him in front of Reeve and the others, but you didn't kill him, although sometimes his smug attitude makes me want to wring his neck."

"But Bryce started the fight. It was clear to everyone that Jamie didn't want to fight," she said.

Gareth let out something that sounded like a laugh. "Once the fight started without any resistance, Bryce thought he would win, establish his supremacy over Jamie, like a dog fighting for his place in the pack." The grimace on Gareth's face left no doubt what he thought of Bryce.

"Laura, you don't understand. Bryce is English and I'm—"

"My Scottish cousin. Emphasis on Scottish, like Richard, Lisbeth, and me." She jabbed her finger at his chest as she said each name. "And we're proud of it. We're proud of you. If he doesn't like it, then the—"

Gareth coughed. She glanced at her father's captain. Heat rushed up her neck and reddened her cheeks.

"If he wants to fight," she said and took Jamie's sword, "I'll give him one and make sure he knows he's gone too far."

A twinkle returned to Jamie's eyes. "You made your point, lass." Jamie took his sword, and stared at her face as if he was preserving the image in his mind. "I'm leaving, but I'll never forget your fierce support, nor will I ever be far away from you."

The sound of rushing water brought Laura back to the moment. Jamie led the group through the high marsh grass that bordered the river and onto the muddy sandy shore of the Annan River.

"We'll rest when we're out of the marsh on the other side." He turned to Laura on her palfrey. "You'll ride across with me."

Laura gave him a cold stare. "I assure you, I can handle my horse crossing a river."

"I'm sure you can. However, it's all about size," he smirked.

She tilted her head and sucked in a quick breath at the double meaning of his words.

"My horse," he said in a husky voice. "Where is your mind, m'lady? He stands several hands higher than yours." He straightened in his saddle. A flash of heat ran up her neck. She wanted to wipe the smirk off his face. She was sure he enjoyed her discomfort.

"There won't be any time to stop and dry your skirts. Unless you want to spend the next two hours wet to your waist. You ride with me."

A command.

The idea of sitting in a wet skirt didn't appeal to her, but only a little less than riding with Jamie.

He reached over and lifted her off her horse as if she weighed nothing, tucked her across his lap, and pulled her close against his chest. She didn't argue. She couldn't if she wanted to. The air had gone out of her lungs and taking a breath to replace it was out of the question. He held her captive, and her senses came to life. Her heart jolted. Surely he heard it. She tried to ease away from him, control the dizzying current that raced through her, but he would have none of that. He drew her back firmly but carefully, as if she was his.

"Hold tight."

His command cleared her head.

"Or we'll both be taking an unexpected bath," he whispered in her ear. Laura wasn't sure if it was his low voice or the picture his words painted in her head that made her heart turn over. It took every ounce of control not to quiver.

His chest rumbled with a chuckle. Heat ran up her neck to her cheeks. She wanted to swat him.

Jamie positioned them by the water's edge. He waited for his men to cross the river and make their way down stream. When they were out of sight, he walked his destrier into the water.

"Gather up your skirts, lass. I'll do my best not to peek." His voice was low and mellow. He took a deep breath and straightened his back, putting a little distance between them.

"The men are away and will not notice your ankles and I'd rather you stay dry. The recent rains have swelled the river and the water is higher than I expected."

One minute he was rude and commanding. and the next, kind and thoughtful. Rather than make an issue of the contradiction, she decided to enjoy his kind, thoughtful side.

Laura gathered her skirts, letting her ankles shamelessly dangle.

"The Annan isn't usually this high. You do know how to swim?" Jamie asked. He took his time and walked his horse into the river and let the animal find his footing. They had gone only a quarter of the way across. "You never know about the river sprites. They may take offense at your humorless expression."

She swung her head around and stared into his eyes. The devilish look made her burst into laughter. "Have I been that difficult? No," she said and placed her hand on his chest. "Don't answer that."

She stared over his shoulder and stiffened.

"What is it?" Jamie followed her stare up river. Riders galloped toward them. They weren't his men.

"We're targets in this swift water." He looked behind him, then to the other side. They couldn't go any faster until his horse found the slope of the river bank.

"It would be faster to return to the near bank, but we'd be separated from my men and any help they could provide. There's nothing for it. We must cross and reach Sean and the others. I should never have compromised your safety for propriety. Hold tight. If you fall, try to stay in the middle of the river. Let the current take you downstream—"

"I'm not going anywhere without you. Get us across."

There was a faint glimmer of humor in his eyes. "Aye, m'lady. As you wish." Jamie clicked his tongue. Getting across the stream was all that counted.

The sound of horses' hooves grew louder.

"Wrap your arms around my waist and try not to lose your seat."

Jamie's battle horse's ears perked. The animal strained and blew hard. Jamie held him back.

"Easy boy, a little farther. As soon as we're out of the water." He coaxed the horse in quiet tones. His horse lumbered out of the river, its head bobbing up and down, straining to take the lead. Jamie loosened his grip on the reins.

"Away." His horse bolted forward. They raced along the muddy river bank, the raiders gaining ground.

"You need to let me down," she yelled at him in the wind. "You can go faster without me."

"Keep down," he said between clenched teeth and pulled his sword. They raced on, the land a blur as they flew by.

The spray of water from his horse's pounding hooves turned into clouds of dust as they came out of the marshland and onto a dry meadow.

How much longer could his horse keep up this pace? It was late afternoon and they had been traveling since dawn.

They reached the area where the river dog-legged to the right and the forest was closest to the water. In the distance, the base of the trees was shrouded in a blanket of unspun white wool that drifted along the forest floor in fleecy clouds as if it was a solid substance. The evening mist would be a good place to lose the thieves.

Jamie veered toward the woods as if he heard her thoughts and let loose his battle cry. In the distance, an echoing cry reached her ears. Relief rushed through her, but they were still in danger. Jamie urged his horse on. The animal gave no sign of slowing down.

Branches flashed by as they raced on, jumping over fallen logs and splashing across shallow pools. Jamie held her tightly against his chest. Out of the mist, his men charged forward. They let lose their roars and headed for the reivers close behind.

Sparks flashed by and confused Laura until she realized Lisbeth's charms hung from the trees. If only The Ancestors could help them. She glanced over Jamie's shoulder and forgot about the charms.

"Rider behind us." Jamie urged his horse on. How much faster and longer could his destrier continue? If they didn't stop soon, the animal would collapse.

Another glance. The rider was close enough for her to see the sneer on his lips.

"He's gaining ground." *Think*, she told herself. The fluid strides of Jamie's horse took them out of the dark forest and into a small meadow. Sunlight bounced off Jamie's sword. A vision of her brother and her practicing drills came to mind. Could it work? She stiffened at the challenge. It had to.

"Put your sword on your left shoulder, then make a quick half-turn to your left. Face the rider. Don't stop. Charge," Laura said as she lay as close to his horse as possible, her arms around the animal's neck, to give Jamie more room to maneuver.

"Don't look. This is not going to be a pretty sight."

She closed her eyes tight. *Please, let this work.*

Her body swayed to the left as Jamie completed the turn. Beneath her, the animal's muscles bunched and exploded as they sprang forward. With the full weight of the charging horse behind his sword, Jamie hit the raider hard, severing his right arm. Jamie's horse turned behind their attacker and advanced. With a quick slash, the man's body fell to the ground. The disembodied head rolled into the mist. Jamie spurred his horse into the woods.

Laura sat up. Trees sped by. "Why aren't we stopping?"

Jamie didn't answer. She began to panic as a tall hedgerow emerged out of the mist in front of them, sparkles from Lisbeth's charms interspersed on the branches.

Their direction didn't waver. Rather than slow down, the animal gathered speed. Jamie crushed her in front of him and held her head against his chest.

"I won't let anything happen to you." The horse's front hooves reached for the top of the hedgerow. Jamie rose in his seat taking her with him. The horse's hind legs kicked out from under him as he carried them over the barrier.

The sensation of flying through the air both frightened and exhilarated her. For three heartbeats everything moved at a funeral pace until they came down with a jarring thud. How they landed without the horse falling or them being thrown was beyond her, but they did.

The horse slowed to a halt. Lathered and blowing hard, its leg muscles quivered from the chase, but she swore the animal smiled. Jamie's men gathered around them. The exhilaration of a safe get away quickly turned to concern. She searched the faces of Jamie's men and let out a sigh of relief. She accounted for every man.

"The raiders didn't want to fight once Donald appeared leading a troop of Robert the Bruce's men. As soon as we joined forces, the reivers turned and ran.

Donald followed them. He should be here soon." Sean helped Laura down. "How did they know where to find us? We covered our tracks well."

Jamie turned at the rumble of horses galloping toward them. He stepped in front of Laura, sword drawn. A troop of men flying an azure lion on a gold field, Robert the Bruce's colors came into view.

"Jamie." The leader, sitting tall in his saddle and dressed in battle leathers, walked his horse into the thicket.

"Donald. You arrived at the right time." Jamie relaxed and sheathed his sword. Donald dismounted and walked over.

"Anything to save your sorry arse."

She stepped out from behind Jamie. Donald looked from Jamie to Laura. Panic rushed across Donald's battle-worn face.

"Oh, I beg your pardon, Lady Laura. I didn't see you with Jamie." Donald's gaze turned tender. "I was sorry to learn of Richard's passing. He will be missed."

"Thank you, Donald. I appreciate your kind words." Donald gave Laura a slight bow and turned to Jamie.

"We followed the raiders. I see you took care of their leader. I didn't recognize him." Donald handed Jamie a battered sword.

Jamie hefted the sword. Laura looked on. The weapon was a light, single handled sword, adequately balanced. The blade, for both thrusting and cutting was badly nicked and rusted in spots. It had not been well maintained. He handed the weapon to Sean.

"A common weapon without any distinct markings," Sean said handing the blade to Donald.

Laura didn't recognize the sword, but she remembered the man.

"He was the innkeeper," Laura said. "He knew where to find us because I mentioned our destination to his wife last night."

The men turned to her. Blood pounded in her temples as she looked from face and face. They didn't hide their hostile stares. She didn't blame them. As soon as she saw the man's sneer she knew what had happened. Her innocent words resulted in a traitorous act, as unintentional as it was.

"I made polite conversation when she served me supper." Her expression begged for forgiveness, but that didn't stave off their anger. "I had no idea... I would never have forgiven myself if any of you had been injured."

"Intended or not, the results could have been deadly." Jamie said. Her cheeks burned at his reprimand. Her mouth slammed shut.

Donald cleared his throat and pulled the men's attention away from her. She was thankful for his assistance, but she had no idea how to make amends with Jamie and his men. Trust was hard to earn once it's been dashed.

"I saw your maneuver. Impressive," Donald said. Relieved, but still smarting, she stepped away from the group.

"You can thank Laura for that." She stopped. "I followed her instructions," Jamie said.

Everyone turned to her and waited. What did they want her to say? She looked to Jamie for guidance. His small nod was all she needed.

"Richard and I practiced that tactic often. The reverse maneuver was a favorite of his. I'm glad it worked." The memories of Richard swept through her along with an overwhelming sense of loss.

"Richard saved the day," Jamie said. He held her hand, providing an anchor. But his simple statement brought back Richard's loss in a rush of agony. Her chin quivered. Jamie squeezed her hand and gave her strength as she fought to keep her composure.

"Laura would make a warrior a good wife," Donald said and set the men laughing, lightening the mood.

"We have some supplies. You're welcome to them," Jamie said.

"Get what you need," Donald instructed his men. "We leave for the border."

"I suspect you're on your way home to Caerlaverock," Donald said to Jamie.

"Yes. Would you like our new warrior to escort you on your journey?" Jamie asked.

Her face colored fiercely and she gave him a hostile stare. The twinkle in his eye assured her he meant to tease.

"Laura would be an asset to any man, but the rest of my journey would bore her. No wild chases or reivers," Donald said.

They walked toward Donald's men, who were mounting up.

"You can save me a trip and give something to Herbert." Donald said.

"What would you like me to give him?" Jamie asked. Donald mounted his horse. His men formed behind him.

"Information." Donald bent to speak to him. "Tell Herbert to watch his back, especially the next several days. I have the information from a reliable source. A traitor is in his midst."

A muscle on Jamie's jaw flicked angrily.

"I will tell him. There are many new faces since moving into Caerlaverock," Jamie said.

"Safe travels," Donald said and straightened in his saddle.

"And may the wind be at your back," Jamie said.

Donald gave his troop a signal. They left the thicket and headed for the English border.

"Do you think his message is accurate?" Laura

asked. Jamie watched the last of Donald's men fade into the mist.

"Donald's sources are never wrong."

Chapter Five

Laura sat upon her palfrey and could not draw her eyes away from the vision before her. The smudge of clouds that gathered around the setting sun were several shades of vivid red against a dark sky and cast a warm glow on Caerlaverock's sandstone walls. The inverted reflection of Caerlaverock and sky in the still moat created a breathtaking view.

The stronghold in the middle of a wide moat had twin towers on either side of the north gatehouse and one tower at the south. Lofty battlements connected to towers with an overly high curtain wall created a unique triangular fortification. Built for defense, the imposing fortress appeared impossible to breach.

The design touched her heart. Along with its strength, the beauty in its lines and position created a grand picture. Put everything together and, as Laura waited for Jamie's order to proceed, she was overcome with emotion.

Jamie came up beside her and moved the group forward. "The castle is impressive even in the darkening sky," Jamie said with pride. "This is your first visit since the building's completion."

"Caerlaverock pulls at my heart with its beauty and purpose. It represents all I hold dear in a person, if that's possible, heart, soul, and strength. I understand why Father was taken with Herbert's plans. He sat with Herbert for hours and discussed the design. After our last visit, he talked about the castle all the way back to Glen Kirk. Mother, on the other hand, hoped the place didn't flood like the old one."

He laughed, deep, warm, and rich.

They crossed a timber bridge and rode through an arched stone gateway, emerging into a courtyard settling down for the night. Behind them, the lattice oak portcullis with metal daggers strained on its chains as it slid down the groove and settled into place with a final thud.

A stable boy helped her down from her mount while Sean saw to the horses and men. She shook her skirts to dislodge dust from their travels, but didn't bother with wrinkles as Jamie escorted her into the gatehouse to reunite with the family.

"Caerlaverock is as fine inside as out," she murmured. They walked into a large solar, a private family room.

"Ah, Laura. How good to see you. When the battlement guards reported a woman with Jamie, I assumed he brought Darla. You are a pleasant surprise." Herbert rose ignoring the papers strewn across his table.

She gave him a peck on the cheek. "I'm sorry to disappoint you, Cousin Herbert. Mother and Father remained at Glen Kirk. They weren't ready to travel yet."

"How insensitive of me. Of course, she's still in mourning. We all feel your sorrow." He put a fatherly arm around her and led her to a chair.

"My wife left with your three cousins and her staff to visit family in Pencaitland. I'm afraid you'll be visiting just with me."

"That's fine," she said and smiled through disappointment. She was familiar with Lady Maxwell's staff and could easily ask them questions about Evan and Angel. Now starting those conversations may be more difficult, but she accepted the small setback. She had every intention of putting Evan's ghost to rest.

"Jamie mentioned Evan and Angel's deaths. I understand a ghost haunts the castle. Mother sent me in her place." She didn't miss the pleading look Herbert gave Jamie. Was he also a non-believer of magic?

"Of course. Your help is greatly appreciated. Why don't you get settled and we can talk about how you can help at supper?" Herbert said.

"I appreciate your concern, but I'm here for a purpose." If her cousin had a pleading look for some assistance before, he downright begged Jamie for support now.

Laura pulled a letter from her pocket and handed it to Herbert. "Mother asked me to deliver this to you as soon as I arrived."

Herbert took the letter and set it on his desk. A soft knock at the door announced a housekeeper. "I'm sure you'll want to clean up before we eat. Mrs. Turner, show Lady Laura to her room."

Mrs. Turner led her out and closed the door behind.

"We met Donald at the Annan River," Jamie said. "He asked that I tell you to watch your back, especially for a few days. His informant says there's a traitor at Caerlaverock."

"Yes. Donald confirms my suspicions. I'm glad I

had Oliver take my family to Pencaitland." Herbert returned to his seat. "I fear no one in the family is safe. Keep close to Laura. If she's anything like Darla, she'll trample anyone else. You know how to handle her."

He chafed at Herbert's order. How could he not see his value in finding the traitor?

"I can better serve you and the family hunting for the traitor rather than playing the courtier to Laura. Perhaps someone on Mrs. Turner's staff would be better suited."

Herbert read the letter. It was from Wesley. "No." He looked at Jamie. "I don't want to worry about her. You'll see to her well-being."

Jamie glanced out the window and spotted Laura and Mrs. Turner crossing the courtyard to the guest house. Why did he agree to bring her to Caerlaverock? The thought died as soon as he acknowledged it. If he hadn't, she would have found another, more dangerous, way.

"Laura said Evan's ghost must be put to rest within thirty days of dying." He turned to Herbert. "That's five days from today. Perhaps I could do both."

Laura examined intricate stonework and relief carvings on the buildings as she crossed the courtyard. The guest house and other structures were built near the curtain wall, with a walkway between the wall and buildings that enabled troops to move. It was clear the primary function of Caerlaverock was defense, not to keep her cousin or mother dry.

"We haven't seen you in a long time. We're all sorry to hear about your brother." Mrs. Turner brought her to a room on the second floor. They waited at the door while two footmen filled a tub with hot water.

"Thank you," she murmured.

Richard. He's everywhere. She should take comfort in knowing Richard's maneuver saved the day. And there was satisfaction in being instrumental in stopping the reiver. She couldn't bring Richard's murderer to the same, but she silently vowed to give Evan and Angel the justice they deserved. That would give some meaning to her mission, put Evan's ghost to rest.

She fingered the beads around her neck and was comforted by their warmth. The truth, she would find justice for Evan and Angel. *So mote it be*, she whispered in her head.

Getting out of clothes she'd worn for two days and soaking some of the soreness from the harsh ride out of her bones—to say nothing of grit—sounded like heaven.

Mrs. Turner led her into a modest-size cozy room with whitewashed walls. Her satchel sat on a single bed pushed against the inner wall. Her other satchel lay across a colorful chest under the window that faced the courtyard. A fireplace, which the footman had lit, was next to the window.

"We were all surprised when Lord Jamie brought us news of Evan and Angel. Mother found it hard to believe Evan would kill Angel," Laura said.

Mrs. Turner opened her satchel and held up a very wrinkled sky blue silk gown. A few hard shakes didn't help the wrinkles at all. Mrs. Turner headed for the door.

"No one knows what to believe. Poor Mary. She found their bodies. The woman is a seasoned soldier's wife, who's seen many a horrible wound, but seeing those two... The image still haunts her. We've all tried to help her."

"Do you think speaking to me would be of any

help?" She hadn't thought about speaking with someone who had been so close to the tragedy. Laura tried to temper her excitement.

"I'm sure she would speak to you. Now get into the tub before the water cools. I'll leave you to your bath with some lavender soap, and take your dress to the laundry to freshen." She closed the door behind her.

A large wooden tub filled with hot water was next to the fireplace. Laura undressed and sank into warm water. She scrubbed the dirt and grit off with lavender scented soap. Done washing, she leaned her head back against a small pillow and let the heat ease her stiff muscles. The crackling fire and warm water soothed and relaxed her to the point of nodding off.

"Excuse me, Lady Laura. I'm Sonia." A young woman entered carrying her dress. "I'm here to help you."

Laura, started awake by the girl, sat up splashing the water. "You saved my life. I would have drowned if you didn't come in."

"M'lady, my sister always falls asleep in her bath after a day at work. Once or twice her head slips underwater, but she come up quick enough sputtering like a fish."

Laura stepped out of the tub and into a linen Sonia proceeded to wrap around her.

"Have you been with the Maxwell's long?" Laura sat next to the fire and combed her fingers through her hair and rubbed it with a silk cloth to dry it.

"Like many others, my parents worked for the family. When The Maxwell moved to here, Mrs. Turner asked if I wanted to join the staff. She said since I was around the kitchen with nothing to do, she might as well put me to work."

Laura stopped rubbing her hair. The girl was

personable. Mrs. Turner was willing to speak about Evan and Angel, perhaps Sonia could provide information. What she needed to do was more than make conversation. She had to be careful.

"I'm sorry for your loss," Sonia said. "Burying someone you love is not easy." Sonia turned away and gathered Laura's clothes, but not before Laura saw the pained expression on the girl's face.

Laura ran her hand through her hair to determine if it was dry enough to be brushed. She put down the silk cloth.

"Thank you for your kind words. I find it difficult to believe Richard is gone. I'm sure it's been difficult here as well with the bad harvest and the appearance of a ghost."

"It's been difficult because of Evan and Angel's murder." Sonia took the brush from the dresser and brushed Laura's hair. She swept it back until the auburn hair glistened and fell into soft waves over Laura's shoulders.

"Murder? You don't think Angel attempted to stop Evan from poisoning the crops?"

"M'lady that is nonsense. Evan's been wrongly accused of both poisoning the crops and killing the woman he loved. He won't rest until the truth is known and the real villain brought to justice."

Was Sonia correct? Evan's ghost is restless for justice, but something else kept poking at her. Not every murderer is brought to justice. This was a good start, but there was more to discover.

"Why would someone murder them?" Laura said under her breath. "Did you mention this to anyone?" Laura asked. Sonia helped her with her chemise and dress.

Sonia straightened Laura's skirt and placed a metal belt around her waist.

"M'lady, they have it in their heads that Evan is the villain in both deeds. They have no reason to look elsewhere." Sonia gazed at her with eyes that glowed with an inner fire. "He won't rest until we find justice for him and the stain is removed from his family."

Laura pulled up the hem of her skirt and stepped into shoes Sonia placed on the floor.

"They won't listen to anyone. They think they have all the information they need," Sonia said. Determination was etched on the girl's face. Laura was sure Sonia believed Evan and Angel had been murdered.

"Could there be something in Evan's background, some dispute with Herbert or his family that would drive him to do them harm?" Laura knew the answer before she finished asking her question.

Sonia lifted her chin. "Never, m'lady. He worked hard for Lord Herbert and was recently appointed the castle Marshal with much more responsibility and people to manage. Their marriage wasn't an arrangement for anyone's betterment. He was excited and loved his Angel. Lord Herbert and both families supported the marriage. Now, they've all tried and judged him. They are so wrong. It makes me... Forgive me, m'lady. I shouldn't go on so. They'd never listen to me." Sonia's shoulders slumped.

Laura knew that helplessness, when nothing one said or did made any impact, even though they had the right answer. Sonia may as well have been a ghost herself. No one would listen to her.

"Calm yourself. I'll speak to Jamie without any mention of you. He'll know what to do."

She took one last glimpse in the polished metal to make sure everything was in place. Laura thanked Sonia and went across the courtyard to the hall for supper.

The great hall was on the first level of the gatehouse. Two fireplaces took the chill off the autumn air. Tapestries dressed the walls and added warmth to the room. Battle weapons were mounted on one wall positioned with the Maxwell's motto, *I grow strong again.* Family banners hung with pride from the rafters.

The room was set for the evening meal with trestle tables arranged in a long row down the center of the great hall. The Maxwell and his guests stood on the raised dais. Plates and tankards were set on the trestles to mark each person's place. Tall candlesticks were arranged on tables, candle light flickering and brightening the room.

"It doesn't flood." Jamie came up beside her. "And the castle cannot be breached."

It can't be breached from the outside, she thought as Jamie walked her to the fireplace. Someone, and not the ghost nor an alive Evan, according to Sonia, poisoned the crops. She scanned the servant faces as they rushed to fill tankards, pull out more trestle tables, arrange benches and pour ale. Who would she speak to first? Mary? And she wanted to look through the pantry. A chill ran up her back. It was a gruesome thought, but it had to be done.

"We have five days to put Evan's ghost to rest. What is our plan?" Jamie asked.

Our plan? She stopped her tart response. Her foot grew sore from her frustrated tapping. She didn't need his help. *Easy.* She took a calming breath and counted to ten.

"I'll help you. I plan to speak to Evan and Angel's families, as well as Mary, the woman who found their bodies," Laura said.

"The situation between the families is volatile." He ran his hand through his hair.

"Your help," she said with as much of a reasonable voice as she could command, then took a calming breath.

"I know you're more than capable to hold a conversation with people." Jamie said.

She took a good look at him: standing with his hands on his hips, inflating himself with importance. She didn't miss the note of sarcasm.

"Both families are on the defensive, their tempers heated. For my well-being, I'll go with you." He didn't ask a question or provide a suggestion. He gave a command and that irked her as much as his tone.

"I don't need someone to protect me. The family has nothing to fear from me. They have nothing to lose, only to gain." She faced him toe-to-toe and didn't flinch. He was not going to intimidate her, or get in her way.

"At this time, only rumors and suspicion swirl among the gossips. If, in your questions and discussions, you come across information that proves Evan, in fact, poisoned the crop, do you think they will let you live? They have much to lose. The family will be tarred and feathered, turned out of the clan as traitors, if not killed. You give a hint of credence to the rumor and innuendo, and they have a great deal to lose."

"That isn't going to happen. It can't." She touched her throat. "Evan isn't guilty." She paled at the picture Jamie presented. The ghost's goal, the gravity of Evan's plight came into focus and it startled her. She believed with all her heart Sonia was right. Evan didn't poison the crops or kill Angel and himself. She still didn't have a clue why Evan risked being dammed to wander this earth for eternity. Until she figured that out she couldn't help him.

"And how do you know that?" His eyes were hard and piercing. She met him blink for blink.

"One of the servants told me, in confidence," she added. "Evan didn't taint the crops nor did he kill Angel."

"And you believe this person?" His smirk made the hair on her arm stand up.

"Yes. Why would Evan taint the crops? What would he gain? He had a new advanced position in the household. Mrs. Turner said he was excited getting ready for the wedding. His family supported his decisions. His new position made him a more ardent Maxwell man."

She touched her beads at her neck. Warm. Besides the beads' confirmation, her conclusion was logical. Why couldn't Jamie grasp that?

He stared into her eyes as if he tried to pull the reasoning out of her head. A glimmer of doubt pass in his eyes, and her hopes soared.

"I understand what you mean. He didn't have a reason. But just because we don't see one doesn't mean a reason didn't exist. I'll let you speak to them."

Laura turned away without a word reining in her escalating temper. "I didn't ask your permission. I was informing you of my decision."

"Yes, I know. However, in case you're not right and you find a reason for him to do kith and kin harm and his family is involved, I'd rather be with you. If something happened to you, Wesley would have my head, and other parts of my body that I truly enjoy. Darla would never forgive me."

She crossed her arms and leveled an icy stare. "Let me understand. You're not accompanying me because you think I may be right or even in danger, but rather to protect your own sorry...skin."

Jamie bit the inside of his cheek in an obvious attempt not to laugh. It drove her to the brink of doing him bodily harm.

"I wouldn't describe it that way."

No, not a smirk. She misread him. His green eyes turned so dark they almost appeared black. Anger. She didn't care what he thought.

Did he have any idea the powder keg they sat on?

If Evan's ghost didn't find rest, the consequences could be greater than the family simply living with an apparition. The drive for justice was a powerful one. She couldn't let Evan's ghost take matters in his own hands. She couldn't predict the consequence to the family. It wasn't only putting Evan to rest that drove her. In the end, Jamie's goal was the same as hers, even Evan's. Protect the family.

Laura had no idea the powder keg they sat on. A traitor was in their midst. Anything could happen and Jamie had no idea where to start his search. Instead, he played her nursemaid following a ghost story.

Not only was Laura feisty and defiant, she was smart. Deep in his bones, he accepted she would to be a challenge to protect. His best course of action was to resolve the situation with the ghost and return her to Glen Kirk.

"Five days are left. I have no choice but to act quickly," Laura said as they took their seats at the table.

"We'll make arrangements to speak to both families tomorrow and follow where that leads us. The sooner we put your ghost to rest, the sooner I can help Herbert with his pressing issues," Jamie said.

He took the wine decanter and filled their cups. He reined in his growing temper. The blame was his. If he hadn't mentioned the ghost at Glen Kirk, he wouldn't be in this difficult situation.

He brought the wine to his lips, but didn't sip. With Herbert gone, what if the traitor's focus turned to Laura? She was English and her family was close to Edward, their king. There would be an uprising if anything happened to her while she visited Scotland.

He drained the cup, and gave her a sideways look. When did her features become so refined, her face so beautiful? When he fostered with Wesley, she had been unconventional and played his squire until Darla reminded her she was a girl. He turned away before she sensed his stare.

He didn't think of her as his squire now. No, Richard would have his personal parts for the thoughts that ran through his head. His protest to bring her with him had been half-hearted. If he was truthful, he looked forward to her company.

He couldn't deny her logic about Evan and Angel's deaths. Both their goals were the same: capture the true murderer. Now a traitor was in their midst. Laura was in mortal danger and he was to blame.

Chapter Six

Jamie walked into the solar. A red and green wool carpet with the Maxwell medallion—a stag, its head raised, lying under a holly bush woven in the center—covered the floor. Tapestries of gardens hung on whitewashed walls. A variety of green and black velvet chairs and leather benches were placed around the fireplace. Herbert sat at the table, eating his morning meal.

"If you're looking for Laura, she's not here. She ran off to speak to Angel's mother and the pantry." Herbert dipped his bread into the honey. "That girl is determined to help the spirit find peace."

"Faith," Jamie ran his hand through his hair, a habit he did when exasperated, which of late happened much too often. "I told her we'd go together."

"Yes, she can be a handful. Like her mother. Darla and I always got into trouble as children. Ask Mara, she can tell you." Herbert broke into a wide smile. "The two of you at odds! When I mentioned you'd be joining us soon, she devoured her meal and made her excuse."

"She's obstinate and headstrong." He stood by the window and stared into the courtyard. "The woman tries my patience at every turn."

"I know a young man who has much the same temperament." Herbert's eyes twinkled. He toyed with the letter Laura gave him yesterday.

Jamie paced in front of a man he respected for his leadership as well as his devotion to his family and people under his care. Herbert understood him better than most, except where Laura was concerned. For years, he'd hid those feelings from everyone. Then, eighteen months ago, he welcomed the opportunity to join Herbert at Caerlaverock rather than fulfill his duty to The Maxwell at Cumgour.

The day before Richard left to serve his king in Wales, people filled Glen Kirk's Great Hall to celebrate his departure, but Jamie's world stopped when Laura walked into the room. He couldn't breathe. His attraction was more than her sky-blue silk gown, the same one she wore tonight that showed off every fine curve of her body. Or the soft cascade of rich, glowing auburn waves that hung over her shoulder. And her face. Everything about Laura attracted him. The afternoon turned into evening and he never had to look for her. He sensed her presence as if she was an extension of him.

"It's not that I don't like her. Truth be told, she attracts me like no other. Even though there are times I want to throttle her." *Other times I want to hold her in my arms and never let her go.* He turned toward his uncle.

"Yes, she's headstrong, but you should have seen her confront Mitchell's men," he said. "She didn't flinch then, nor when the reivers' attacked. Laura may have been scared, but she didn't let anyone know." Any man would be proud to have her, but she was not for him. "She'll make a warrior a good wife."

"You're a warrior."

Jamie turned on his heel to face Herbert. He hoped to God he wasn't a warrior. He didn't have the stomach for it. He handled disputes with discussion and negotiation. Violence was a last resort.

"I'm a farmer."

Herbert let out a long slow breath. "There are times farmers need to be warriors."

Jamie had nothing to say to that. He straightened his shoulders and cleared his throat.

"She's Richard's sister. I can't think of her that way."

"Are you so sure? She's not a child. She's four years younger than you. Laura is a beauty, and from what you tell me, a very capable woman. Regarding Richard, you're probably the only person he would trust with his Laura. Think about that." Herbert put the letter he held on top of a pile of papers on the table.

Laura. She cheered him on at every turn. Could there be more to their friendship? Until this journey, they'd spoken easily to each other. Now, she challenged every word he uttered. No. Her interests weren't with him. To Laura, he was a distant relation and Richard's close friend. It would never go well. They'd kill each other before their wedding night.

"I said Captain Oliver has returned and I've new information concerning our other issue."

Jamie gave Herbert his full attention.

"The unrest grows in the villages along the Nith River. The day you left for Glen Kirk, two suspicious fires destroyed as many granaries. For some reason, the villagers blame me. I'm accused of taking their grain and setting the fires to cover up my theft. The fact that the grain and land are mine is lost to them."

Herbert passed him warm, crusty bread, honey, and the decanter of wine. Jamie tore off a piece of bread and dipped it into the honey.

"I sent grain to the villagers out of concern," Herbert said. "They complained I didn't send enough. I gave them as much as I dared. I can't deplete the castle's stores. They accuse me of quarreling with neighboring lords and bringing my disputes down on them. To protect them, Oliver organized a patrol, but the villagers twisted that as well. They grumble that my men watch them and report back to me. Some even harass my men."

"No matter what you do the villagers find fault. Have you spoken to any of your farmers?" Herbert was vexed for good reason. The villagers' behavior was unusual.

"Oliver is busy putting down disputes. I plan to speak to Jack. However, with Evan's death, now is not the time. I can't imagine a more painful blow for a father than losing a son, or any child, under any circumstances."

"It all must be to stir people against you. But why?"

"Caerlaverock stands in a strategic position, now an invincible building close to the English border." Herbert gave him a knowing glance.

"You play the role of a border guard."

"I like to think of my role as a keeper of the peace, not only at the border. Whoever holds the castle, gains easy access to both England and Scotland. Caerlaverock is a desirable stronghold."

"Donald warned the traitor worked within the castle walls. I want to work with Oliver to find the betrayer. We cannot waste time."

Herbert stared at his table. Didn't the man understand he was more valuable looking for the traitor than holding Laura's hand?

"I'm glad to see Laura." Herbert continued to stare at the table as if the answer was carved in the wood.

"For her own safety, I'd rather she remained at Glen Kirk."

Jamie had a sinking sensation. He didn't like the sudden turn in the conversation. Herbert shook his head. "Until we get to the root of the matter, we need to keep Laura inside our walls. She's titled and English, a bigger target than me. The fact that the reiver gave his life to get to you and her worries me. I appreciate your desire to take a more active part in the search for the traitor, but I cannot do that. And before you say anything, I want you inside the walls, as well. Your neutral position with the English is well known. It's not a far jump to sympathetic, especially with Cumgour a short walk to the border. You're as vulnerable as she is." Herbert tapped the edge of the table. "You have my decision. We'll keep Laura's vulnerability between the two of us. She doesn't need to know."

"Yes. I understand." He should be honored The Maxwell thought so highly of him. He should be glad he stayed behind the wall. He was a farmer, not a warrior, so why did he bristle to be in the thick of things?

The very nature of a traitor was to draw one in, earn trust, a most sacred thing, then use that trust against their opponent. To him, traitors were scum with no place in his world.

Jamie took a piece of bread and rose to leave.

"You'll find her in the pantry. I gave her the key. She's exploring the room for my whiskey. It's gone missing."

Jamie gnashed his teeth. Would the woman ever wait for him? He may have to tie a rope around her. Jamie tried to disguise his annoyance.

"I find it interesting. Our ghost appears to be shy of late. He hasn't materialized since you and Laura arrived. Maybe all we need to do is keep her here."

Herbert's soft chuckle echoed in the corridor as Jamie went down the stairs. He marched across the courtyard and entered the kitchen area.

"We don't talk about it, I tell you." Lewis, a seasoned soldier and Angel's father, pushed past him.

Laura was with Celia. Angel's mother fidgeted with her apron, her face a combination of sadness and pain.

"He loved his Angel. Now, he won't talk about or even mourn for her." The woman's expression hardened. "Evan, that bastard. She told me everything. Everything, but mentioned nothing of his treachery. Why did she speak to him? Why didn't she come to me or her father?" The hardened expression on the woman's face collapsed and quivered. "Why didn't I protect her?"

Silence spread. After several long seconds, Celia, with her head bowed, let out a heavy sigh. "I was cooking and she went on and on about the wedding and examining the stones in the leather pouch he made for her. To get some peace, I sent her to the pantry for more onions. Evan came in with a barrel of ale, kissed me a good morning. I told him to put the ale in the pantry. I left for the great hall. The next thing I know, Mary comes running for me. She found Evan and Angel," she said and let out a halting breath, "dead in the pantry."

"I know this is difficult for you. Was anyone near the pantry?" Jamie asked softly. Laura's head whipped around.

"People are always about. The ale and perishable food stores are kept by the pantry." Celia started to dismiss the idea then stopped and wrinkled her brows in thought.

"No. I don't remember who. I didn't take notice. I sent her to the pantry." Celia lifted her head and gazed at them with tears ready to overflow. "I sent her to her death."

Celia's face was blank, although her chin quivered

and she struggled to hold back tears. Every instinct in Laura wanted to ease the woman's pain, but she had no words that would bring Angel back, no actions. All she could do was listen.

"I'm sorry for your loss," Laura said as she put her arm around Celia. "The words are so inadequate. I know. I lost my brother recently." Celia's head snapped up to Laura. The pain in Celia's face mirrored her own. For days, Laura played the strong one, not only for her parents and sister, but for the men at arms and villagers. Everyone else. Now, she let her emotions rise to the surface and shared her pain and tears with Celia in a moment of profound understanding.

Jamie waited next to her, silent. After a few moments, he gently cradled the small of her back.

Celia took a steadying breath and nodded at Laura. A thank you? A slight smile touched the woman's lips as she stepped away.

"You'll want to speak to Mary. She's in the garden getting me some herbs." Celia hurried off to the kitchen.

The pain would always be present. Laura understood that now, but having shared her loss made it easier to bear.

"Where's the herb garden?" Laura asked.

Jamie threaded her arm through his and led the way beyond the kitchen. "You should have waited for me before you spoke to Celia."

"Yes, yes, I needed protection from a cook with a wooden paddle."

The tendons along his jaw tensed. Her reaction was a bit too tart, although she had to applaud him for having the good sense not to respond. *Wait for him.* Was he insensitive to what she shared with Celia? A pang of loss overwhelmed her. Her eyes widened as she hoped to stop the threatening tears.

A thought struck her. Was that how Jamie coped? Not tears, but action? Yes, that's what she recognized in his face. How could she be so blind?

"I hoped Celia would be able to tell us what the two argued about," Jamie said. There was irritation in his tone.

"But she couldn't confirm they argued. To the contrary, they were very happy." Laura bit the side of her cheek. She tried to make sense of what Celia said.

"If they argued someone must have overheard, or took note of the others near the pantry," he said. His words echoed her confusion.

They made their way through the courtyard, weaving around tables erected under an arcade that ran along one side of the castle wall. Farmers with fresh vegetables had set out their goods. Her nose told her they'd find the tanner at the far end of the marketplace. People from the village and nearby farms casually strolled or moved along with a specific purpose. The crush of people and noise made it difficult to walk and to hear.

"Where were you when they found Evan and Angel?" Laura asked.

"Say again," Jamie shouted. "I didn't hear you." She could barely make out what he said over the chatter and hawking that filled the courtyard.

"I said," she leaned closer to him, "where were you when they found Evan and Angel?"

He led her past the stable and around to the back of the kitchen. The noise subsided considerably. At least now she could hear herself think.

"I returned from patrol and nearly ran Mary down when she rushed through the courtyard. Before I could get off my horse, she grabbed Captain Oliver. They ran toward the kitchen collecting a trail of people behind them. By the time I arrived, I couldn't find a place to stand."

He held open a gate, and she stepped into a modest kitchen garden filled with herbs and flowering plants. She took a deep breath and enjoyed the familiar earthy aroma of basil, chives, mint, and sage.

"Good day, Mary." Jamie and Laura approached a woman. Mary wore a dark brown dress with a blue apron fastened around her waist. Her fading red hair was a disarray of unruly curls. Her face was fair and her features plain, but honesty and sincerity were her greatest attributes.

Mary wiped the dirt on her apron, and picked up the basket of fresh herbs at her feet. "Good day, m'lady, Lord Jamie."

"Lord Jamie told Mother about Evan and Angel. The news upset everyone. Mother's in disbelief and is sure something was overlooked. After speaking with Celia, I feel the same way." Laura pushed a wayward strand of hair from her face.

"Every so often, I still see their faces, those poor children. Angel's lifeless eyes stared up at me. Her pretty lips tinged blue." The woman shuddered. "Everyone loved the girl, such a light spirit. Never a nasty word or raised tone. Kind and generous she was, gave out trinkets to the soldiers. For protection, she said. Like the charm you wear around your neck." The woman motioned toward Jamie.

Laura lifted her gaze. Jamie wore one of Lisbeth's charms. She hardly noticed it any more. She patted her pocket and felt another charm. Lisbeth gave them to everyone.

Laura waited. Mary's soft smile turned to a tearful quiver. "Evan made her a small pouch to hold them. He worked with the tanner for weeks, even burned an angel into the leather for her. It was around her neck when she died. They were so loving and caring to each other. He couldn't have kill her."

"She didn't raise her voice? Someone mentioned they had a loud argument. Isn't that why you went to the pantry?" Jamie asked as he started them walking back toward the kitchen.

"You wouldn't be able to make out a shouting match at that time of day. The pantry is an active part of the house around mealtimes. It's more difficult when the men come in for their ale. I didn't go to the pantry because of any noise. I went to get some candles. That's when I found them." She quaked as if overcome with a chill.

"Who was near the pantry?" Laura asked as they came to the kitchen door.

"Three soldiers. Jermyn, Brian, and Thomas were getting ale from the barrel by the pantry when I arrived. If anyone overheard an argument, it would be them."

"Thank you for your help." Laura and Jamie were in front of the pantry. Mary went off and got halfway to the kitchen before she wheeled around.

"There is something else." Heavy lines of concentration deepened along Mary's brows and under her eyes.

"The floor was covered with blood. I didn't know someone could have so much."

Mary stared, a haunted look about her eyes. Jamie remained still. Laura realized the woman didn't see them. She was someplace else, back to that day in the pantry.

"Evan was covered in blood. He must have dragged himself through the pools on the floor to reach Angel. I had little hope for him. When I found only a little blood on Angel's dress, I thought, I hoped she was alive." Mary's eyes cleared. Agony etched her face. "She was also gone. When I picked up her hand, I found skin under Angel's fingernails. I thought she clawed someone. There were no marks on Evan's face, arms, or hands. I told someone who came into the room, but nothing came of it."

"Did Angel scratch herself?" Jamie asked.

"I didn't find any scratches on her."

"Were Evan's lips blue?" Laura asked.

Mary thought for a moment. "No. His lips were white. He didn't kill her and he's not a traitor to The Maxwell." Mary picked up the corner of her apron, wiped her eyes, then headed toward the kitchen. "Celia, here's the parsley and spring onions you wanted."

"I'm getting anxious. We have a lot to do in five days," Laura said as she fumbled for the pantry door key.

"Why don't we divide and conquer. You look through the pantry. I'll speak to Evan's father. Jack stood by the stable when we crossed the courtyard. Afterward, I'll meet you here."

Surprised by his willingness to cooperate, she agreed, even though she wanted to be with him at the interview. She gazed at Jamie as he walked to the stables. For all his obstinate resistance and teasing, he was a compassionate man.

"Are you lost, m'lady?" Sonia came into the corridor and followed Laura's gaze. "Oh, Lord Jamie," she said with a knowing smile.

"What about Lord Jamie? He's gone to speak to Jack. I wanted to make sure he didn't get distracted along the way." *Liar*, she told herself licking her lips. One look at Sonia and she knew she hadn't fooled the girl.

"He's an honest and trustworthy man."

"Yes, he is, but to him I'll always be Richard's little sister," Laura whispered.

"I don't see that when he watches you when you're not looking. I don't think he sees your brother at all." A soft curve touched Sonia's lips.

Laura touched her necklace, her fingertips warmed

by the beads. The warmth could only be from the heat that rushed up her neck.

"Mrs. Turner is coming." Sonia headed for the courtyard door. "I must be on my way before she scolds me for wasting time."

"Go on." She shooed the girl out the door. Sonia vanished in the crowded courtyard.

Laura slipped the key into the lock, slid the bolt, and swung the door open. She wasn't superstitious, but she needed a moment. It was easy to be brave when one knew what they faced. It was something else when they had no idea what to expect.

The open door provided the sole source of light. Laura tentatively entered the room and looked at the floor. To her relief, someone had scrubbed the stones. There was no sign of blood.

She lit the pantry lantern and hung it on the peg in the center of the room. The dim light revealed rows of shelves to her left lined with tins and small wooden crates. Larger crates and barrels stacked to her right. Several large barrels, filled with salt, flour, and cheese flanked the door. Several bottles of wine were on shelves.

She faced the back of the pantry. With the limited light, she found it difficult to see past the line of stacked crates and barrels that divided the pantry.

She looked at the room with its shelves and barrels and created a plan. The bodies were found by the door and it was likely that anything related to Evan and Angel's deaths would be in the front, not beyond the divide. Perhaps she'd look in the back last, if she went back there at all.

She began to search the shelves. The hint of a breeze ran across her cheek. The breeze didn't come from the door, but rather from behind the shelves. She peeked around. No windows. Perhaps another door?

Mist gathered, shimmery and soft. Mesmerized by shifting wisps and curls, she gasped as the vapor throbbed and expanded, and a young man stepped out of the mist.

She brought her hand to her lips as the young man's jerkin moved and revealed his blood-stained shirt. "Evan?"

His eyes widened and he gave her a respectful bow.

"Why are you here?" The apparition lifted his head and said nothing. He pointed to his lips and shrugged his shoulders. She noted a faint note of pleading in his face before he began to fade away.

"Your murderer. You want him brought to justice." She stepped toward him.

Evan hesitated and nodded as he disappeared.

The ghost was unable to speak. A complication. If he appeared again, her questions needed to be restricted to yes no answers. This was progress.

She spent the next hour looking through the shelves while she waited for Jamie. The only item that appeared out of place was a small decorated vial. She put it into her pocket and continued her search.

"Did you find anything?" Jamie called, walking into the room.

"No, but Evan paid me a visit," she said, putting the tin she examined back on the shelf. "He didn't say anything. I don't think he can speak."

"Is that usual for ghosts?"

Laura spun to face him. At first, she thought him sarcastic until she noted an open smile. He leaned against the door jamb. She smiled back and inclined her head.

"Mother could answer that question. She is the expert on ghosts. You arrived at the right moment. I can't get to the shelf behind this barrel. I promised Herbert I would thoroughly check every shelf for his whiskey."

Jamie moved the cask. She brought the lantern around.

"Hmmm," she rummaged in her pocket, pulled a small container out and showed him.

"What is it?" Jamie examined the closed vial she put in his hand.

He lifted the small bottle to his nose and snapped his head back. "A rather unpleasant pungent odor." He pulled out the stopper and dabbed his finger on the rim of the purplish liquid.

"You're not going to taste that?"

Jamie didn't acknowledge her. The tip of his tongue flicked at his finger. He pulled his hand away and put the stopper back on the bottle.

"Deadly nightshade." he said.

"Poison. But why—" No one stores poison in with the food.

"Perhaps someone plans to poison the stock, the tips of arrows..."

Or The Maxwell. Jamie didn't fool her.

"At Cumgour, we keep the poison locked away. This vial is decorative, something a lady might keep. Let's keep this to ourselves until we gather more information. I don't want to start a panic. Perhaps there's a logical reason the vial is here," he said and slipped the vial into his pocket.

Was he trying to convince her or himself? "Very well. You spoke to Jack. Was he any help?"

"He had little to add. He never heard Evan or Angel raise their voices even when they argued. He swore Evan was loyal to the family. I'm a reliable judge of character. I believe he told me the truth." He waved his hand in a dismissive gesture.

"We can't confirm there was an argument. They were likeable and we found no one had any reason to kill either one." She ticked off each item on her fingers, more confused than ever.

"If Evan did turn against The Maxwell…" Jamie said. She mentally added the possibility to her list.

"All we know is the two of them are dead. Stabbed." Laura tried to put the pieces together. She was good with people. Live ones.

"Evan's stab wound was mortal. The amount of blood he lost proves that. Angel's stab wound—"

"Why did she have so much less blood? And blue lips. Mary mentioned Evan's lips were white." She drew her brows together, frustrated she didn't know more.

"If a wound is made after the person dies, it doesn't bleed." Jaime's expressive face changed and grew somber.

"That means she wasn't killed with a knife." Laura turned to Jamie who looked as if he weighed her statement.

"No, she wasn't."

"When did he stab her? If Evan killed her in anger, then regretted it enough to kill himself, would he stab her after she was dead?"

He stroked his chin, deep in thought. "No, that doesn't make sense." He walked toward the door.

"Where're you going?" She locked up the pantry and followed after him. Looking through the rest of the pantry could wait.

"To the barracks. I don't think there's any more we can find here today." Jamie turned abruptly and Laura slammed into his chest. He had to admit her tenacity brought him around. Her explanation may actually have merit. He continued on, his long strides eating the distance as she struggled to keep up.

"Jermyn, Brian, a moment if you will," he called to the two men in front of the barracks.

"You were by the pantry the day they found Evan and Angel. Tell me what you saw or heard," Jamie said.

"Nothing out of the ordinary until Mary called us." Just as he thought. At last they were making progress.

"When you went inside, what did you see?" Jamie tried to restrain his excitement.

"Evan and Angel on the floor," Brian said. Jermyn nodded in agreement.

"Did they argue? Was anyone near the pantry?" Laura blurted. He put his hand on her back, hoping to keep her quiet. He didn't want her giving any ideas.

The two men stared at each other. "No, no one other than Thomas. I didn't hear anything, did you?" Jermyn asked Brian.

The soldier shook his head.

"Thomas was on guard duty by the gate today."

They thanked the soldiers for their help and moved on toward the gatehouse.

"I thought I heard something and asked the others to hush. It turned out to be nothing. A few minutes later, Mary went in and came rushing out telling us not to let anyone in. We stood guard at the pantry while Mary got the Captain. Oliver had us join him. It was a sad sight." Thomas shook his head. "Perhaps Holger can give you more information. He was standing guard in the pantry when we entered."

Laura and Jamie stared at each other. The tinker, one of those silent souls you overlook while they go about their work.

"Had he been there long?"

"He must have been bringing crates into the pantry. He was sweaty and wore only his under-tunic."

"Where can we find him?" Laura asked.

"He's visiting the villages along the Nith River. He should be back by the end of the week." A crofter and his wagon pulled up to the portcullis.

"Many thanks for your time." Jamie drew Laura into the courtyard. "Now all we can do is wait."

Chapter Seven

"I wish I had more to tell you. I didn't go by the pantry. I can only tell you what I know about my sister." Angel's older sister, Marge, sat across a small table from Laura in the castle kitchen, hands clasped in her lap. Laura didn't doubt her sincerity. Heartache, loss, and frustration were written on the woman's face.

"Tell me about Angel. What was she like?"

Marge's shoulders eased. Her lips turned up into a serene smile. "Her name wasn't a mistake. My sister was an angel with a soft way about her, yet able to hold her ground when she had to. Not everyone is good with people, but she had a special way with them. She soothed and cajoled the angriest temper and laughed and celebrated with others. Oh, she could be stubborn, but she was fair. I don't know anyone who could say a bad word about her."

"You make her sound more saintly than angelic," Laura said.

Marge looked down at the table and sighed before she returned her attention to Laura. "She grew to be a wonderful, thoughtful woman. Angel worked hard, was honest, and truthful. She didn't gossip. But saint... no. Although Evan would disagree."

"It was a love match?" Laura asked.

"Our families are close and as children, Angel and Evan were always together. They grew up liking each other and often turned to one another for advice. They had a lot in common. Some things they never realized, but more than anything, they cared about each other.

"Their friendship changed about a year ago. She didn't hear when I spoke to her." Marge laughed. She had a beautiful loving smile when she spoke about her sister. "Angel didn't hear when anyone spoke to her. Off in a daydream about him. Evan acted much the same. They only had eyes for each other.

"Of course we all knew what was happening. Neither one had any idea they were perfectly matched. They had such plans..." Marge stared at her hands in her lap.

Laura didn't want to break the silence, but a question hung heavy in her mind. Why were Evan and Angel dead?

"He didn't kill her. Evan would never hurt her." Marge's words were sincere. No one wanted to believe someone close to them could do something so horrible. Perhaps Angel hid things from her sister. As much as Laura loved Lisbeth and as much as they shared with each other, there were things she kept from her.

"He'd do anything to protect her. I'm sure he gave his life for her." Laura was startled by Marge's words.

Much like you would for Jamie. The admission dredged from a place of logic, reason, and love. Marge's words were synonymous with her thoughts about her and Jamie.

Laura's fingers toyed with the beads, warm on her neck. But were they warm for Angel or for her?

"There you are. Ready to finish examining the pantry I suspect. I think this is all a plot by Mrs. Turner to have us clean the pantry for her." Jamie said from the bottom of the gatehouse stairs. She stifled the bubble of laughter that threatened to erupt and marched past him.

"Yes. I'm ready. No, I don't think this is a ploy by Mrs. Turner. Are you coming? You still need to find Herbert's whiskey." She glanced over her shoulder as he came up beside her. She walked a little faster.

"We've spent two days searching through tins and crates. I think you told me about Herbert's whiskey only to get me to help you."

"I did not." She couldn't help but widen her smile. "You were there when Herbert said his favorite bottle is missing. If you spent more time helping me—"

"Now, lass, when not searching with you, I've been questioning Evan and Angel's families, though I don't know why I bother. They tell the same tale. There is no new information." She ignored the irritation in his voice. They both were frustrated with the little progress they made.

They found their way around the crowded corridor.

"Every day more crates and barrels fill the area. It's difficult to walk," Laura said.

"The passageway is better than using the storage rooms down by the dungeon," Jamie said. He hefted an apple in a basket by the door and replaced it while he waited for her to unlock the door.

Jamie followed her inside.

The last two days of moving boxes and sweeping the floor had been hard, but pleasant. The distance between them caused after months of absence melted away.

"I'm as puzzled as you are," she said.

"We've searched every shelf," he said.

Laura led the way to the back. One-by-one, Jamie pulled the barrels away from the wall. She sprinkled a few drops of water to keep the dust down before she began to sweep.

"According to Mrs. Turner," Laura said, "the family used the pantry for storage while they moved into the castle. They stored everything from her ladyship's personal things to supplies for the barn in here. Some of these crates and barrels haven't been opened in a year.

"I have no idea if we'll find anything, but I... I don't know where else to search. I keep hoping Holger will return soon." She sprinkled a bit of water. "Then there's Evan's family."

"Half his family is in mourning and the other half disowning. Evan's cousin is sure Angel corrupted Evan." He pulled a barrel away from the wall.

"Yes, I heard a similar accusation from someone in Angel's family, Evan corrupted Angel." She ran a broom behind the next barrel. Nothing.

"His family shared information, but gave me nothing we didn't already know."

"Marge was very clear. Evan loved Angel very much, since childhood. Their friendship grew into love." Laura kept sweeping, anything to avoid looking at him. She could easily be speaking about their relationship. *Don't be silly.* He gave her no indication she was anything more to him than little Laura.

"I have to speak to Herbert. You coming along?"

She stopped sweeping mid-stroke and raised her chin. She wished she had better light. His face was in the shadows. Her mind floundered. *Stop hoping for something that doesn't exist. It will only lead to disappointment.* Where was that ruthless woman who faced things head on?

"Something wrong?" he asked.

She shoveled what little debris she swept into a barrel and put the broom to the side. "No, nothing's wrong. You go on. I'll finish up here and meet you in the great hall."

She walked with him to the outside door and watched him cross the courtyard. A graceful man. He commanded attention without saying a word. She admired that he knew who he was and his worth. When he wanted, he was a sensitive man, an oddity for sure. He had a knack for giving her his full attention and making her believe no one else mattered.

Halfway through the courtyard, he stopped and looked over his shoulder. Her breath caught as his stare met hers. She should turn away, but couldn't. He gave her a knowing smile and a slow nod, then disappeared into the crowd.

Laura wasn't sure what had just happened, but her heart pounded. She thought she was past her girlhood fascination. A deep sigh escaped her lips. She resisted touching her beads. She didn't need to confirm her blatant thoughts. She went back to the pantry.

"Do you have a moment? If you're busy, I can speak to you another time." Jamie waited at Herbert's solar door.

"Come." Herbert rummaged through papers in his hand.

"I have questions about Evan and Angel before you leave for Parliament."

Herbert motioned to an empty seat across from him. "I'll be away at Scone until the end of the week and wanted to speak to you before I left. You start while I finish packing."

"Aside from being dead, what were the conditions of Evan and Angel's bodies?"

"Their bodies were moved." Herbert put down the papers and closed his satchel. "That's what I wanted to tell you. Oliver said he didn't let anyone into the pantry until I arrived. When I entered, Evan was on the floor, his body and hands covered in blood. A blood smear was painted across the floor as if he had been dragged. I thought perhaps Evan pulled himself over to Angel, but I didn't find any hand prints. There should have been hand prints."

"Mary mentioned three things I found odd. First, as you mentioned, she found a lot of blood in the pantry and on Evan. She never mentioned anything about his hands, but she did say she found very little blood on Angel. Her wound hadn't bled much. Second, Angel's lips were blue. Third, she found skin under Angel's fingernails and no marks on Angel's or Evan's body."

"I don't remember seeing marks on Evan's body. The sight overwhelmed everyone. Some of what I witnessed came to mind days later." Jamie rose and paced the room.

"I believe someone suffocated Angel before she was stabbed. That would explain her blue lips and why she didn't bleed." His sixth sense said he was right.

A cloud of dust and clatter of wagon wheels by the gatehouse caught Jamie's attention. The tinker and his wagon rolled in. Holger. Now he and Laura could stop rummaging through the pantry and get some answers. He peered toward the kitchen and searched for Laura, but didn't see her. Jamie turned to Herbert, anxious to finish their conversation. He had to speak to Holger.

"Evan didn't murder Angel in a sudden rage. Evan is as much a victim as Angel. Both were murdered by someone else."

"Why would anyone want to kill either of them?" Herbert sat back in his chair.

"We found this in the pantry. It must have rolled amongst some baskets." Jamie handed him the vial.

Herbert examined the vial then took a whiff. He gaped at Jamie.

"The vial is my wife's. Some time ago, I gave her six bottles filled with rose water when I returned from Edinburgh. She complained a bottle was lost when we moved her belongings into Caerlaverock. My wife is not—"

Jamie touched Herbert's arm. "Someone has this planned to put blame at your doorstep."

"This is deadly nightshade." Herbert hefted the vial in his hand.

"I believe Evan and Angel were innocent victims. They surprised someone who planned to poison the food. They paid with their lives. This proves Donald's warning was correct." Surely now Herbert would use him to find the traitor.

"Walk with me to the stable." Herbert picked up his satchel. "As a member of Parliament, some of my decisions are not popular and make me a target, which is something I deal with every day, but this takes a serious turn."

"You mean traitor." Jamie spit the words in disgust.

"I want to discuss securing Caerlaverock while I'm gone." Jamie followed Herbert to the stable.

Laura watched Jamie's back as he crossed the courtyard to see Herbert. Jamie's gaze sent a shiver of desire through her. Why would he do that? She didn't want to speculate. *Back to the pantry.*

She picked an apple from the basket and sent several cascading onto the floor, rolling every which way. Annoyed by her own carelessness, she scurried after one that rolled into the pantry.

Sonia appeared at the pantry door and placed the basket with the other escaped fruit back on the barrel.

"Many thanks." Relieved, Laura put the escaped apple in the basket and bit into one she had taken.

"Come, m'lady. You shouldn't be here, not alone." Sonia, her brows pinched, reached out for Laura. Sonia's feet shuffled close to the edge of the door sill, careful not to cross the threshold.

"Sonia, I'll be fine. Why are you so upset?"

"You mustn't be in the pantry. It's dangerous. I'll not leave until you come out of the room." Sonia glanced at the kitchen, then focused on the courtyard doorway and wrung her hands.

Herbert was right. Villagers were a superstitious lot. Sonia must be apprehensive being in the area because of the deaths. To ease Sonia's mind, Laura stepped out of the room.

"Much better, m'lady. The pantry is not safe for you." Laura walked with Sonia to the courtyard.

"You go on before Mrs. Turner catches you." Laura kept watch as Sonia navigated around the growing crowd on her way to the guest house. The aroma of meat pies wafted through the corridor and made her mouth water. Hefting the apple in her hand, she took a bite, sweet juices filling her mouth.

The sky was blue and clear, the air crisp with a hint at colder weather to come. It was September, and winter snows would come before too long. By the time they did, she hoped to be back at Glen Kirk.

Standing around admiring the view served no purpose in getting her home any faster. Laura returned to the pantry eating her apple. Sonia's reaction to the pantry wasn't unexpected. She shook her head. How superstitious people were. If she wanted to stop their foolish fears, she needed to find the answer to the murders and put Evan to rest.

She put her half-eaten apple on top of the salt barrel inside the pantry door. She'd finish it later.

An empty crate-width space created an entrance to the back portion of the pantry. Laura took the lantern off the barrel, picked up the broom, and side-stepped through the small opening. Searching this area satisfied her compulsive need to be thorough even though her efforts would probably yield nothing other than possibly finding Herbert's lost bottle of whiskey.

Laura held the lantern high and let out a sigh of relief. She found a few crates stacked on extra pallets, not much else. With the lantern settled on the barrel in the middle of the small space, she swept the floor.

She swept around a crate tucked into the corner, tight against the wall. There was something jammed next to the wall. Curious, she teased the piece out and found a dirty cloth.

She set the cloth next to the lantern and pulled it open. Laura stared. The dim light bounced off a glittering jeweled brooch.

Boxes scraped the floor on the other side of the waist-high wall. "Mary? Jamie? Is that you?"

No one answered.

She wrapped the brooch in the cloth and turned to leave. How strange, she must have gotten turned around in the dim light. The space that led to the front of the room was filled with crates. At least she thought that was the way out. She turned in a circle, a mild panic building. Laura pushed against the crates searching for the way out. Nothing moved.

An odor wafted through the air. She stepped back against the boxes and sniffed again. Laura screwed up her nose. Spoiled eggs? She stepped back and her calf hit the wall of crates.

Yanked off balance from behind, Laura's hair combs flew in every direction. She raised her arms to loosen the grasp of whoever pulled her hair. Her attacker tried to pry the jewel from her hand. Laura held tight. The aggressor pulled her head back further. Laura threw the gem and rag onto the floor and used both hands to pry the person's hands from her hair.

Bent backward over the crate, her attacker forced a cloth over her mouth and nose. Laura's stomach cramped from the nauseating order. She pulled at the hand holding the cloth. Her heart raced and her vision blurred. *Stay calm. Fight the instinct to breathe.*

Her attacker tugged. Thrown off balance, her foot shot out from under her and kicked the barrel. The lantern flew off its perch and crashed against the wooden boxes, splashing them with oil.

She couldn't hold her breath any longer. Laura meant only to take a small breath. Instead, she gasped for air and took in gulps of sickening poison.

Wisps of smoke spiraled up from the small space. The snap of flames grew larger. Whoever held her shoved her to the floor.

Stunned and disoriented, she grabbed on to the edge of the box and pulled herself up in time to glimpse a man's silhouette in the doorway before the door banged shut and the bolt slammed into place.

Trapped and coughing, she pushed the box. It didn't move. Smoke thickened, making her eyes tear. She kept blinking trying to focus, but everything moved as if she peered through murky water. Best keep her eyes closed. She needed fresh air. Her strength waning, Laura managed to roll onto the top of the waist high box that separated the two areas. The smoke was worse here. There was no relief. Laura grabbed her skirt and covered her mouth and nose, but the smoke was already deep in her chest. Even small breaths sent her into spasms that were like knives stabbing her chest.

Disoriented and dizzy, she turned onto her side and threw her legs over the edge. Her chest ached from the incessant cough. *Don't stop. Keep going.* Laura gathered her strength and slid down the other side onto the floor.

She lay on the cool floor. A draft of fresh air bathed her face. *Follow the draft.* Her eyes closed, she used her hand like a blind person to find her way. She crawled along not knowing the course she navigated and hoped it led to the door.

The draft was stronger and cooler. Her eyes popped open and she caught a glimpse of light along the floor. The door. She staggered to her feet and pulled on the handle. It didn't budge. Flames erupted, working up the crates on the other side of the boxes.

Her back against the door, she tried to think. Stop the fire or at least slow it down until she found a way out. No water, no blankets. There had to be something. Through her coughing, she pulled tops off crates, and searched for anything that would slow the fire.

She touched a barrel top and found her half eaten apple. A spark of hope burst inside her. She wrenched off the barrel's lid and scooped salt into her skirt. Laura stumbled toward the fire with renewed determination and threw handfuls of salt at the flames. The fire subsided. Still she threw handful after handful of salt until her skirt was empty.

Weak and lethargic from exertion, smoke, and poison, she thought a man pulled a bottle out from behind a crate against the wall—whiskey. Jamie? Laura tried to get to him, but she couldn't get her legs to work. She slid to the ground like a stuffed doll. Her hand touched a rag. The jeweled pin. She grabbed it before everything went black.

Jamie paced in front of the fireplace in the great hall waiting for Laura. He had gone to the pantry and found it locked tight.

"Come quick," a woman called.

He stopped and turned to the door. No one was there. "Whose there?"

"Come quick. The pantry," the woman shouted.

"Wait. What's this about?" He hurried into the corridor. Had she rushed on? Smoke. Coming out from under the pantry door. He immediately lost interest in the woman.

"Fire," he yelled and pulled the bolt. It didn't budge. He ran into the kitchen and searched for anything he could use. A mallet, used for setting stones, leaned against the wall. He grabbed it along with a bucket of water that sat on the table and rushed back to the pantry door.

He pounded the bolt until it released. With great care, he opened the door. Overwhelmed by smoke, he covered his mouth with his shirtsleeve and stepped into the room.

Billows of smoke rushed at him from the back of the room. Laura must have left the lantern. No one else could get in here, he reasoned. She was the only one with the key. He'd get the fire under control then search for her. She must be off speaking to someone about Evan or Angel. Yes, that's what she doing.

He raised the bucket to dowse the fire, but stopped upon seeing an outstretched hand on the floor.

Laura.

He threw the water into the smoldering embers. Quickly, he picked her up and carried her into the courtyard. Fresh air. She needed fresh air. Oliver and soldiers rushed past him in such haste that water from their buckets sloshed and created a small stream from the trough in the courtyard to the pantry.

He held her in his lap and pulled her hair away from her face. Black soot edged Laura's lips. A fine powder mixed with soot rimmed her nose. He tore her petticoat, ripping off a strip of linen. Gently he cleaned off the soot, then shook her face.

"Laura," he said, straining to keep his tone even, controlled. She didn't answer. He cursed. The thought of her being harmed turned his anger into a scalding fury.

Her eyelids twitched, but didn't open. He bent close, then sat back. His left brow arched a fraction. Was that whiskey he smelled on her breath? He leaned close again. Had she fallen into a drunken stupor and neglected the lantern?

"Laura. Open your eyes," he demanded.

Her eyes fluttered open. "Jamie?"

He breathed again. He could hardly hear her through her choked and hoarse voice. She tried to sit up, but was overcome with a coughing spasm.

"Stay still." He held her back.

"Fire's out. Someone had their wits about them and spread salt to dowse the flames." Mrs. Turner came up next to him.

Glistening crystal specks on Laura's skirt caught his attention. "Salt?" Jamie asked Laura.

"From the pantry barrel," Laura said between coughs.

Mrs. Turner took cloth from Jamie and gently removed soot around Laura's eyes. As she worked, her expression darkened.

"Deadly nightshade," she whispered. "I can see the signs in her eyes."

The housekeeper stared at Jamie, then rushed toward the kitchen, pushing Oliver and his men out of her way.

Poison. His chest heaved. Who would dare? Alarm and anger rippled up his spine. His head throbbed with a dull deafening beat. He took deep breaths, one, then another as he fought to keep the berserker within him buried deep. There would be plenty of time for him to let him loose once Laura recovered.

Mrs. Turner ran from the kitchen carrying a cup of whiskey.

"This is strong. Drink slowly." The housekeeper knelt beside them and held the cup. Laura pushed the cup away.

"No, no more," she said.

"A little more. There isn't much left," Mrs. Turner said. "Lord Herbert's wife uses deadly nightshade to brighten her eyes. I keep whiskey, an antidote close by in case she uses too much."

"That explains the vial we found in the pantry. Lord Herbert identified the bottle. How deadly nightshade got into it puzzled us both."

Laura's cough came in spurts and her ashen face turned pink. Mrs. Turner rose, a look of satisfaction on her face.

"She'll recover," Mrs. Turner said.

"How did you get locked in the pantry?" Jamie asked.

"It's the ghost, I tell you," Mrs. Turner said.

"No," Laura said. "He knew where to find Herbert's whiskey. He gave me a sip before I fell unconscious."

"I'm sure The Maxwell will be happy to learn that his whiskey is safe. Right now, I want to know what happened to you in the pantry." He struggled to keep calm. His anger diminished somewhat when she looked up at him with a warm smile. Her trust humbled him and wore away some of his rage. At the moment, his arms ached to hold her close and keep her safe.

"Someone came into the room." She turned to Mrs. Turner. "I thought Mary, you, or Jamie, had come to help me. I couldn't see in the dim light. I was attacked from behind. I never saw him. He grabbed my hair and held a cloth over my face. I struggled and pulled at his hand. When I lost my footing, I turned over the lantern. That's what started the fire."

Oliver came into the courtyard. "I found this on the floor." He held out a smelly, sooty linen.

Jamie took the rag from him. He brought the cloth to his nose to discern the odor. Rotten eggs. His head snapped back is if someone slapped him.

"This must be what he held over your face. Did the attacker say anything? Did you see anything? His hand? His clothes?"

"No. The room was dim. I caught a glimpse of him when he stood in doorway. The glare behind him made it impossible to see more than a silhouette before he shut and locked the door."

"You're sure the silhouette was a man?"

"Strong hands held me and the shadow wore pants."

"Jamie, the castle gates have been closed for some time. Whoever attacked Lady Laura is still here," Oliver said. "I'll take a group of men and search for the intruder."

"You go ahead. I'll join you when I'm done."

Oliver hurried off.

"Mrs. Turner, take Laura to her room and stay with her." He held up his hand to ward off Laura's argument. "I need to know you're safe while I work with Oliver. Besides, someone should be with you until we're sure the effects of poison are gone."

"I'm fine. Really. I can help you." She rose on wobbly legs. Jamie grabbed her before she fell.

"I'll tell you everything, but I need you to be safe." He held her in his arms. "Go with Mrs. Turner," he said softly.

She grabbed Jamie's sleeve. "Don't let anything happen to you, do you understand?"

His hand caressed her face. Her eyes closed at his touch.

"I can bear anything, but something happening to you," she whispered.

"I will do as you command, lass. I will always do as you command." He kissed the top of her head.

"Come with me," Mrs. Turner said. "I'll get you cleaned up and comfortable. Whiskey helps, but you need rest. You gave me a fright." Mrs. Turner took Laura by the arm.

"I gave me a fright," she mumbled

"Before you leave." Laura and Mrs. Turner stopped. "Did you find anything in the room?" Jamie asked.

"Only this. The intruder tried to take it from me." She opened her hand.

Jamie unwrapped the pin from the rag. He stared at the brooch with the black gem in its center, then handed the jewel to Laura. He thought nothing of the jewel's wrapper at first until he spread open the cloth.

Laura gasped. In the center was a bloody handprint. The little finger on the left hand was crooked.

Chapter Eight

Laura either buried under blankets to get warm or threw them off to cool down. Evan. She needed to get out of bed and help him. She tried to sit up several times only to be encouraged back onto the pillows and falling into another fitful sleep.

Faces loomed before her: the innkeeper's wife's treacherous glare, Mrs. Turner's watchful eye, Bryce's scowl, her Mother's concern, and Sonia's anxious expression. She didn't have strength to speak to them. Instead, she closed her eyes tight and waited for them to leave her alone.

The touch of a cloth cooled her forehead, a trickle of water eased her parched throat, and a soothing baritone spoke to her even though she couldn't make out words. His gentleness calmed her and at last she fell into a restful asleep.

The thud of a falling log in the hearth startled her awake. The fire was the only source of light in the room. Groggy, she took a deep breath, then screwed up her nose at the nauseating odor of rotten eggs.

An unusual misty haze gathered by her door. She lifted onto her elbows and tried to focus. Laura was mesmerized by the moving mist, Evan's ghost slowly took form.

Her heart broke. She had nothing new to tell him. The poor boy was different today, a troubled expression about his eyes screamed urgency.

"I don't know what to do. We've spoken to everyone."

He didn't move. Did he understand? He started to fade.

"Don't go. There must be something more we need. I vow I won't give up until I know who murdered you and Angel." Tired and weak, she collapsed back onto the bed. Breathing hard, she turned toward him.

He shook his head. With a soft smile, he tapped his head with his forefinger.

"Think. What do you suppose we've been doing?" she said through a moan.

He grew larger. Or had he stepped forward? He tapped his head more insistently.

"Think?" She tried to sit up, but couldn't muster the strength. "Are you telling me we don't need any more information? We have all the information we need?"

He nodded, then faded away.

"Wait, I didn't thank you for the whiskey." She closed her eyes. "Thank you."

Her eyes too heavy to stay open, she fell into an exhausted sleep.

Laura opened her eyes and stared at the ceiling. Sunlight filtered in between partially closed curtains. She blinked to focus and struggled to make out wood beams on the coffered ceiling. She concentrated for several more minutes to remove the cobwebs from her head. She stretched, rolled onto her side, and threw her legs over the edge of the bed. Her arms braced behind her, she sat on the edge of the bed. The room spun until she thought she would faint. Deep breaths helped. The spinning slowed and finally stopped. There was no time to put up with this inconvenience. Looking at shadows against the wall, she estimated it was late morning. Only a peek out the window would confirm her suspicion.

With great determination, she rose on wobbly legs. She grabbed onto the bed post for balance. *Work. Damn you.* She reached for the back of a nearby chair. From there, she slid her feet along. She looked from side to side searching for something to grasp. Nothing. If she wanted to reach the window she had to cross the floor without support.

"Straighten your shoulders and take a deep breath," she said. "Yes. Now step toward the window."

The tips of her fingers strained to remain on the back of the chair. Another step. Good. She was steadier.

"Don't get over confident, you're not there yet." She removed her hand and took another step.

Her legs started to wobble. *Don't panic. One foot in front of the other.* She dragged her foot and moved one step farther. She reached out for the wall. She wiggled her fingers as if that would make the wall closer. Almost there. *Again.*

Her legs more steady, she took one more step and reached the wall. She took a breath, pleased with her accomplishment. She peeled back the curtain and leaned her forehead against the cold pane. After a few steadying breaths, she looked out at the activity. Her head cleared. The tremors in her legs eased. People rushed about the bailey. The sky was clear, the sun past its high point. She had slept the morning away.

She made her way to the chair with almost no difficulty. She wrapped a shawl around her shoulders. Fragments of her dream about Evan surfaced. His sense of urgency made her anxious. He must sense time slipping away.

Sitting here was a waste of time. Best she dress and start her day.

"Lady Laura. You're awake." Mrs. Turner came in carrying a basin of fresh water. "Should I call for a bath?"

"No, I'll wash up and dress. Where's Lord Jamie?"

"He's in the solar. He'll be glad you're awake."

She washed while Mrs. Turner took out her clothes.

"We didn't expect you to be out of bed so soon after such a fever and sleeping so long."

"A fever?" She washed and put on her chemise and hose. She was familiar with fevers. Jamie wouldn't be concerned unless the fever was serious.

"Yes, after the effects of the poison was gone." Mrs. Turner helped her on with her dress. She held on to the back of a chair for support and slipped on her shoes.

"How long did I sleep?" Her mind spun trying to grasp what was happening. She waited for Mrs. Turner's answer.

"Three days." Mrs. Turner straightened the back of her skirt.

Laura whipped around. "But—"

"Let me finish." Mrs. Turner spun her around, draped her shoulders with her wool, and kept it in place with a black gem from the table. "There. You're ready. I suspect you're hungry. I'll bring you some fresh chamomile tea and bread with honey. It's in the solar."

"That won't be necessary. I'll join Lord Jamie." She'd wasted three days. Hopefully Jamie had some success.

She made her way from her room into the solar with Mrs. Turner. Jamie was at the table. He raised his head and stood.

"Laura. You appear well this morning." He stood as she entered.

Jamie, on the other hand, didn't look his usual self. Dark patches circled his eyes and he moved a bit slower.

"Did you find Evan and Angel's murderer? Why did you let me sleep so long? Three days." How many days since they left Glen Kirk? She concentrated, forcing her sluggish mind to function. A jolt of realization struck her. "We must find our answer before... midnight tonight."

"First, no, we didn't find your attacker." He counted his fingers as he went through a list. "Second, you obviously needed your rest or you would have woken sooner. Third, I've looked at everyone's hand these last three days and did not find one with a broken finger on the left hand. And fourth, Evan's ghost will wait."

Laura walked to the window. His first three items were upsetting, but she quickly put that those aside. That didn't mean she would give up. The fourth item, Evan's ghost, was another issue. She had no right to be disappointed Jamie could easily put Evan aside. She could not.

Mrs. Turner whispered in her ear. "We kept you awake until the effects of the poison had worn off, but when the fever started, Lord Jamie stayed by your side. He wouldn't let anyone near you, not even me."

Mrs. Turner poured her a cup of tea, then left the room.

He gave nothing away in his stance or expression. He handed Laura her cup.

"We interviewed everyone. No one gave us any

information that could help find your attacker. The castle gate closed after we found you. Your attacker no doubt fled to the village."

"I wouldn't let anyone near you. You were too vulnerable. The only way I could keep you safe was to stay with you myself. Oliver made sure there was no mention of an attack, only that there was a fire and you tried to dowse it. Many already blame the ghost. The last thing we need is a rumor the ghost is attacking people. It would start an uproar and put Evan's family in the middle." He ran his hand through his hair. "We need to resolve this before Herbert returns. Once he's back, he'll be in danger, too."

She stirred her tea, stepped to the window and peered out. Her spoon clattered onto the saucer.

"The tinker." She spun toward him. "He's returned. Did you speak to him?" She sipped the warm liquid. She breathed in the earthy, daisy-like fragrance of the tea. A sip of the sweet flowery liquid soothed her throat and warmed her.

"I had other things on my mind." Jamie shook his head and stared at her with guilty eyes. "I never should have left you alone. What would I tell Darla and Wesley?"

Is that what drove him to protect her? Was she nothing more than an obligation? She had hoped... She swallowed around a knot in her throat and pushed the thought down.

"It was as much my fault," she said. A wave of nausea hit her. Not from the poison. That was long gone. One deep breath, then another calmed her stomach as much as her thoughts. Childish dreams of Jamie flew away and left her empty. "If we spend time placing blame, we'll never move forward."

She put the tea on a nearby table and headed toward the door.

"Where are you going?"

"We've no more time. I'll speak to Holger." She turned too fast and stumbled. Jamie rushed to her side and caught her.

"Are you sure you're recovered?"

Laura pushed away from him.

She needed to be as far away from him or she'd look like a fool. Stretching to straighten her back, she brushed imaginary wrinkles out of her skirt.

"Yes. I'll be fine. When you report to my family, you can report I'm quite well." Laura gathered her pride, glad she hadn't made a fool of herself and turned to make a quick escape.

His arm shot out in front of her, braced against the window jamb and barring her way. She struggled to fill her lungs with air and tried to object. His closeness, so close she could see the vein pulse in his temple, unnerved her. She made the mistake of looking up. Her breath caught. She stared into his eyes, dark green and filled with passion.

"I'm not concerned about your family. I'm concerned about you. Have you any idea how I worried? I thought I lost you. I won't let that happen again."

His nearness made her senses spin. She closed her eyes and savored his words. She was back riding tandem with him racing away from the reiver. The fright and exhilaration when they flew over the hedgerow surged through her, but this time, the sensation nestled warm between her legs.

Jamie bent close. She didn't move. She didn't breathe. She didn't want to.

He covered her mouth with his and captured her lips in a passionate possession. Heat swept away any remnants of doubt. Her only thought, to be in his arms.

Her heart thumped wildly and echoed in her head.

His kiss was surprisingly gentle. His hands slid up her arms, then brought her closer. She arched against him. The feel of his hard body against her made her step closer until she didn't know where she stopped and he began. Strong arms tightened around her. Lost in his kiss, her heart raced faster.

Laura wound her arms inside his jerkin and around his back. Her fingertips ran along his muscles. He drew her closer, deepened his kiss. She was on fire. A building frenzy excited and alarmed her. She pushed against him, but he wouldn't release her. He held her fast. The fire built until she flew apart.

He released her lips and held her close, cradling her head on his chest. His heart pounded as hard as hers. For long minutes, he stroked her hair as she regained her composure. How often she'd dreamt of his touch, his kiss. His kiss, his arms were better than she imagined.

"We must find Evan and Angel's murderer," she said and moved closer and molded into his side.

"Yes, Evan and Angel. Are you sure you've recovered?" His chest rumbled. Jamie smoothed back her hair, then tipped up her chin and kissed her nose.

His soft kisses didn't hide the worry on his face. How had she not seen his tenderness before? "I've never felt better."

"Me neither. I've wanted to kiss you for some time."

She closed her eyes and reveled in his words. "Mrs. Turner said you stayed with me."

"I wouldn't let anyone near you. I watched you battle nightmares and was helpless. All I could do was keep you comfortable. We need to discuss—"

"Yes, but not now. Evan has so little time," she said.

"We'll do this together. No more going off on

your own. I may have doubts about ghosts, but not about a very real murderer. We need to sort this out before Herbert returns tomorrow. Someone has to speak to Holger. Now."

Reluctantly, she stepped out of his arms.

He took her elbow and directed her down the stairs.

"While I slept, I dreamt of Evan's ghost. He indicated we don't need any more information. We must find the right way to put the pieces together. What have we overlooked?" She stopped mid-way down the stairs.

"Why don't I like that smile?"

She stared up at him. "What smile?" She forced her smile to be more dazzling.

"The one on your face that tells me I'm not going to like what you're thinking."

"I trust you more than anyone." The action they needed to take was clear to her. Jamie would be her biggest obstacle.

"Yes, but I still don't like the look in your eye." His brow wrinkled. She continued down the stairs.

"We have what the murderer wants." She touched the black pin on her shawl. "All I need to do is have him see it."

"Oh, no. You're not going to be bait." He came to a halt at the bottom, and pulled her around to face him.

Determination locked his features. She had to make him listen, then she could concentrate on persuading him. "Herbert returns tomorrow, there is no other way."

"He tried to kill you. No, we can leave the pin in the pantry and wait for him to come for it."

"That's a good plan if we had a lot of time, but we don't."

"I'll wear the pin." He held out his hand. She took

a step back and placed her hand over the gem. Was he daft?

"You wear it? You're as big as a tree. He won't steal it from you. He'll wait and kill you."

"We may need to uncover a murderer, but I'll not allow you to be in danger. You've taken too many risks already. We'll let people know that an item has been found and is locked in Herbert's desk. I'll station myself nearby and wait. You and I will find the murdering bastard. I promise."

"But—"

"Don't look so miserable. Your attacker knows you have the gem. I'm sure Mrs. Turner will accommodate us and pass along that an item found in the pantry is now in Lord Herbert's desk. This will keep you out of danger and serves our purpose. While you dine tonight, I'll keep watch." He held out his hand.

"What?" She knew what he wanted.

"The pin." Reluctantly, she took it off and handed it to him.

"Come, I'll take you for a walk through the market."

She wouldn't get much farther with him. Mrs. Turner, while not a gossip, would know whose ear needed to be bent. But she wanted to be involved, not a bystander.

"I agree, but only if I can search for the person with the crooked left pinkie and we still need to speak to Holger."

"Yes, we'll speak to Holger and while we go through the market, look for the person with the crooked finger."

She grinned, quite satisfied. He took her hand and moved on with their little conspiracy.

Jamie stopped long enough to give Mrs. Turner her instructions.

"I'm glad I can help. Before you're halfway through the market, people will know about the brooch," Mrs. Turner said. Jamie and Laura were about to leave.

"Mrs. Turner." The housekeeper gave Laura her attention. "You knew Evan well. Do you know if he had any broken fingers?"

"No, he didn't have any broken fingers or other bones."

The early afternoon weather was crisp. She pulled her wool tightly around her. Relieved the handprint wasn't Evan's, the problem remained. Whose was it?

There was a subtle difference in her relationship with Jamie, a combination of excitement and adventure. She didn't want to talk about their kiss. Not because of Evan, although that was a good reason, but rather she wanted the magic to linger. Was his kiss an impulse because she had been ill? Right now, why he kissed her didn't matter.

"Lord Jamie, can I help you?" the tinker asked.

"Holger, I'm making inquiries into the deaths of Evan and Angel." Jamie glanced at the man's hands. No crooked little finger on either one.

Holger pulled his cap off and averted his eyes.

"Bad thing that was. And I thought they were such a loving couple." The man's unconvincing sing-song voice struck her as insincere. Laura touched her beads. Cold as the biting breeze.

"Tell me what happened."

"What happened?" The tinker turned toward Laura and nodded.

The hair on her arms stood and she struggled not to shiver. Jamie must have sensed her discomfort. He stepped in front of her, blocking Holger's view. She took the opportunity to examine the wares on the wagon and still hear Holger answer Jamie's questions.

"Thomas said you were in the pantry when he entered with Brian and Jermyn."

Holger stiffened.

"Yes. It was awful. I went to put a barrel of salt into the pantry. I heard Evan and Angel arguing something fierce. She wasn't any angel with the words she tossed about. I didn't want to interrupt them and decided to go back when they were gone. When I returned with Mary, they were both dead."

"What did they argue about?" Laura, holding a pot of fragrant spices, leaned closer to hear.

"They may have had a lover's spat. All I heard was noise. She probably accused him of being unfaithful and he denied everything, of course. What else would a woman argue about? I'm sorry I can't give you more information." His words sounded unconvincing. Her beads confirmed his words a lie.

"If you remember anything else, make sure you tell me." Holger nodded and Jamie stepped over to Laura.

"You didn't want to question him about the argument? With all we know about Evan and Angel, you don't really think they had a lover's spat?" Laura asked.

"Not at all. He's just a man with his prejudices, making assumptions."

"I overheard several people mention something was found. Mrs. Turner was right. The news is spreading quickly," Laura said.

"Did you think our murderer would hold up his hand and say the pin belongs to me? No," he said and snorted.

"We found out that Evan didn't have any broken fingers. I was sure the handprint on the rag was his. Someone must have seen or heard something."

"If you're well enough, I thought we'd walk

through the market. Afterward, I'll take you into the hall, then lock the pin in Herbert's desk as planned. Hopefully, before supper is over, we'll capture the murderer, have his full confession and you'll be able to put Evan to rest."

Any place he wanted to go was fine with her.

Chapter Nine

Laura sat at the high table while Jamie hid in Herbert's solar waiting for the murderer. The plan sounded good at the time, now she wasn't sure.

She pushed her uneaten baked salmon, the second course of the evening meal around her trencher. Her stomach was tied in knots. She had no patience to hold a conversation and avoided everyone.

Laura glanced out the window across the courtyard. Nothing and she didn't know if that pleased or disappointed her.

Unable to sit still, she fidgeted like a restless child. A quick look around the hall and she found Sonia in the shadows. The girl put a lot of faith in her to help Evan. She bit her lip hard. What was she going to tell Sonia at midnight? What would she tell Evan? The holes in their plan were evident now. What if the murderer didn't come for the pin? What if Evan was the murderer? Laura couldn't concede to failure. Not yet.

Laura pushed her plate away. She had picked the salmon apart until it looked like a battle area. Restless, she drummed a dirge on the table. The Maxwell cousin next to her placed her hand over hers to silence her fingers.

"Forgive me, Cousin. I'm a bit distracted this eve." Laura put her hands into her lap and twisted her linen handkerchief.

What had she and Jamie overlooked? Evan was adamant no more information was needed. She went over every piece of information again and again without any answer.

"Lady Laura, you seem anxious this evening." Her Maxwell cousin gave her a scathing stare. Laura followed her stare. Her rebellious fingers once again tapped.

Laura returned her hand to her lap and glanced toward the window, again.

"Mrs. Turner, is there any more ale?" her cousin asked, holding an empty pitcher.

Mrs. Turner was behind her struggling to keep hold of a platter of meat.

"I'll fill the ale pitcher," The housekeeper had enough to do, besides she had a hard time sitting still.

"No, you needn't go. I'll send one of the girls," said Mrs. Turner.

"You and your staff have enough to contend with this evening." Laura was halfway to the kitchen corridor.

"Bring the pitcher to the kitchen. They'll know what to do." Mrs. Turner gave her a wide smile. "Take care on your way. Crates are stacked in the hallway. The passage is narrow."

Laura took the pitcher and hurried out of the room. She sidestepped around servants rushing out with hot food and others returning with empty platters. The passageway was choked with people and crates. She navigated the narrow path that passed the stairs to the well and reached the kitchen.

"More ale is needed," she said as someone took the pitcher without a word. No time for pleasantries.

The kitchen was controlled chaos. One cook carved a roast, while another rushed to remove fowl from a spit. Seasoned vegetables were moved to a serving platter. A cauldron hung in the fireplace, bubbling with an aromatic stew. She breathed in the aromas, but nothing enticed her appetite.

Out of the noise and bustling servants, a baby toddled toward the stairs in tears. Laura moved fast to bar the child's way.

"Where are you going?" Laura spoke softly, trying to calm the child. "The steps are not safe."

Laura picked up the little girl. Drool ran down her chin, and she quieted. Pudgy baby fingers touched the shiny gems of Laura's necklace.

"She's cutting teeth and is a bit out of sorts," a woman said, handing a platter of vegetables to another servant and hurried to Laura.

"Not to worry," Laura said to the anxious mother.

"See, Mummy's here." The baby unexpectedly dove toward her mother without letting go of Laura's necklace. The woman tried to pry the child's hand loose, but with a final tug snapped the delicate chain.

The baby pointed to the beads and laughed as they slid down Laura's bodice and bounced on the floor.

Laura scrambled to keep the beads from falling. Only able to catch two, she put them in her pocket, then listened in horror as the remaining six scattered across the floor.

Consequences. Lose a bead, lose something precious, Lisbeth warned. She pushed aside the warning. Frozen in place, a cold chill ran up her back. Jamie was most precious to her.

Lose him. How? His love? His life? Now wasn't the time to panic. She took a steadying breath.

Recapture the six remaining beads and all will be well.

"Don't move." She held her arms out and brought activity to a halt. "I must find six beads."

A squire came rushing into the hall. "Stay back." Her shout stopped the poor boy where he stood.

"Here, m'lady." A servant handed her a purple bead.

"I found another, here by the wall." Another gave her a bead. Two. She found a third close by. She tucked those into her pocket. That left three still missing. She searched the floor.

"Here, m'lady. Maybe this will make the bead sparkle." One of the girls gave her a candle.

She methodically went over the floor. Her skirt swished as she turned near the top of the steps.

"Careful, m'lady," the woman holding the child shouted.

But her warning came too late. Pinging echoed down the steps as one-by-one three beads cascaded to the bottom.

"I'll bring them to you," the baby's mother said. "I need to bring up a pitcher of water."

"No. You can't go down with the baby. I'll bring you the water." She raised the candle and started down the narrow spiral staircase.

"Be careful, m'lady. Take care, the steps are not all the same height and are difficult. Stay close to the inner wall. The footing is best there." The baby let out a cry, punctuating her mother's concern.

Light from the main level diminished and the shadows deepened the farther she descended into the lower level of Caerlaverock. The small circle of light from the candle pushed against the darkness and lit her way.

Deep in solid rock, the dampness of the lower level along with the chill created a slick icy film on the stones steps. Laura hugged the wall, and, with care, picked her way down. She had gone down a dozen or more steps, and tried to see what was below. Nothing. The inky blackness yawned before her and brought her to a halt. She peered behind her and made out a dim flicker of light.

Consequences. She should have been satisfied with staying with her Maxwell cousin. A deep breath and she went on. She stepped onto the next stair and her foot slid out from under her. Laura reached out and grasped at the edges of the stone wall, searching for anything to cling to.

She found her footing. A tumble down these steps would be fatal. She said a small prayer of thanks. Stay to the inside. She moved tentatively and continued down until she came to the bottom.

Laura raised her candle high. An unlit torch was in a bracket next to the well room door to her left. She touched her lit candle to the torch which sizzled, then flared to life. Relieved with more light, she searched the floor. A purple agate bead twinkled in front of her. Encouraged, she picked it up. Six.

The other two beads couldn't be far. The well room door was ajar, held in place by a crate. At the far end a passageway went deeper under the castle to the dungeons and storage rooms.

She searched every inch of the floor, but found nothing. The beads had to be there. She straightened up and glanced toward the upper floor. Or had only one bead fallen down the stairs? Tired and frustrated, she leaned against the crate. It moved a few inches, pushing back the heavy well-room door. Startled, she looked down. Half-way underneath the door, the seventh bead gleamed.

Laura searched across the room to the passageway and realized she was at the lower end of the room. The bead couldn't roll in that direction. She turned to the well room. Perhaps the bead bounced its way inside.

Holding the candle in front of her, she entered the small room. The well, level with the floor, was in the middle of the room covered with a wooden board. That was a relief.

Rows of buckets and pitchers lined the wall. Ropes curled neatly on the floor. One full pitcher waited to be brought to the kitchen.

A glint of light caught her eye. The last bead had rolled next to the well. She set down the candle, picked up the bead, then took the others out of her pocket and counted. Satisfied she had all she returned them to her pocket. Eager to return upstairs, she picked up the heavy pitcher, splashing water down the skirt of her gown.

A chill crossed her shoulders, and she froze. Someone's eyes were on her.

"Jamie? I was just getting some water."

"Lady Laura. Are you here alone?"

"Holger, is that you?"

Get out, a warning voice echoed in her head. The urgency to leave grew stronger. A sheer black fright swept through her. She bolted for the door, not bothering with the candle.

He blocked most of the doorway. She took a breath to control her pounding heart and squeezed past him.

The heavy pitcher began to slip out of her hands. Holger caught the water jar, but not before water spilled and doused his shirt, plastering it to his chest. The torch flared, and an outline of a leather pouch exposing a raised engraving of an angel.

Holger glanced at his shirt. Slowly, he lifted his head, his face set with a wicked grin.

Laura pushed past him. "*Get out, get out, get out,*" the voice shouted in her head. The pitcher smashed to the floor. She rushed through the puddle tugging at her heavy wet skirt. Between icy steps and her skirt twisted at her feet, she struggled with her footing as she hurried up the first few steps.

The tinker grabbed her arm. He dragged her down and swung her around to face him.

"Give me what's mine."

"I don't know what you're talking about. I don't have anything of yours." She pulled her arm away and stepped closer. With all her heart, she prayed challenging him, as she did with Bryce's men would work with Holger.

Holger held his ground.

"How dare you touch me?" Her scream bounced off the stone walls. She doubted anyone would hear her. Perhaps, if she was gone too long, Mrs. Turner would send someone after her. If the woman realized she was gone.

"My brooch. And don't say you don't know what I'm talking about. Everyone knows you and Lord Jamie have it." He pushed his face close to hers. "The brooch is mine."

"Your brooch?" she said with an edge of disbelief. "How do you have a jewel like mine?"

For a moment doubt clouded his eyes. Was it possible she had succeeded? Did he believe she had the brooch twin?

"A barter. Your life for your pin." Her ploy didn't work.

"Jamie. Now. Laura." A voice reached inside his hiding place and echoed in Jamie's head. *"By the well,"* the deep male tone insisted.

Jamie stepped out of his hiding place, physically shaken. Laura? Forgetting his mission, he ran through the courtyard into the crowded kitchen passageway to the stairs.

Danger. The air snapped with it, radiated from the depths of the castle. He treaded down the stairs, listening for any hint of what he had to face. Halfway to the bottom, voices filtered up. He stopped.

"How do you have a jewel like mine?" Laura. There was indignation and command in her tone. The same tone she used when they encountered Bryce's men. His anxiety level lowered, but only a notch.

"A barter. Your life for your pin." Jamie straightened to his full height. Holger?

"My life? Do you think you will live if you harm me?"

"They'll all think the ghost is the murderer." He let out a snickering laugh. "You have no idea the jewel's value, especially to certain people. Much more than your life."

Jamie pressed his back against the stairway wall, tormented by the sound of a scuffle. He inched down the steps until he came upon the last turn. He stood still so as to not give away his position. With care he peered around the last bend.

His instincts said go forward, but if he acted now, Laura could be hurt and the element of surprise would be lost. He peeked around the curve.

Holger held Laura around the waist, arms pinned to her side, a candle in his other hand. He dragged her down the dark passageway toward the dungeon.

Jamie fisted his hands as his breath came in ragged bursts of powerless anger.

"Wait," the voice in his head ordered.

He came down the last steps as feet shuffled in the distance and candlelight faded. He stayed in the shadows and followed.

Holger nudged open the door to the storage room

and dragged Laura inside. Jamie followed. Crates and barrels haphazardly stacked filled the area.

The tinker put the candle on a barrel. "I want your pin."

Laura said nothing.

Holger raised the back of his hand, but hesitated. Instead, he threw Laura to the ground. "One way or another, you'll give me the pin."

Jamie stepped out of hiding. His fist cocked and ready, he grabbed Holger by the shoulder and swung him around.

Holger's eyes widened in surprise.

"Now," the voice whispered in Jamie's ear.

Jamie threw his full weight behind his punch. Holger's head sprang back. His body followed and collapsed in heap on the floor.

Jamie stood over the man. "On your feet." He could stand anything, but nobody touched Laura. He nearly killed Bryce all those years ago when he threatened to harm her.

Jamie lifted Holger off the floor, and pulled his arm back, ready to hit him again.

"Jamie." Another voice reached through the rumble of noise in his head. "I'm all right."

Jamie's heart hammered, his breathing ragged.

"He didn't hurt me," Laura said.

Jamie threw Holger against the wall. He saw the outline of the leather pouch around his neck.

Jamie pulled his shoulders back and stepped closer. He loomed over Holger. Jamie was large and used every device at his fingertips to intimidate Holger. He didn't raise his voice. He stared at Holger. The vile scent of fear leaked into the room, Jamie could almost taste it.

"Where did you get this?" Jamie poked at the leather pouch.

"The pin is mine." Holger's chin tipped up, defiant, but his eyes betrayed his fear.

"Another item you bartered for?" Laura asked.

Something in Laura's tone made Jamie pull up. Her determined look and quick, precise movement of her fingers startled him. She tied imaginary knots in the air. Did she think her games would work?

"Yes." Holger sneered at Laura.

Jamie's head snapped back to Holger. "When?" He grabbed the man's jaw with his thumb and forefinger and yanked it so all Holger could see was his face. "When did you barter? Angel wore the pouch when she went into the pantry."

Even in the dim candle light, the tinker's face paled. His eyes darted everywhere but at Jamie.

"When?" Jamie demanded, pinching the man's face in a vise-like grip.

"I was outside the pantry. Those two were yelling at each other. Something about not wanting to marry. She would have none of that. He told her to be quiet. She kept screaming. I walked away. Thought I would come back later. I got back to the pantry as Mary ran out. So I went in. That's when I saw her with the linen over her face. He was on the floor with a knife in his chest. The pouch was no good to either of them, so I took it."

The strings of the pouch around Holger's throat tightened. Jamie glanced at Laura, her face intense and determined. He had never witnessed such an expression before. Her fingers worked faster. Was it possible? He thought the movement only childhood games she played with Lisbeth. He brought his attention back to Holger. The man clawed at his neck.

"The truth," Laura whispered. "You took the pouch, but Angel fought for it."

Jamie pulled off Holger's shirt. Scars of deep scratches were on his chest and neck.

Holger pulled at his throat.

"Make her stop," he begged.

"The truth," Laura said. Holger looked from one to the other.

"The truth," Jamie said.

"Evan left the pantry, straightening his clothes, so I went in to see his tidbit. I found the girl alone. I thought to have some fun. After all, he just had his." Holger stopped.

Laura's fingers kept working. Holger's face turned red.

"I grabbed her from behind and put my hand over her mouth. She fought me. I pushed her to the floor. She kicked and scratched. I reached under her skirt, She found my dirk and pulled it out.

"I got the dirk from her. She started to scream. I held one of the sacks over her face and I told her to stop screaming. When she stopped I took the sack off. She didn't move. I tried to wake her. That's when Evan walked in. He went mad."

Jamie knew how Evan felt all too well.

"Evan didn't know how to fight. I broke his finger, but he kept coming at me. I couldn't let him win. He'd tell the others. Evan had to die. I killed him.

"There was blood everywhere. Evan grabbed at me, his bloody hands all over my shirt. He held on tight. I stabbed the girl to make it look like Evan killed her. That's when I heard someone coming. I pulled off my shirt forgetting the jewel was attached. I hid behind a row of crates and stuffed my shirt beside some crates. I pretended I followed Mary in."

"You didn't try to retrieve the pin?" Laura asked.

"I didn't know it was missing until I left the castle. By the time I went back, the pantry was locked."

"And the poison?" Jamie asked.

Holger didn't answer.

Laura's fingers worked another knot.

"The innkeeper at Cannonbie paid me to poison

the grain and light fires. Make it look like The Maxwell did it, he told me."

A soft gasp escaped Laura.

Jamie nodded to Laura. She flicked her fingers and the invisible string around Holger's neck loosened. She picked up the candle, and Jamie shoved Holger out of the room. "Sir Herbert will deal with you."

Holger pushed Jamie into Laura and swung the door shut. The candle went out, sending the room into darkness. The slap of leather against stone echoed through the room as Holger ran through the passage.

"Laura," Jamie called, scrambling to his feet.

"Go after him. I'm not hurt."

Jamie shouldered the door, and ran toward the stairs. Laura followed close behind. Halfway to the stairs, the quiet was broken with a terrifying shriek that echoed down the stairs.

Jamie pulled Laura into his arms.

"Holger?" she asked. Jamie held her close and stared at the staircase.

The muffled sound of something tumbling down the steps grew louder until finally, the tinker's body landed at their feet. His neck was broken. He stared at them, his face a frozen mask of fear.

Justice. The word echoed in Jamie's head, not only for Evan and Angel, but for The Maxwell, the clan, and Laura. It was a just end for the murdering traitor. He felt no remorse, just relief.

Laura strained to see Holger.

"You needn't look," Jamie said.

"Evan and Angel's deaths were senseless. They had everything to live for. If Holger hadn't fallen down the stairs I would have happily pushed him," Laura said.

He led her past Holger to the steps.

"I'll stay here. Tell Oliver to bring some men. Then, go to Herbert's desk and take the pin. Holger was adamant about its value." He pulled the pouch off Holger's neck. "Perhaps your ghost is looking for this. We'll give the pouch back to its rightful owner."

Laura smiled at his conclusion then rushed up the stairs.

Oliver jumped out of his chair and sent it flying behind him. "What is it, m'lady?"

"Quick, bring some men to the well. Jamie needs you."

Oliver left with several of his men. She rushed to Herbert's desk to retrieve the pin.

"Lady Laura. You're safe," Sonia said outside Herbert's room, her relief evident. "I was afraid he wouldn't reach you in time."

"You sent Jamie. How did you know?"

"I had some help when I noticed the tinker go down the stairs."

"You were right. Evan didn't kill Angel. Holger killed them both." Laura opened Herbert's desk and retrieved the pin. "We even found..." She spun to tell Sonia about Angel's pouch, but she was gone.

Laura hurried into the great hall. Jamie and the men brought in Holger's body.

"Here's your murderer." Jamie dropped Holger's body on the floor. "He thought to lift Angel's skirt, but Evan walked in. He was valiant to the end trying to protect her."

He held up Angel's leather pouch. "I found this around Holger's neck."

"Maybe that will satisfy Evan's ghost," someone from the crowd shouted.

"Give the pouch to me," Angel's father said. "I'll take care of my girl. As for him," he said and nudged Holger with his foot, "he can rot."

"He will," Oliver said. He pointed to his men.

"Take him to the battlements."

The men took Holger by his legs and pulled him out of the great hall.

Jamie and Laura walked with the families to the graveyard gate.

"That's..." Jamie stopped dumbstruck, looking at a woman kneeling by a grave outside the cemetery wall.

"Sonia. She's the woman who told me we had everything wrong. Whose grave is she sitting by and why is the grave outside the wall?"

"She's been helping you? Interesting. She's at Evan's resting place. They wouldn't bury him inside the graveyard." He stopped and inhaled.

"What is it?" She faced him, drawing her brows together in concern.

"Sonia is the woman's given name. Her father called her his angel," Jamie said.

"I had no idea she was... You didn't recognize her?"

"I haven't seen her for four weeks." His tone was filled with awe and respect. He turned to her.

Laura was too startled by his words to say anything. Then, another piece fell into place. "Gather the others. I think I know what has to be done."

In the mist, before midnight, they reburied Evan next to his Angel. Words of praise were spoken of his honor and sacrifice. Lewis, Angel's father, buried the small pouch with her.

"In my heart of hearts, I knew he would never hurt our Angel. These last four weeks, she's come to me at night to tell me I was wrong. She never lied to me. Let's leave them both in peace." Lewis put his arm around Celia and led the way back to the castle.

Jamie and Laura stood at the graves. "Your magic is powerful. I'll never doubt you again. I'm glad we found the true murderer, but why did you go down to the dungeon?"

"I couldn't sit and wait any longer. I needed to do something. I thought to help Mrs. Turner." She put her hand into her pocket and felt each of the eight beads.

"My beads tumbled down the stairs. I couldn't lose them."

The mist behind the gravestones swirled. When it settled, Angel and Evan were behind the markers.

"Thank you," Evan said, his left arm around Angel, his little finger clearly crooked.

"I couldn't see or speak to Evan." Angel gazed at Evan. "I never would as long as he stayed outside the graveyard. I couldn't bear being separated from him."

"Hush, love." He put his finger to her lips. "I knew Lord Jamie—"

"And Lady Laura," Angel said.

"And Lady Laura would make it right." He faced Laura and Jamie. "My Angel did her part. She watched over Lady Laura."

"That's enough. Tell them," Angel said with an urgent nod toward Jamie and Laura.

"Give me a chance." Evan broke into a knowing smile. "I have a message. Richard loves you both almost as much as you love each other. He gives you his blessing."

Tears trailed down Laura's cheek. "Thank you," she whispered. She had never seen Jamie stand so still. His chin quivered, he couldn't speak. He didn't have to.

Jamie turned to Laura. Her eager affection reflected in the passion in her eyes. She stepped willingly into his arms as if it was something she did every day.

He closed his eyes. She was his, at last. He kissed the top of her head.

"That's the greatest gift you could give us," Jamie said to Evan.

"There is one more thing before we go, Lord Jamie. Treachery still lurks. The pin, keep it safe. Follow its ownership. Let no one take it from you."

"I understand," Jamie said with pulse-pounding certainty.

"Come, Angel. It's almost midnight." Evan took Angel's hand, and, without a backward glance, walked into the night.

Jamie and Laura returned to the castle.

"I've changed my mind," Jamie said as they entered the courtyard. He turned to face her and stared into her eyes. "It is magic."

Chapter Ten

"Fire?" Jamie stood on Caerlaverock's battlement. He flared his nostrils wide to sniff the air. The acrid odor of burning wood alerted him. Where was the fire? From his vantage point, high on the wall, he sought out the kitchen area, most likely place for a fire. Nothing. He directed his attention toward the blacksmith. Small tendrils of smoke rose from both hearths. He leaned over the wall and concentrated on the forest. The animals would rouse if there was a fire. All was quiet.

"You smell smoke, too." Oliver came up next to him. They both scanned the horizon.

"There." Jamie pointed east. A plume of smoke spiraled over the trees and smudged an otherwise clear sky.

"Fire! The village. Mount up. Raise the portcullis," Oliver bellowed to his men below. His alert quickly spread through the castle.

Jamie and Oliver raced from the battlement.

Jamie was aware fires were not uncommon. They ate wood houses with a voracious appetite and in their wake they left death and destruction. He had walked through many charred remains of villages and observed people scouring debris for anything that could be salvaged.

"I'll get the men to the village," Jamie said. "You bring the women and wagons." Oliver nodded and rushed to the castle kitchen where the women had already started to pack wagons with supplies to help the victims.

The bailey was a tangle of activity, horses being saddled, wagons loading, and soldiers mounting up.

Jamie took reins from a stable boy and swung into his saddle. His horse sprang ahead and raced over the bridge, Sean at his side. Oliver fell in behind him. Stragglers would catch up.

Jamie rode hard and kept going past the first buildings. Men with leather buckets broke away from the column and rushed to the well to join the human chain that passed water buckets along from the trough to the fire.

Jamie and others raced on. He could see flames leaping above the tree tops. He took a deep breath and the odor of burnt grain confirmed his fear. The granary.

Determination hid his anger. Yesterday Holger confessed to setting the fires. Unless his ghost set this one, someone had taken up his cause.

Jamie rode through the village. The grain supplies were already low. How much more strain could the people take?

Controlled confusion ran rampant in the village. He rode past a tide of people with anything that could hold water rushing to help. Others carried small children and belongings away from the inferno.

Jamie and the men wove their way through the maze of lanes, dodging people and riding around carts. The smoke wafted toward them. The granary wasn't much further now. He came to the last turn and burst into the granary yard and dismounted before his horses came to a halt.

The smoke and heat were oppressive. He squinted to see the condition of the building. A portion of the granary roof was in flames. Black smoke belched out the door, covering the granary yard in a gray haze.

The yard, choked with people, became the center of activity with everyone either pulling sacks of grain out of the building and stacking them at the blacksmith or loading grain onto waiting wagons.

"Take the horses out of here," Jamie said. Two village boys grabbed reins and pulled horses away.

"I'll have my men relieve the villagers and get on the bucket line," Oliver said. "The blacksmith organized the older children. He had them create their own line to pass the empty pails down the line to be refilled."

Wagons from the castle rumbled into the yard. Sean steered them to the side. Laura and the other women unloaded supplies and began treating those who needed help.

All around them, a frantic pace prevailed.

A man staggered from the building and grabbed on the door frame. "A beam. Came down. Someone is pinned."

Laura reached the man a few steps behind Jamie and grabbed him under his right arm. Jamie took the man's left side. Propped between them they walked him away from the building.

"There's—"

"Don't try to talk," Laura said.

"I couldn't see who was under the beam." Jamie could hardly hear the man, he spoke in a whisper. Stumbling, Jamie and Laura helped him to the ground.

"You're in good hands with Lady Laura." Jamie faced her. Every bone in his body said Laura was in mortal danger in the middle of this chaos.

"You go on. I'll be fine." She searched her sleeve and handed him a square of linen. A spout of coughing drew her attention back to the injured man.

"My boy. Have you seen my boy?" A woman pulled Jamie's sleeve. "I told them he was too new to guard the granary. I can't find him anywhere." Her words tore at his heart.

"What's your son's name?" A burst of relief lit the woman's face.

"Ned."

"Go help Lady Laura, Mother. I'll bring your Ned to you." He gave her a warm smile. If Ned was inside, there was no telling his condition. The woman's watering eyes were filled with trust. Jamie would bring Ned to her. He hoped the reunion would be joyful. The woman hurried off to Laura.

He put Laura's cloth around his mouth and hurried into the building.

The dim light from the open door didn't penetrate the dense smoke. He let his eyes adjust.

Burnt fragments of grain, thick smoke, and another odor filled the air.

"Ned," he called out, stifling a cough. No response. The only sounds were the snapping flames overhead, pounding of water thrown against the walls, and the resulting hiss of steam.

"Ned," he yelled louder.

He turned to the left and stepped toward a ladder that led to the upper level. He hesitated a heartbeat, not sure why.

"Here," a gravelly voice filled with pain followed by a coughing spasm said. "By the wall."

Jamie moved toward the wall amid ropes, slats of unfinished wood for storage barrels, and empty sacks. More fuel for the fire.

In a few steps, he was in front of a pile of smoldering wood that had once been part of the storage platform. Held up by four beams, two beams were down. It was only a matter of time before the rest of the storage platform came down.

Jamie was sure the voice came from here. He pulled the wood off piece-by-piece until a hand reached out to him. "Ned?"

"Yes," the man said.

"Your mother sent me to find you. She told me to tell you to come home now or you'll get no dinner." A strained chuckle followed by coughing relieved Jamie, but only for a moment. The rest of the storage platform above them creaked.

Ned pushed Jamie's outstretched hand away.

"Go, before everything falls on your head. My leg is pinned. I can't move."

"Don't give up now." Jamie rushed a few steps away and picked up two slats and rope. Hefting the rope in his hand, he threw it down. That wouldn't work. The rope was too thick.

The wood above creaked again. Jamie squeezed under what was left of the platform and supported it with his back.

"You'll have to do this yourself," Jamie said, straining to keep the platform from falling. "Put these slats on either side of your leg. Take off your belt. Bind the slats on tight with your belt."

He had no idea how much pain Ned was in, but the man didn't argue or complain.

"Done," Ned said.

"Give me your hand." Jamie said and grabbed Ned's forearms.

"We must move fast. On the count of three." Ned's grip tightened.

"One... Two... Three." Jamie strained and pulled Ned out. Wood erupted all around them. Ned stood on wobbly legs next to him.

"Go. Toward the door," Jamie commanded.

Ned staggered forward and disappeared into the smoke and dust.

The loud snap of wood and splatter of sparks and cinders were the only warning he had. In a deluge of fire and pieces of the roof showered down, striking the platform.

Jamie grabbed the edges of the wood on his back. A loud snap roared through the building. He heaved the wood off and dashed toward the door. Wood came down in a crash and cloud of debris.

Jamie rushed and caught Ned under his arm. They walked out of the granary as if propelled by a cloud of smoke.

"I never thought I'd get out of there," Ned said and turned to Jamie. "Or eat my mother's cooking."

"What happened?" Jamie looked at the boy. Ned was on the cusp of becoming a man, tall with thickening muscles most likely from farm work. Jamie had seen grown men give up in grave situations. Not Ned.

"I guarded the granary as I was told. I was tired. I'm not used to standing idle for so long. I walked around the building to keep awake."

"Where was the other guard?" They reached the edge of the yard. Jamie helped him to the ground.

"Other guard? I was the only one."

Jamie struggled not to react. "Go on."

"I got back to the front of the building. The hair on the back of my neck went up. I went inside. I thought an animal got inside. I checked under the platform and the next thing I knew everything came down on me."

"Ned." They both turned at his mother's shout. She ran to her son and threw her arms around him. The woman raised her face to Jamie. "I don't know what I would have done if..."

"He won't be on guard duty for a while." He knelt

next to the pair. Ned was smart, asked questions and took his job seriously, all good traits for a farmer and a warrior. "Ned, when you can't sit still any longer, find me at the castle."

"Many thanks, Lord Jamie. I—"

"Take care of your leg and enjoy your dinner," Jamie said. He rose and surveyed the building.

He needed to inspect the damage and find the cause. He doubted the fire started naturally. One of the villagers came up to him. The man was broad shouldered. His muscular arms were bare, smudged with ash.

"The fire is almost out. The building is too hot to go inside." Under the man's beard, Ned's likeness shone through. "You have my gratitude."

"You would do the same for me," Jamie said. He tilted his head toward Ned. "So would he. I'm glad I was able to help."

"I couldn't understand why anyone made him guard the granary by himself." Ned's father scratched his head. "It didn't make sense, a boy without experience. He's big and smart, but why did they have him guarding the granary alone?"

"I agree." Jamie said. "I told him to see me once he recovers."

He gave Jamie a curt nod before he went to his family.

"Jamie," Sean called. "Lord Herbert's back. His guards took him to Caerlaverock. Everyone has been accounted for. Only scrapes, a few burns, and Ned's twisted leg. The fire could've been worse."

Soot smudged Sean's face and clothes. The man appeared exhausted.

"Don't look at me like that. You don't look much better." Sean tried to dust the soot off his clothes and gave up, throwing his hands in the air.

"Ned shouldn't have been guarding the granary. Certainly not alone. Find out who gave him his orders." Jamie and Sean walked through the yard. Soldiers and villagers picked up discarded buckets and placed them to side to be claimed.

"I want to examine the building as soon as it cools. I'll go back and report to Lord Herbert. Do you need my—"

"I'll be fine here," Sean said. "I'll get the wagons and our men back to Caerlaverock."

"Jamie," Oliver said, approaching. "Lord Herbert is back."

"Sean told me. I'm on my way to speak to him."

"Tell Lord Herbert I posted guards. No one will be allowed into the building until we do a thorough search. Most of the grain was saved. We've moved it to the blacksmith's barn." Oliver started to walk toward the barn. "Guards will be posted there, too," he shouted over his shoulder.

"This could have been a disaster. I'm not sure who to trust. Ask questions and tell me what you can find out." Sean agreed, then went off to help the rest of Jamie's men.

"You're deep in thought. Oliver told me everything was under control. Has he misspoken?" Laura asked.

"No, nothing is amiss. We need to return to the castle. Herbert's returned and we have much to tell him."

Laura nodded.

"Now that we put Evan to rest, when do you think we can leave for Glen Kirk? I'm eager to return home."

Jamie didn't answer. He planned to speak to Herbert after he told him they caught the traitor. But now, he didn't know when they would go home.

"I notice we have a new decoration on our battlements." Herbert let out a joyless laugh, sitting with Jamie and Laura in his solar.

"I find it hard to believe Holger murdered Evan and Angel. He was shrewd, maybe even sly, but to kill two of my people and attack Laura—" Herbert's face flashed red with anger.

"Please, don't upset yourself. I'm fine." Laura laid her hand on Herbert's to calm him. He patted her hand with assurance.

"I never believed Evan killed Angel or that he turned against the family. I'm glad you solved that mystery and put Evan's ghost to rest. Maybe now things will go back to normal."

"I don't think Holger acted alone. Not after what I witnessed at the granary," Jamie said. "Ned is too inexperienced to guard the granary alone."

"Alone. Oliver knows better than that." Herbert slammed his hand on the arm of the chair.

"Yes. That surprised me, too. We focused on getting the fire out and saving the grain. I left Sean to find out what he could."

"I thought Holger was the traitor." Laura searched Herbert's face. "I thought we were leaving for Glen Kirk."

"No, Laura. No one's going anywhere right now, especially you." Herbert's words left no room for an argument.

"But—" Her eyes pleaded with Herbert.

"Herbert's right. The reiver and Holger came after you," Jamie said.

"How do you know I was the target? You were on the horse, too. And Holger wanted the pin, not me."

Her face morphed from shock to anger and finally to fury.

"The truth is we don't know what the reiver or

Holger or whoever set fire to the granary wants." Herbert looked at Laura and said to her more gently. "I'm not willing to jeopardize your safety in any way. I will get you home as soon as it is safe."

Laura looked from Herbert to Jamie. Both were in agreement.

"I want to inspect the granary in the morning," Herbert said.

"Is that wise?" Jamie ran his hand through his hair. "Let me and Sean search the rubble and bring you a report. I don't think you're safe in the village."

"It may not be safe, but you know I must show my strength. To cower would only make things worse. I won't let my people suffer. My people. Most of them are family. I promised to protect them and I will. The villagers will be arriving soon with their petition for grain. Come with me to the great hall."

Laura glanced at Jamie's profile as they walked to the hall, the familiar lines of his face, tilt of his shoulders, he was Herbert's man. She let out a heavy sigh. Honorable and trustworthy. Herbert would always be first. Isn't that why he remained here instead of returning to Cumgour? She didn't want to stay at Caerlaverock with all its intrigue. She didn't belong here.

Flanked on each side by Maxwell standards, the ceremonial carved chair, symbol of the Maxwell clan, was centered on the dais. Shafts of sunlight came through leaded windows and made a pattern on the floor in front of the chair. Her father had told her about this room. The window placement had been intentionally designed to coordinate with the sun. The sunlight illuminated the specific spot were villagers and farmers petitioned the Maxwell for grain.

Herbert took his seat. She and Jamie sat on chairs provided. She looked from the dais to the door. The long walk was intimidating. She laughed at the drama.

Herbert nodded to the sentry. The door opened and two women entered. Laura recognized the older woman, Mara. Herbert spoke of her fondly. She had served in his nursery when he was a boy. She walked with pride and a little difficulty, her daughter Rhona by her side.

"Greetings, Mara, and to you, Rhona," Herbert said.

"Lord Herbert. My mother has served the Maxwells for most of her life. She didn't want to come today, but I wouldn't have it. She cared for you, your wife, and your sons. We come to you for assistance."

Herbert gazed kindly on the old woman. "Mara, you look well."

"Lord Herbert, she is young. Forgive her curt—"

"Don't make excuses for me. I ask for none."

Startled speechless at Rhona's rude behavior, Laura's chest heaved as she formulated her response. Before she could give it voice, Jamie lightly touched her arm. She glanced at him. He raised his finger to his lips and signaled her to stay silent.

Herbert ignored Rhona's outburst and kept his focus on Mara.

"I'm well." She shuffled closer to him. The woman tilted her head toward Laura as she passed.

Mara's fingers flashed. She made the sign of protection. Laura took in a quick breath. What or whom did Mara need to protect? Surely not her.

"I haven't forgotten all you've done for us," Herbert said, his voice soft with concern.

Mara laughed an odd dry laugh. "I taught you well." Her daughter stepped beside her. A show of strength or protection?

A heartfelt smile spread across Herbert's face. "Now that Caerlaverock is complete, there is no reason for you to stay in the village unless you want to. I can make good on my boyhood promise. Your room is ready, should you want it."

Mara stepped in front of her daughter. "It is a generous offer, and perhaps when Rhona remarries and moves away, I'll come to you."

"Mother." Rhona stiffened, and Mara went into peals of laughter.

"Jamie, take Rhona and make sure you load her wagon with a barrel of grain." Herbert turned to Mara. "I wish I could give you more, but that's all I can give you."

"You are a generous man, Lord Herbert. May you lead us to peace."

Jamie and Rhona went ahead. Laura led Mara down the stairs toward the castle storehouse.

"Take this." Mara put a stone in her palm and closed her fingers around it. Before Laura looked at the stone, she grasped what it was.

"Why do you give me a charm for protection?"

"An aura surrounds you. Something is out of place. I don't know to what degree, but I know you need the stone more than me."

Laura touched her throat, but it was bare. The broken strand was in her room. "I appreciate your concern, but I don't know what you mean."

Mara's penetrating stare held Laura's attention. The woman's eyes shined with a worldly wisdom.

"No, you don't. You coming to Caerlaverock is... a journey to greatness. You will see. Your opportunity will come when least expected. Be ready. It is your destiny. But your way is not without tests. Some will be difficult, but it will be worth the fight. The stone of protection only goes so far. The rest is up to you." Mara shuffled away. Laura was left behind staring after her.

Mara turned. "Not everyone is as they seem. Keep that in mind."

Mara made her way to the wagon where Rhona waited with Jamie.

Destiny? Fight? Deception? Laura gazed at the stone. She looked up as Rhona drove through the gate and on into the village.

She didn't want a great destiny. She wanted Jamie and she wanted to go home.

Chapter Eleven

"Are others in Parliament anticipating similar problems?" Jamie asked. He and Herbert walked through the remains of the burnt granary.

"Caerlaverock is not unique, but our troubles are greater. Our proximity to the border and the tension with the English King are all reasons why I built Caerlaverock into an impenetrable fortress. However, with the building's defensive beauty, the castle has become a target. Whoever can take Caerlaverock will demoralize the Scots."

Herbert inspected the damage to the granary's interior and let out a heavy sigh. "We need a new roof and the platform is gone." Herbert bent down and picked up a damaged sack, brunt grain lay beneath it. He threw the sack to the ground.

"I spoke to the villagers. With winter coming, they fear food will be scarce. I don't blame them. I assured them there would be enough grain for everyone."

Jamie grasped Holger's brooch in his pocket. The tinker had been eager to retrieve it. Jamie needed to find out its significance. He hoped Herbert had the answer. He waited for the right time to ask the question.

"Where are you taking my grain?" a villager demanded. "Burning our food wasn't good enough, now you're going to take what little remains." Men and women, who helped with the aftermath, stopped what they were doing.

Outside, villagers and soldiers took salvaged sacks and barrels of grain from the blacksmith's barn and loaded them onto wagons.

Herbert looked out what was left of a window. "Who is the man making the accusations?"

Jamie released the pin. His questions would have to wait. He stared at the tall man, large arms and crumpled clothes, like any other highland farmer, yet something was familiar. He couldn't place the man, but he'd remember.

"I say we take the grain back from these thieves," the man continued. Villagers salvaging what they could inside the granary took note and came outside. The group grew larger, their grumbling louder.

Herbert leaned against the burnt window frame. Jamie pulled him back. All he needed was the instigator to have words with The Maxwell. "I've never seen that man before."

A breeze barreled down between the buildings and ripped off the man's hat.

"I have," Jamie said. "In Cannobie." Jamie scanned the crowd and located three other men who had been sitting behind him at the coach house.

The men were speaking to the villagers. It was an old tactic, encourage people to be discontent. He had to act with haste to smooth things over before they got out of hand.

"I'll take care of this. Stay here." Jamie didn't give Herbert a chance to answer. He made his way to Oliver.

"Here let me give you a hand." Jamie picked up a barrel, put it on his shoulder and placed it into the wagon. The rumbling hushed.

"Don't let me stop you," Jamie said to the troublemaker, then picked up another barrel. Soldiers followed his lead and continued to load the wagon.

"We will if we need to," the agitator said. Jamie put a barrel into the wagon, then turned to the man.

"Which Maxwell are you? Because I know everyone in my family and I don't recognize you." Jamie tilted his head to the side and stared at the man.

The man swaggered over to him. With a meaty finger, he jabbed Jamie in the chest. "Why do you want to know?"

Tension rose and the buzz of whispers spread through the enlarging crowd. Jamie knew this tactic, too. Pick on the biggest man and beat him. Everyone else will be docile. It would only work if you beat him.

"Friend, we are all Maxwells here. You must be new to Caerlaverock. The planted farm land and woods are not for the taking. This is all Maxwell land. We work alongside Lord Herbert's men, planting and caring for the land. The family takes care of each other and The Maxwell takes care of his family, protects them, and shares a portion of the grain." The rumbling crowd agreed.

"You're taking the food out of our mouths," one of the agitator's allies shouted.

"Ah, you brought a friend. Come, where we all can see you." The crowd parted. The man stood exposed. His gaze shifted from one person to another as he looked for support. Jamie glanced where the other two men had been, finding their backs as they walked toward the tavern.

"Another thought to interfere with The Maxwell. Maybe he's a friend of yours, too. Holger, he was a tinker. You can find him on our battlements."

Jamie faced the two men, but spoke to the crowd. He was lucky he was able to contain the men's attempt to stir up the villagers against The Maxwell.

"The granary has been damaged. The smithy hasn't room to store the grain. Caerlaverock has a new clean and dry storeroom. Lord Herbert will make sure his family is protected and provided for as he always has."

Jamie turned to the agitator. "He'll make sure he takes care of you and your friend." The smile he forced didn't reach his eyes. Jamie was sure his meaning was understood.

"Let me help you," a villager called out. The man grabbed a sack of grain and put it into the wagon.

Jamie watched as the agitator marched toward the tavern, his friend a few steps behind. Jamie went back to the granary.

"Nicely done. I hadn't anticipated outward unrest." Herbert's face grew solemn and thoughtful.

"Fighting the man would get out of hand and bring about more anger. With Holger hanging from the battlements, I hoped the threat of a traitor and the outsiders stirring internal unrest had ended. Everyone is aware of your concern for them and your interest here. Now, you need to return to the safety of the castle," Jamie said.

"Yes, but before I leave I want to show you something. While you did verbal battle with our friend, I found something very interesting." Herbert led Jamie to the wooden post where Ned had been pinned. The two men squatted and examined what was left of the damaged beam. Jamie ran his hand over a smooth, even edge.

"The beam's been cut." He stared at Herbert.

"My thought as well. I want you to stay here and search what's left. Report to me when you return. Did you or Laura find anything of interest in the pantry?" Herbert brushed off his hands.

"Yes, Holger was willing to die for the piece." Jamie removed the jeweled brooch from his pocket and handed it to Herbert. "He told Laura people would kill for it."

Herbert turned the brooch over in his hand. After several minutes, he gave the jewel back to Jamie.

"The workings of the clasp and the cut of the stone are old. Maybe even ancient. The filigree work around the edges remind me of a clan piece. If you look with care, the stone had a carving. I can't make it out. Only a part of the marking is visible. If I had to guess, I'd say the stone contained a herald. Keep the brooch safe. If Holger wanted the gem, it must be valuable."

Jamie pinned the brooch inside his jerkin.

Herbert, with Oliver and his soldiers, returned to the castle. The breeze picked up, and Jamie went back into the granary.

Jamie examined the fallen beams. Each showed signs of being cut. He examined the two beams that remained standing and found deep cuts on them. Someone tried to saw through. He searched what remained of the first floor and found nothing.

The fire had started on the second level. The stairs were gone. Jamie covered his mouth, then pulled down the last standing beams. The platform crashed down.

Once the dust and ash settled, he had a clear view of the roof. Holes. He climbed on top of the wood pile and scaled as far up the wall as he was able. He was close enough to see no charring on the edges of the hole, but rather, clean chop marks. He retraced his steps and jumped down the last few feet.

He walked through the debris. The smell of wood and ash filled his nostrils along with something else. He remembered it now. He picked up a piece of partially burnt wood and took a deep breath. Oil.

This puzzle wasn't difficult to solve. Ned, an

unskilled soldier, guarded a highly strategic building without any support. The beams and roof had been deliberately destroyed. He threw the wood to the ground. Even though he had arrived at the same conclusion earlier, he was angry. The fire had been purposefully set.

"Anyone in here?" a woman's voice called from the doorway.

He dusted off his hands and walked outside. "Rhona."

"I thought it was you going into the granary. When I heard the crash... well, I thought you might need help." She put down her basket, walked up to him, and took a cloth from her bodice, then proceeded to wipe soot off his face. Her eyes followed where she cleaned, his cheek, his hair line, his chin. She hesitated as she wiped his lips.

"Don't move. There's definitely something on your lips." She smirked but didn't take her eyes off his mouth. "It's quite expressive, your mouth."

He stilled. His eyes never left her face. Her intimate touch didn't interest him, but her actions did. He knew Rhona for years. Their relationship was cordial, certainly not one in which they would blatantly tease. The woman was calculating. What did she want from him?

She worked down his neck. She spied the brooch and her heavy lashes that shadowed her cheek flew up.

His heart raced at her recognition. What was her interest? He quieted his thoughts, and pulled his jerkin closed, covering the brooch.

"I thought you were back at your farm," she said and stepped back. "I wish I could go back to mine, but mother insisted on coming to the castle. Reivers already raided our stock. Mother insists staying without someone to protect us was too dangerous."

"Lord Herbert provided room for you and your mother. I would think you'd be comfortable."

"Take away our home? You don't believe that, do you? You do understand what The Maxwell is doing. First the grain, then he'll take our farms."

"We all have our duties," he said. He focused on staying relaxed and not making her aware she'd struck a nerve. He should be in Cumgour helping with the fall harvest and hunting instead of leaving it to his cousins. His responsibility included making sure the farm was defended and prepared for winter.

Home. Not a grand place, but the stones were strong and the rooms comfortable. The view from his solar window included the entire valley spread out before him. He took a deep breath as if he could inhale the fragrance of Cumgour. Instead, burnt wood and ashes filled his lungs.

"My duty is to my mother and she's waiting for me at the tavern. I'm glad you weren't hurt." She picked up her basket.

"Let me take that for you." He lifted the basket out of her arms and balanced it on his shoulder.

"That's really not necessary." Her coy reaction didn't fool him. She wanted him to go to the tavern. That was why she had the basket with her. He was more interested in finding out what she knew about the brooch.

"Where is your farm?"

"Cumgour is in the northeast, by the English border." Where the woods are lush and the streams run cold and fast. A person can walk for miles or sit on the cliff and enjoy the valley. Would he ever see home again?

"Is Cumgour much different than here?"

"My farm is similar to Caerlaverock, but not as vast. I enjoy peace and quiet, as well as working the fields."

"Peace and quiet. What I wouldn't give for that. Here, you must watch your back and what you say. I would do anything to make Caerlaverock like your Cumgour." They walked into the tavern. Jamie put her basket on the floor.

The room was cozy with a warm fire in the grate. Tables were scattered around the room. Most of them empty. Mara sat near the hearth with one of the agitators. Jamie looked around. The other men were not to be found. Interesting.

"Join us for an ale?" Rhona asked.

She looped her arm in his. Her other hand rested on his chest. She gazed at him with adoring eyes, except when he looked deep, he detected cold determination. She was softening him for something.

The man with Mara kept his head down, but Jamie caught him staring at Rhona. The two of them were connected and this man was doing his best to stay still.

Would they lead him to the traitor? It wouldn't take much for them to believe he was disgruntled and had turned against The Maxwell. He'd be playing a dangerous game, one he would have to keep from Laura and Herbert.

"Sure. I'll join you for an ale." Jamie got comfortable at the table. Rhona took a seat next to him, her thigh against his.

Chapter Twelve

"Good morning." Laura entered the solar, a bright yellow ribbon in her hair. She sniffed the air and followed the delicious aroma to the morning buffet. She filled her plate and took her usual seat next to Jamie.

Herbert, who sat at the head of the table, was well into his meal.

Jamie nodded and launched into a conversation with Herbert. She touched his arm. He gazed at her hand, then at her eyes with a cold expression. Her small touches had always been eagerly received. She pulled away as if burned by a hot ember. Her brow creased, she had no idea what had Jamie so irate.

"Good morning, Laura," Herbert said, his voice tired but cheery.

Confused, she focused on Herbert. Perhaps he held the answer, but his demeanor gave nothing away.

"Lord Herbert. Mrs. Turner said you wanted to see me." Oliver entered.

Herbert rose from his seat. "If you'll excuse me,"

he said to her and Jamie. He put down his linen. "Oliver come with me."

Jamie started to get up.

"No, you stay and finish your meal with Laura. We'll speak later." Herbert left.

Jamie relaxed in his seat. He pulled a piece of bread off the loaf.

He refilled his plate from the buffet, then stood by the window and ate. He had a perfectly good seat at the table, next to her. He said nothing, but his demeanor said everything. He had no desire to be with her and didn't try to hide it.

Now that she thought about it, he had returned from the village yesterday with Mara and Rhona, laughing, his arm draped around Rhona. He never came to the table at the evening meal, nor sought her out. Her heart thudded. He avoided her.

They had a long history. She couldn't remember a time without Jamie. Before he fostered with her father, the two families enjoyed time together. Afterward, Jamie was one of the family. Their relationship was an easy one.

She never hesitated speaking her mind, until now. One minute, doubt stabbed at her, and the next, her anger raged. Ridiculous. This was Jamie.

"I waited for you to tell me what you found at the granary," she blurted out, hardly aware of her grudging tone.

"The fire was not an accident." With his plate half full, he put his plate on the table. "We've worked very close the last week. And the situation between us may have gotten a little out of hand. I had no intention of…"

She gasped. "Making me feel foolish?"

His head snapped up and his cheeks reddened. "If you'll excuse me."

He didn't wait for her response. Instead he rushed out of the room as if he couldn't tolerate her company any longer.

She sat at the table, not understanding what happened. She went to the window. Jamie came out of the gatehouse and crossed the courtyard. She started to turn away until she saw him put his arm around Rhona.

Unable to pull her gaze away, she stared as Rhona cuddled into that warm space next him. Did he hold her tighter? Place a kiss on her head as he did with her?

Short breaths struggled around a hot knot in her throat. Still, she couldn't turn away.

Jamie and Rhona walked toward the great hall. He turned and glanced at the solar window. Her senses dulled, she couldn't move away quick enough.

Their eyes locked. Even at this distance, she recognized his disinterest, his silent rebuke. She took in a strangled breath. His indifference stabbed at her heart, but she couldn't look away. Instead she hoped she misread him.

Rhona followed Jamie's gaze to Laura. She pulled him away. He crushed her next to him and they walked on.

Laura stared at the space. Tears threatened. She leaned against the window jamb. He kissed her here, slowly and deliberately.

She let out a deep breath and banished the vision of his passionate eyes, his soft lips, his strong arms.

"Enough." She gathered her wits. What did she expect? She should have listened to the women at Glen Kirk. Ninnies, Ann called them. And she was the biggest ninnie of them all.

But his sincerity. Maybe it was working closely to find the murderer or grieving together for Richard. Who knows what moved him. She left the solar and went to meet Mrs. Turner in the kitchen garden.

Jamie entered the battlements, empty except for Sean, the only person aware he played a double game.

"I didn't think this deception would be so difficult. But the hurt in Laura's eyes this morning was almost too much to bear."

"We discussed the best way to protect Lady Laura was to distance yourself from her." Sean turned and faced Jamie. "If they had any idea you were close to her, they'd use her against you."

"I know, but I don't have to like it. It makes me feel… dirty. You didn't see the hurt in her eyes, how hard she held back her tears. I've given Rhona enough encouragement. I'll not do that again." He slammed his hand on the stone.

"Lady Maxwell didn't want tallow candles in the new castle. Too much smoke. Thank you for your help." Mrs. Turner sat at a table and cut wool string for wicks.

"My pleasure." Laura took lengths from Mrs. Turner and tied the wool to a stick. She held the stick at the end so the wicks could hang down while warm beeswax was poured over the wicks.

"Have you seen Lord Jamie and Rhona?" the servant stirring beeswax asked another girl. "They make a nice pair. I always thought she was cold and remote."

"Not when she's with him." The stick and tied string began to waver. "Lady Laura, could you steady the stick, please?"

"Of course," Laura said. The two servants began to ladle wax over the string. Laura didn't want to listen to gossip, but couldn't move.

"As long as Lord Jamie's been here, I never seen him with anyone. Not that every woman hasn't tried to get his attention. I think that's why The Maxwell keeps him here. To marry a Scots woman."

"I say good for Rhona," the other servant said. "With the loss of her husband and three brothers, it's about time her luck changed. The wax is too thick. I'll heat it."

"I'll shape the candles and put them in the sun to bleach," Laura said. Anything to get away.

Laura brought the candles to the herb garden. The low gate wall gave her a view of the courtyard. Laura nodded to some passersby as she shaped the candles.

Across the courtyard, she spotted Jamie hand something to Rhona. She didn't mean to look, but her gaze sought him out. She paid a heavy price. Rhona stepped into his arms and kissed him. The unbearable ache in her chest held her in place.

Mrs. Turner came up beside her. "I... I thought you and Lord Jamie..."

"So did I." Laura put the candles in the sun and left. She forced herself to walk, although all she wanted to do was run as far away as possible. Anyplace was better than here.

She slipped around the guard at the gate. Lost in the crowd of villagers leaving the castle, she let the flow carry her along. Voices buzzed around her. She didn't hear anything. As soon as she was able, she left the path and headed for the forest. Alone. She needed to be by herself.

He looked down and caught a glimpse of her yellow shawl. He leaned over the battlement. Where was she going? He searched the crowd. Alone.

"What is it?" Sean came up next to him. "Isn't that—"

"Laura." Jamie raced down the tower stairs and into the throng of people. He pushed past everyone and worked past carts and wagons. At the bend he caught a flash of her shawl before she vanished into the forest.

What was she doing? He told her not to leave the castle without an escort.

Jamie found the impressions of her shoes in the soft ground and followed her trail deeper into the forest.

The area was familiar. Rhona had brought him here last night to the meet the others. Were they still here? Had she stumbled upon them? His heart quickened. Was she safe? He knelt for a closer view of the impressions. No, the tracks were all hers.

She must have been pacing. He scanned the area of disturbed leaves. Her footprints were all over. The breeze shifted, and in the silence, he heard sobbing. He froze.

He had hurt her more than the taunts she suffered from Bryce when they were younger. He hated himself for it, but he couldn't do anything about it now. *"You did this to keep her safe,"* he said over and over. But the words didn't take away the guilt or pain. Separating from her was for her own good. He had to make her hate him, if she didn't already.

He stomped around the boulder and stopped. Ten yards beyond, he spotted her back.

"Laura." His voice made her jump as he moved to her side. "What are you doing here?"

She stiffened and didn't turn. God help him, he wanted her in his arms as much as she wanted to be there. He wanted to tell her...

She turned to face him, composed. Her red swollen eyes betrayed her misery.

He scanned the area to make sure none of Rhona's friends were about. She followed his gaze.

"Are you expecting someone?" Her words hung heavy in the air.

She had no idea he followed her. She suspects he's here to meet... Rhona. He schooled his face to hide his thoughts.

Be proud of yourself. She thinks little of you? Isn't that your goal. You went to great lengths to give her that impression, the voice in his head said.

Proud? Why did he feel dirty? His betrayal shook his very core.

"Why are you here?" he asked, his voice soft and inviting. He stepped close enough to see the gold flecks in her eyes.

"I came here for some fresh air. It was too close in the castle."

He gently brushed a tear from her eye with a shaky hand. How she didn't hear his heart hammering was beyond him. Every one of his muscles screamed to hold her, love her.

He nudged her chin up with the crook of his finger. "You shouldn't be here. The forest isn't safe. I'll bring you back."

Laura didn't hide her thoughts well. They were written on her face as she tried to make sense of the last few hours. Sean was right. To protect her, she had to hate him.

"Thank you, but no. I can take care of myself."

He spun her around and held shoulders.

She pushed him away and didn't look him in the eye.

"Can you now? If so, why the tears? A lost love perhaps. You didn't take us seriously," he said in a teasing tone, his hand running down the side of her cheek.

All color drained from her face. He wanted to take her in his arms and make it right, kiss away her tears, and take her away from Herbert and the castle. More than anything, he wanted to go back to the way they were in the solar, tender and caring. Instead, he would be her villain.

"No," she said and let out a deep breath, then raised her chin. "Not a lost love. A departed brother who should have come home to us today for father to give him his portion. You remember your good friend, Richard."

Forgive me, Richard, for what I'm about to say. Jamie gave her his best blasé look.

"Richard is gone. A senseless loss, but life goes on for everyone. Wesley, Darla, Lisbeth, you, and even me. I prefer the carefree life, not warring for someone who has no concern for his subjects or their well-being. I don't want to be shackled to anything or anyone."

A red flush raced up her throat and settled in her cheeks. There was no mistaking it for embarrassment and anger.

"Ah, Saint Richard. Will you measure all men to his standard?" He held up his hand to ward off her answer. "That is for you to decide and none of my concern. Although, I'll warn you, idealized saints, even ones exonerated for murder, won't keep you warm at night or put a babe in your belly."

She stepped forward, her breasts heaving.

He caught her hand before it landed on his cheek. Their eyes locked. He twisted her arm behind her back and drew her close to him. His lips were inches from hers. She didn't struggle.

She would never be in his arms again. He opened his senses intent on remembering every detail. The scent of lavender that announced she was near. Her soft touches that told him she cared. The warmth of her body that said she was his. He pulled her closer and searched her eyes, slightly asking for forgiveness. Silently telling her everything. He brushed his lips against hers. She didn't resist. He deepened his kiss.

He pushed her away and grabbed his lip. "You bit me!"

"That you mention yourself in the same breath as Richard is vile, and to speak about an incident that happened years ago and that you know so little about is despicable."

He died on the inside. Bringing up the death of the Harmon Gualter was a cheap shot, but there was no other way. He couldn't give her hope. For him, the memory of their kiss, her soft lips, her warmth and understanding, even her devotion was all in the past. It had no place in his future.

Her icy stare went through him. She walked past him and out of the forest.

"I'm sorry, Richard. There was no other way," he whispered. He stood at the forest edge and made sure she returned safely to the castle.

She knelt in the kitchen garden and spent an hour pulling weeds. The intensity of her anger waned and left her empty and exhausted. She'd never raised a hand to anyone before. She wanted to believe she was wrong about Jamie. He made it clear where he stood in their relationship. Their relationship? There was no relationship, there never had been. Only a childish dream.

She scooped the weeds into a pile with other kitchen debris. She shook out her skirt, dusted off her hands, and went to the kitchen.

"You'd better hurry, Lady Laura. It's almost time for the afternoon meal. Do you need any help getting ready?"

"No. That won't be necessary." She went up to her room. Preoccupied, she bumped into a servant coming out of Jamie's room.

"Oh, excuse me." When she glanced up, she stared into Rhona's smug face.

With all the dignity she could muster, Laura moved on to her room. Rhona hurried down the hall.

Rhona didn't belong in the house. She didn't work in the castle. She didn't belong in the house, unless invited.

Numb, she had seen too much, witnessed too many painful scenes. Feeling sorry for herself didn't get her anywhere. She needed a diversion. She'd completed her mission here. It was time to return to Glen Kirk. She'd petition Herbert again. If he said no… Well, she'd leave without his consent.

Laura glanced into the looking glass and stared at the agate beads around her neck. Truth. Her hand hovered, a question on her lips. She hesitated. The truth. Confirming it would be—painful.

"Coward," she said to the mirror. She didn't need to ask the beads when the answer had presented itself in the forest. Nothing would change. She glanced at the deep lines set in her forehead and tried on a tentative smile. That wasn't too difficult. She broadened it a bit. That was better.

Laura picked up her shawl and left her room for the great hall.

"Finally, 1 was waiting for you. Herbert asked that I escort you in." Jamie held out his arm.

She looked at his arm with distaste. "No need. Why don't you escort Rhona? She appears to be your new attraction."

"Rhona?"

"Yes, I stumbled into her when she left your room. I thought you were more discrete, if not for yourself, for her." She moved past him. "Captain Oliver, would you escort me in?"

"Of course, m'lady." She took Oliver's offered arm and swept into the room.

Why was Rhona in his room? Most likely searching for information.

"Excuse me, Lord Jamie." Rhona came up next to him and placed her hand on his arm as if she declared him her own. "Sunset, at the tavern."

He moved his head slightly to the side and glanced over her shoulder. Laura stared at him for a moment before she looked away.

"I'll be there." He entered the great hall and walked onto the dais as Oliver handed Laura to Herbert.

"I need your help," Herbert said to Laura. "Guests are arriving, and with my Lady away there is no one—"

"Say no more. I will gladly be your hostess." Laura straightened her skirt. "When will they be here? How many guests do you expect and how long will they be with us?"

"I received word from Duncan, asking me to host a party of fifteen. They should be here anytime. Duncan didn't say how long they would be with us."

"Is that wise?" Jamie asked Herbert. "A visitor now, with a traitor loose and who knows what else? There could be dire consequences."

"It appears the Earl of Fife is having a housing problem. His wife's family is ensconced and his rooms are filled. I told his messenger yes, but he neglected to tell me who to expect. For all I know, it could be the King of England. Come and sit. We'll have our meal and wait for our guests to arrive."

They were through the first two courses. He and Laura hadn't exchanged a word.

"Lord Herbert, the Earl of Huntingdon," Herbert's steward said.

Herbert glanced toward the door as a tall man and four of his men walked into the hall.

"Reeve. You are my guest," Herbert said.

The drone of the people stopped and everyone turned to the door.

"What a pleasant surprise. Come join us. The meal just started."

It had been years since he and Reeve were in the same room. They both preferred it that way.

Reeve walked through the hall with an air of authority and the appearance of one who demanded immediate obedience.

Women found him handsome, and men who didn't get in his way enjoyed his company. His straight black hair hung at shoulder length and framed a thin chiseled face with dark eyes that gave nothing away. Reeve cultivated his ruthless side, which he often displayed growing up. Now his reputation as a bully preceded him.

"Where are the rest of your retainers?" Herbert asked.

"I came ahead. They'll join me tomorrow. I thought I would take the opportunity to see your new Caerlaverock. What little I've seen is impressive and solid."

Herbert nodded. "So you came to spy on me. I heard you were preparing to build a fortress of your own. You know everyone here."

"Collins." He nodded, dismissing him. He turned to Laura. "M'lady. I wouldn't have recognized you."

"It's been some time, m'lord."

Jamie knew Laura didn't like Reeve any more than he did.

"We've been friends for a long time... Laura. Please, you once called me Reeve."

Laura's smile began to melt. "Of course, Reeve."

The exchange appeared civil and pleasant. Why were his hackles up?

Reeve and his older brother, Harman, and Bryce trained with Gareth at Glen Kirk. The three were the same in attitude, disposition, and mannerism, although, he thought Reeve was the best of the lot. After the accident and Harman's death... He refused to let that memory take hold. He sealed it up where it belonged. Forgotten.

Dinner over, everyone talked in small groups scattered around.

Jamie wasn't in a talkative mood. He grabbed a tankard from a passing steward and downed it in two gulps. It dulled the memory of the accident but not enough. It had been a long time since that guilt engulfed him. It was never far away. He may have learned how to tame the berserker, but not the memory.

"Lady Laura seems to be taken by Reeve." Sean was next to him. Jamie studied her discreetly, certain that every laugh, toss of her head, and smile was meant for him to witness. He must stop this torture. She may be his in his heart, but he made it clear he wanted nothing to do with her.

"I'm glad Laura is here to entertain our guest," Herbert said, joining them.

"Why do you think the Earl of Huntingdon is here?" he asked.

"He campaigns with every house for a seat in the Scone Parliament."

"An Englishman," Sean blurted out. Conversation around him stopped.

"He has claims on both sides of the border."

"The Earl's claim in Scotland is by recent title and land won playing cards. It's nothing like the long history of The Maxwells and Scotland." Sean walked away.

"Yes, our allegiances are well defined. Reeve's are not. He has a tendency to shift with the wind when the need suits him. His father taught him well." Herbert sipped his ale.

"He was like that as a boy. He's an Englishman who tolerates Scots. He and Harmon sided with Bryce most times." It made Reeve his natural enemy. He didn't like Reeve then. Now, he liked him even less.

The man still held Laura's hand, his mouth hovering over her knuckles as if he would eat them. He wanted to march over to her and... do nothing.

"Parliament is concerned about England's influence," Jamie said. Herbert nodded. "Your comrades at Scone must be relieved he sought you out, rather than deal with him themselves."

"Precisely." Herbert let out a heavy breath. "He must be here to soften my heart and move me to his side."

Reeve lowered Laura's hand, but held on. "I was sorry"—he bowed his head before he gazed up at her, his face morphed into a pained expression— "to hear about Richard. We were separated on the battlefield. I admonish myself for not staying with him to protect his back."

She pulled her hand away and leaned toward him, touching his arm. "It wasn't your fault."

Laura clucked at him like a hovering mother hen soothing her chicks. It made Jamie's blood boil.

"I'm sorry to cause you pain. Come, let's console each other." Reeve led her to a private seat by the hearth.

Jamie stood with Herbert. He drank his ale, but looked over the rim of his tankard at Laura and Reeve. Their heads were together in soft conversation. Their friendship easily re-established.

Not once did she glance at him. Reeve stood, gave her his arm, and escorted her to the balcony outside.

Quiet conversations filled the room as small groups scattered about. He drained the tankard for a bit of courage before turning to Herbert.

"Relieve me of my duty and let me return to Cumgour. You're armed sufficiently and with enough trained soldiers, you don't need me. I am needed home."

Herbert scowled. "No. You will stay here until I say you can leave. I made that very clear."

"Home," Jamie said and raised his voice. The conversations around him stopped.

Herbert didn't back down. Jamie counted on that.

"I have no idea what you are about, but you will do as I say. Do. I. Make. Myself. Clear?"

Jamie threw down his tankard to the gasp of those around him. He was sure the news of his argument with Herbert would speed through the castle and village. That was fine with him. The sooner he found the traitor, the sooner he could go back to Cumgour and be a farmer.

He marched out of the room and headed for the tavern to meet Rhona.

Chapter Thirteen

The scent of ale and the woodsy fire filled the tavern when Jamie arrived. It was a cozy, familiar place. Somewhat empty in the early evening, this was the gathering place. Soon there wouldn't be an empty seat, and finding a place to stand would be just as difficult. Jamie sat at a table with Rhona, and drank his second ale.

"You're deep in thought." Rhona sat close with her own tankard.

"Yes, nothing for you to worry about." He emptied his mug and motioned to the innkeeper for another.

"When will you realize your Lord Herbert does not intend to let you go back to your Cumgour? He has too much to lose if he does."

"You don't know what you're talking about. I fulfilled my obligation to serve The Maxwell." He took another sip and stared at the table. He wasn't drinking to drown his anger. He wasn't drinking to erase the pain he saw on Laura's face. He drank to erase the sight of her with Reeve.

"Only for one year. Why has he kept you here?"

He turned to her, a playful smirk on his lips. "I'm his nephew—"

"Where are his sons? Three grown men hiding with their mother. He keeps you here because you're expendable. Open your eyes. He cares as much about you as he did for my husband and brothers, all lost in senseless fighting. I would do anything to stop it." She laid her hand on his arm. "Anything."

"Almost as much as I would to leave this place." He drained another tankard. He left Cumgour to get away from Laura, now he would do anything to get back home for the same reason. He chuckled, finding his situation humorous.

Rhona glanced behind him, she nodded, and another tankard of ale appeared. Chairs and benches scraped across the floor. More people filtered into the tavern.

A pipe played the delicate lilt of a melody. A steady drum beat joined in. An infectious beat, he kept cadence on the table. The din of voices subsided and the drum beat synchronized with his heart. His pain subsided as his body responded to the music and the ale.

The music grew louder, feet stamped, and the words of a drinking song bubbled up. One man grabbed a serving maid and twirled her across the room to everyone's delight.

Within short time the entire room filled with music, dancing, and song. And Rhona was in his arms.

Laura didn't need to see him go to know he was no longer in the room. The void his leaving created left her empty and cold.

"For you, speaking of Richard is painful. You must

understand his loss disturbs me, too. I kept away from Glen Kirk for a long time, since Harmon's accident. Distancing myself from Glen Kirk gave me time to heal."

She didn't say anything. Still pre-occupied with Jamie, she forced her attention to Reeve.

"I understand the accident wasn't Richard's fault, although he carried the blame for some time," Reeve said.

"That feud wrenched our families apart. We were very aware that nothing we said or did would bring Harmon back. When your father came to attack Glen Kirk, we understood why." She let out a heavy sigh. "We all feared the worst."

He took her hand, his head bowed. "Your father was brave that day."

"Mother said he was insane. Not everything was settled over a tankard of his ale." A small snicker escaped her lips.

Reeve chuckled. "It did that day. I was amazed when they went alone to Wesley's hunting lodge and came back two days later reconciled, almost happy."

"Father swears by his ale. But even with that reconciliation, it was never the same."

"When Richard brought him to his room, Harmon was barely conscience. What made them fight that night is beyond me. Richard told us they came to words and Harmon got the worst of it. Let's not dwell on it. Harmon's unfortunate death is in the past. I want to start our relationship anew."

"Agreed."

"Can you still sit a horse, let loose a blot, and make your target? I won't admit this to anyone but you. I was jealous of your ability with a horse and bow. I could have used you as my secret weapon in my last campaign."

"I ride, but my weapons training was cut short after I came to an evening meal bandaged from a mishap. Mother screeched at Father and demanded my training be switched from deadly weapons to courtly etiquette. She held my training could prove just as fatal."

"Yes, Darla would say that. I have missed you." He picked up her hand and kissed it.

Laura glanced at him as if she was seeing him for the first time. His touch was tender, his attention gallant, and his words gentle. A welcome diversion. Perhaps he could help her return to Glen Kirk.

The lower tables in the hall were being moved against the walls to make room for the night's entertainment.

"Ah." Reeve rose, and drew her up with him. "I convinced Duncan's troubadour the audience is better here."

"A song, m'lady?"

"Not now, Beneto." Reeve tossed the man a coin. "Treat Lord Herbert to a song about King Kenneth MacAlpin. The one you sang last night."

The minstrel gave them a graceful leg and pulled the mandolin that sat snug against his back around. He moved to Herbert.

Reeve poured Laura a goblet of mead, and together they listened to the tales of the king, then a long ballad about the Pictish kings from the fourth century and King Talorg.

The entertainment went by quickly, and the mead and ale flowed easily. Barriers that had taken years to build between Reeve and Laura seemed unimportant, and, over the course of wine and music, crumbled.

She clapped her hands to the beat and swayed as Herbert's guests danced. Reeve got up and extended his hand to her.

She looked at it as if it were an odd thing. He didn't wait for her to answer. He took her hand and pulled her onto the dance floor.

Lost in the music, she danced with Reeve and joined him singing old songs. He serenaded her with the most humorous lyrics that brought her to peals of laughter. Even Herbert smiled his approval.

"I must sit or I'll fall down," she told Reeve. He escorted her to a heavily draped window seat. He adjusted the curtains to block out the noise, then handed her a full goblet of mead.

"Comfortable? We're more secluded here." He tipped up her goblet and she took more than a sip. The sweet wine refreshed and soothed. She stifled a giggle.

"May I sing a song for you, m'lady?" Beneto appeared in front of her.

"I have no coin for you." Laura laughed. Lightheaded in the congenial company, she hadn't felt so free and joyful since... She let out a breath. Even thinking about Richard now didn't seem as painful. She tipped up her goblet. *To you, Richard.*

"I'm sure you'll enjoy his songs. I'll play your banker." Reeve took her hand, put a coin in her palm, then closed it up, his hand covering hers.

She laughed at his jest.

"But beware, m'lady. I may ask for payment—— with interest."

She raised her head to say something clever, but got lost in his gray eyes. She never noticed the color before, or the warmth. Before she reacted, he leaned forward and brushed hair from her eyes. Laura froze at the intimate gesture.

Reeve guided her hand toward Beneto. She gave the musician the coin.

In the quiet corner of the great hall, Beneto sung about a beautiful maiden and her stalwart knight. How he pined for her. He sung about the knight's dream of kissing lips that tasted of sweet berries, touching soft breasts, and how he longed to settle between her legs and make her his own.

She closed her eyes, swayed to the music, mesmerized by the pictures the rich baritone voice painted.

Soft tender lips covered hers. The beating of the drum, the seductive words, the soft breath and manly fragrance that surrounded her, held her in a place she didn't want to leave. She was wanted and loved and that was all that mattered. She parted her lips.

"Laura," Reeve whispered in her ear.

His warm breath sent chills down her back. She pulled away and opened her eyes.

"Beneto is long gone and the others are leaving the hall." He signaled to someone behind her. "Mrs. Turner will help you upstairs."

Without saying a word, she rose and went with the housekeeper.

"Laura."

She glanced over her shoulder at Reeve.

"I'll collect my payment soon."

She turned and left humming Beneto's song and seeing Reeve in a much different light.

Laura sat at her mirror as she finished her morning toilet. The tragedy of Richard's death was tolerable, although her anger at him for dying still surfaced. But not this morning. This morning, she dwelled on the lightness of the prior evening and not the pounding in her head, her uneasy stomach or her parched throat.

Reeve's attention was enjoyable. She touched where he kissed her. His kiss had been the last thing she remembered before falling asleep, and the first when she awoke. A knock on her door brought her back to the present.

"M'lady, The Maxwell is asking if you're feeling well," Mrs. Turner said, walking into her room with a steaming plate. "It's well past the morning meal."

She sniffed the air, and the odor of boiled cabbage hit her. Her stomach was unsettled and she was hungry, but not for cabbage.

"Lord Reeve suggested I bring this to help with your... headache and your stomach. I enjoyed your dancing and singing last night. You reminded me of Lady Darla." She put down the plate.

"I hope I don't regret it the rest of the day. But it was lovely." She picked at the cabbage and ate it with a warm slice of bread. This wasn't her choice for a morning meal, but she was well aware of the cabbage's medicinal affects. She toweled off her hands and took one last look in the mirror before she walked across the courtyard to the great hall.

"M'lady." Reeve met her outside the hall. His eyes twinkled. She couldn't help but smile.

"Many thanks for your thoughtfulness. Cabbage isn't my usual food for starting the day." At least Mrs. Turner had a knack for cooking cabbage with little odor.

"I thought you would benefit from the vegetables' medicinal attributes." He bent close. "I did it for a very selfish reason. I wanted to ask you to ride with me today."

Herbert and Jamie kept her a prisoner in the castle. She was familiar with almost every stone in the castle wall and the number of steps between the gatehouse and the great hall. Riding across the meadow with the wind in her hair sounded like heaven.

"I'd like that."

He straightened to his full height. "Wonderful. I

took the liberty of having Mrs. Turner prepare a basket for us, without cabbage. Our mounts are ready. Shall we?" He directed her to the stable.

For three weeks, riding with Reeve became a daily event. After breaking their fast, they visited the now abandoned old castle with its pools of water or rode through the woods to the Nith River and sat on the river bank to watch wild swans glide by. They even rode across Solway Firth and rested on the lowland hills to peer out at the Irish Sea.

The days sped by. After each excursion, she returned to Caerlaverock eager to see where he would take her the following day.

He didn't kiss her again, although, his tender lingering touches assisting her on and off her horse had her wanting more.

By the end of the weeks, their relationship was re-established. They were comfortable and playful. Reeve was a surprise. The dark moods she remembered were history. His authoritarian manner that made him impossible was gone.

But dinners were difficult. Each night, she sat at the dais with Reeve to her right and Jamie's empty chair to her left. Rumors of his liaison with Rhona had gone around the castle. She saw him in the courtyard from time to time. They acknowledged each other, but nothing more.

Intellectually, she realized her attraction to Jamie had been a part of her childhood. He would always be special to her. She had made her peace, and like him, she had to move on.

Dressed for her morning ride, she hurried to the great hall.

"Many are vying for Glen Kirk Castle because of

its closeness to the border. That is what is driving me. Would you rather have an ally on the other side or someone less in favor of Scots?" Reeve said.

She started to barge in, but hesitated.

"You should speak to Wesley. Not me." Herbert's stern tone made her uncomfortable. Was Glen Kirk in trouble? "Without an heir, he would listen to your petition."

"Time is of the essence. Money hungry courtiers are now conjuring ways to seek their fortune at Wesley's expense. It doesn't really matter. Edward sanctioned *my petition* as you call it. Acting now, will keep the peace and stability as well as everyone happy."

"So, this is why you're here."

Reeve offered no reply.

"What petition to my father?" Laura said and walked into the room. The two men turned.

"You're looking quite well this morning." Reeve gave her a warm smile. "I hope you slept well. I, for one, did not."

"It must be the mattress." She held back a smirk.

He came up next to her and took her hand. He kissed her palm. "Yes, of course. The mattress. Several times I thought to seek you out to fill my wakeful night, but then thought better of it."

She pulled away. "What petition, Reeve?"

He took a deep breath. "I wanted to spare you this. There are rumblings in London. Glen Kirk Castle holds a strategic position. Your father planned to give Richard his portion when he returned from Wales. Wesley is a good leader and soldier, but with these troubles, a younger man is needed. It's time for him to step aside. It's the natural order of things. With Richard gone, Glen Kirk and the entire border area is vulnerable."

"Step aside? How ridiculous. A man doesn't give

up his home because of age. Father need only call up more soldiers," she said.

"That won't work. He needs more than men. The castle needs to be under strong leadership. Edward suggested me."

"You? And what about my family?"

She felt like a rat caught in a trap. Reeve was bold and boastful, but not as good a leader as Richard or her father. Or Jamie for that matter.

"Edward suggested we marry. The solution will keep your family in residence and the opportunists at bay. Those that are inside England, as well as in Scotland."

"Marry? That was what your attention was all about these last weeks?"

"Of course not. It was a bonus. But I have used up all our time."

"Our time? What do you mean?"

"Edward wanted me secured at Glen Kirk by the end of October, next week. Tomorrow, you must give me your answer."

She could only gape at Reeve and his proposal to marry her. She searched his eyes, but the soft gray she had seen these last few weeks was gone. It had been replaced with a hardness she remembered.

"There really isn't anything to decide," Reeve said. "We must do as the king decrees. I hoped we would be fortunate and like each other and possibly have more than that in time. That remains to be seen. For now, you alone can secure the well-being of Glen Kirk and your family. No one else."

The idea should have given her a sense of power and duty. The reality of Reeve's true intent didn't cloud his recent attentions. He intentionally manipulated the situation and she, the rejected lover had been easy prey. Was he wrong to try and soften the blow? Was she so obsessed with Jamie that she couldn't see Reeve's thoughtful and kind actions?

"Yes. I understand. But I would like my father and mother with me."

"Travel at this time for you or them is dangerous. I wouldn't want to put any of you in jeopardy. We'll marry here, and as soon as we are able, I will bring you home."

"My family is in danger?" What had happened in the last several weeks? Glen Kirk was a formidable castle, not easily taken. Her father's troops were some of the best, trained by the King's standard. She couldn't stay here, abandon them when they needed her most.

"Yes. Before I left England, I sent troops to secure Glen Kirk to keep your family safe. I'll give you some time to yourself. We can be quite happy together, in spite of the circumstances."

Stunned, she said nothing. She stared at his back as he left the hall.

"Oliver can secret you away to Glen Kirk," Herbert said. "It would be dangerous, but you would—"

"No. I never thought of Glen Kirk as a strategic position, only my home. If I can keep my family safe and Glen Kirk intact, then marrying Reeve is a small price to play."

"Is it? Living with a man as harsh as Reeve will not be easy. As a father, I would not let my daughter marry him, no matter who decreed it." The words exploded from him in such anger that spittle flew everywhere. "What do I tell your mother? She sent you here to rid me of a ghost, not marry you to a fallen knight."

"Reeve harsh? No, he's not. I've spent the last weeks with him. He may be demanding in managing his business, but that's to be expected."

"Laura." Herbert raised his voice, his face turning red. "He's not what he appears. You've been aware of his true nature for a long time. Don't let him fool you. He is out for himself and no one else."

"Calm yourself. Mother and Father will intercede. I will find a way to convince him the wedding must be at Glen Kirk."

"Where have you been? I sent Sean to find you hours ago." Herbert threw the quill on his desk and bolted out of his chair, turning it over in the process. Maps with strategic markings went flying to the floor.

"I came as soon as I heard the rumors. Reeve is taking a wife. I pity the poor girl." Jamie leaned against the door jamb. Now that he looked at Herbert, the man appeared unusually upset.

"The poor girl," Herbert muttered. "I've sent a message. God knows how long that will take, and by the time we get a response, the deed will be done and sealed."

Jamie stepped into the room. He picked the maps off the floor and tucked them into the leather binder on the desk. "Why are you agitated?"

"Reeve." He slammed his hand on the desk, disturbing more papers. He sank into his chair. "He's marrying our Laura."

Jamie was too startled by Herbert's statement to offer an objection. Finally, he found his voice. "She can't marry him. Wesley would never permit it."

"That's the thing." Herbert lifted his head and glanced at him with tired eyes. "It seems this is a decree from Edward. To hold Glen Kirk, Reeve said. I sent Ned with a message to Howard, the king's man in London. He's close with Wesley, and can be trusted."

"Hold Glen Kirk? Reeve's a man with poor judgment. His father left him a thriving earldom that he managed to piss away on war campaigns for Edward.

Now he has nothing but an empty title and heavy debts. The man has no sense for politics, or strategy, for that matter." Reeve taking Glen Kirk was one thing. The castle would always be recaptured, but Laura married to Reeve? Reeve was after something else. He needed time to puzzle it out.

"Reeve believes he understands both sides of the border argument," Herbert said. "He always has thought himself more capable then he actually is. His shortcomings are obvious to everyone, even his king, but him. That's why I sent Ned to England. I don't think Edward granted Reeve this petition."

"He thinks his father's name is all he needs. He hasn't got half his father's ability." Jamie paced the small space in front of Herbert's desk while he tried to think of ways to prevent the marriage, short of killing Reeve, although, that option wasn't beyond consideration.

"What's been going on between you and Laura?" Herbert asked.

The question brought Jamie up short. "Nothing."

"Don't tell me nothing. I have eyes. You two were mooning over each other and now all of sudden, Rhona?"

Jamie couldn't tell The Maxwell what he'd been doing. Not now when he was so close.

"Ever since her brothers and husband died—"

"Killed," Herbert said. "Don't glorify them. They were murdering thieves, not heroes as she would like to believe. They didn't only steal livestock. They brutally murdered farmers and left women and children defenseless. I know, because I picked up the pieces. No, not heroes at all. How can you think—"

"Laura is not for me. She never was. How can I marry her—" Thoughts long hidden came to the surface. Painful thoughts. Guilty ones.

"You still think you killed Harmon. You forget, I was with you and Richard. We walked in and saw Harmon attacking Laura while she lay unconscious. I don't want to think about it. The picture is burned in my head. He was experimenting, he said." Herbert righted his chair and sat.

"I pulled him off her," Jamie said. He was back in the small room at Glen Kirk. "Harmon had a crazy look on his face and a bottle in his hand. I had never seen such a devil. After that, I didn't see or hear anything."

"I watched it unfold as if every step took minutes instead of seconds. You held back until he drew his knife and threatened Laura," Herbert said to Jamie.

"I was a man possessed. My only thought was to stop Harmon. No, I had to kill him, and the only weapons I had were my fists," Jamie said.

"Yes, Richard and I had some time pulling you both apart," Herbert said.

"I poured that concoction he gave Laura, the entire bottle, down his throat," Jamie said.

"Thank the saints Lisbeth knew what to do for Laura. She has no memory of the incident. You wouldn't leave Laura's side. I had Richard take Harmon to his room." Herbert rubbed the back of his neck. "We never told Darla or Wesley."

"Harmon went to sleep and never woke up. I killed him. Not only that." Jamie turned to Herbert. "Richard took the blame."

"He did it gladly to—"

"Protect me. Yes. Harmon could die at the hands of another Englishman and it was considered an unfortunate accident, but at the hands of a Scotsman, my life was at stake."

"You didn't kill the boy," Herbert said. "She can't marry Reeve."

"I can't marry Laura. She's better off with someone else."

"Dammit, Jamie. Not Reeve. She's meant for you. She always has been. Reeve doesn't want her. He wants Glen Kirk to swell his coffers. Reeve will use her until there is nothing else for him to gain, just like he's done with others. Don't you understand?"

He did understand, but now she was beyond his reach.

"She thinks she's doing something noble. She's sacrificing herself. We can't let her marry Reeve," Herbert said.

Chapter Fourteen

"I didn't realize how much your company means to me. Not seeing you yesterday was... difficult."

Laura was with Reeve near the hearth in the solar. "Oh. I hardly noticed." In truth, she searched for him all over the castle and grounds yesterday. He was nowhere to be found.

He clutched his hand to his heart. "I am wounded. I must make you notice me." He nudged her against the wall. She didn't protest. He braced his arms on either side of her head, trapping her. His gaze traveled over her face and searched her eyes.

Her heart pounded in her chest. She closed her eyes as he lowered his lips onto hers. Anticipating a rush of heat, when she realized his lips were on hers and there wasn't any tingle her eyes sprang open.

She gave him the most passionate gaze she could muster, then ducked under his arm to gain distance.

"You made your point. One day without my attention and your passion runs cold. I shall take note of you from now on." He moved away from the wall.

"The last few weeks have been wonderful, but marriage is a lifetime. Do you really think we're well suited?"

"What you want for a husband and who you marry may be two different things. You and I are not free like the villagers to marry who we want. We marry for other reasons. To strengthen our family."

She still found it difficult to believe Glen Kirk, tucked away as it was, held any strategic advantage.

"With Richard gone, every knight is vying to secure Glen Kirk. I see you haven't thought about it." He laid her hand on top of his arm and walked her to the windows that overlooked the formal garden.

"Glen Kirk is idyllic, and Herbert has created a beautiful sanctuary at Caerlaverock, but don't be fooled. Both castles are fortresses for war. And war is eminent. We must protect ourselves."

"You give Glen Kirk much too much importance," Laura said.

He swung her around to face him. "Look and see what a warrior sees. Glen Kirk is strategically placed on the England Scotland border. Whoever rules Glen Kirk, rules a way into Scotland. Who do you think would be best owning that space? An Englishman who hates the Scots, or an Englishman who sympathizes with them. You certainly can't put a Scot in charge, can you? That alone would start a war."

Her mind turned over what Reeve said. A Scot in charge of Glen Kirk. Jamie. Reeve knew where her sympathies were, if not her heart.

"King Edward wouldn't let anything happen to Glen Kirk or my family."

Reeve let out a deep breath. "You are naive and I blame your family for that. Politics outweigh personal feelings. Edward needs a strong hand. Edinburgh is a two-day ride from Glen Kirk. One day, if you press hard."

"Are you saying we are just pawns in the king's chess game?" she asked.

"Ah, think of me more as your knight that comes to his queen's rescue." He said it with such flourish, she burst out laughing.

"We are suited and will deal well with each other. To allay your fears, I received a report that the troops I sent to Glen Kirk arrived. My captain assures me your family is well and the castle is secure."

"Father and Gareth can protect Glen Kirk." She resented his insinuation that her father lacked the ability.

"Of course they can. My men are in Glen Kirk to augment Wesley's soldiers. Nothing more. Besides, it was Edward's suggestion. I assure you I took no liberties. Will you defend me as adamantly when we're married?"

"I can't give you an answer." For several heartbeats, his eyes were cold and hurtful before they softened with understanding.

"I had hoped the answer would be easy for you. Your struggle is unfortunate and useless, and in the end, won't matter. We will be married. I can only be generous until Edward makes his demand. I must know by tomorrow if you go willingly to the alter. If not, other arrangements will have to be made."

"Other arrangements?" What would he do if she said no?

"Instead of a joyous celebration and our intimate moments private, we would marry with your father's consent instead of yours." He hesitated and gave her a hard stare. "For your sake, I would rather not have a witness at our marriage bed."

She paled at the alternative. He started to say something, but instead turned and left her standing by the window. All her life, with guidance and nudges from her family, she was free to choose her own way. She gazed down at the garden. The wind pushed the fallen leaves across the flowerbeds. Now, the wind at her back was the King of England.

From her vantage point in the solar, she could see merchants filling the market area. In the distance, she spotted the jeweler, a welcome distraction. She had waited for him since her agate necklace broke. Her chain was beyond repair, a new one needed.

She left the solar and crossed the courtyard. The chilled breeze caught her unawares. It would storm later in the day. She wasn't the only one who felt the weather changing. Merchants hawked their wares, eager to sell their goods before the rain. She hurried along and made her way through the stalls.

"Lady Laura, how can I help you?" the jeweler asked.

"I broke my chain and need it repaired." She took out the beads and remains of the chain and laid them on a black velvet cloth.

"These are old stones," the jeweler said as he examined each one closely. "They're all from the same large stone. See here," he showed her the inside of the hole where the chain had been threaded. "A fine gold has been applied."

He looked up at her. "It's an ancient technique. I haven't seen it often."

The jeweler put down the beads and picked up the chain.

"I can't fix the chain. These beads are heavy and need a special chain. I have exactly what you need, but I don't have one with me. I'll have one for you tomorrow."

She took the beads and broken chain. She headed to the spice merchant when she spotted Jamie three stalls away. He bargained with a seamstress for a lovely shawl.

He was tall and broad. She licked her lips and realized it was his lips she wanted on her mouth, his arms around her, his... For a heartbeat, she imagined the exhilaration when she and Jamie jumped the hedgerow with his strong arms holding her, protecting her. The idea of never being close to him again was almost as painful as losing Richard. No, God forgive her, worse. Richard had no choice. Jamie walked away.

She took a step and a flash of skirt came into view. Rhona flew to him. He held her and wrapped the shawl around her.

Laura couldn't move. Large drops started to pelt her. Within minutes, people around her closed their stalls as the drops became a torrent. The crowd thinned. She hurried to the gatehouse and up the stairs into her room.

Leaning against the door, she breathed hard. Moments later, his door opened. She moved into her room, the bottom of her skirt soaked and dripping. She was startled by a knock on her door.

"Laura?" Jamie. She froze. What would she say?

"Laura, are you there? Open the door."

Her chin quivered. She couldn't speak to him. What would she say? I love you? He would laugh and think nothing of it.

"Laura, I know you're in there. Open the door." *Go away, please.* At last, his footsteps retreated. The final click of his door was the sound of her heart breaking.

The rain had let up by the time the evening meal was over. Mrs. Turner had servants clear the trestles and benches. Conversations during the meal were low. Everyone focused on the warm food. At least that's what Laura did. She didn't hear the minstrels soft singing, nor much of the conversation around her.

Jamie's chair remained empty, although he walked the hall and sat at a table with Mara. She searched the room for Rhona, but she wasn't there.

All this was a distraction from the real issue at hand. She was caught in a trap, but it was tolerable. She glanced at Reeve's profile. More than tolerable. If the king thought Reeve was the man for Glen Kirk she would abide.

Reeve's hand appeared in front of her. Startled, she gaped at him.

"You seem pre-occupied this evening. I'm sorry to have caused you discomfort. That was not my intent."

She placed her hand in his and walked down the dais. "It is not your doing."

Reeve brought her next to Herbert and went to speak to one of his men.

She fought against the constraint of having her life directed. If Reeve was going to command Glen Kirk in the name of the king then she should go with him, in a position of power. Richard served the king as warrior. She would serve the king as a wife.

"Laura?" Herbert bent toward her. "Reeve told me you're hesitant. I leave for Scone in the morning. Don't make your decision until I return."

His concern touched her heart. "I appreciate your concern, but I see no other way."

Reeve returned to her side. He gave her a wide smile.

"You've been very understanding with me concerning your proposal. I'm sorry I wasn't more gracious in my...acceptance."

Reeve drew in a quick breath and squeezed her hand. "You won't regret this."

Herbert stepped close. "Are you sure, Laura?"

Laura nodded. How could she tell Herbert she was anything but sure? Her decision was good for the family and that's what mattered. Would he do any less?

She could never have what her heart wanted, and Reeve didn't speak of love, only responsibility and friendship. She should be happy and excited.

Then why did she want to run away and cry? She plastered on a smile and faced the room.

"Everyone," Reeve said, not giving Herbert the opportunity to address his guests. The room quieted.

In the corner, Laura spotted Jamie leaning against the doorway to the kitchen.

"I have asked Lady Laura Reynolds to be my wife." A flurry of excitement and noise rolled through the hall. "She has," he said and waited for the noise to die down. Her eyes were fixed on Jamie, and his on hers.

"Said yes." The crowd moved toward them, but she kept him in her sight. He dipped his head and smiled. Out of nowhere, Rhona appeared next to him in her new shawl and they left the hall.

Jamie truly had no affection for her. How many times would she look for a different answer before she accepted there was none? What had she expected him to do? Rush through the crowd and declare her as his own? Silly notion. Silly girl. But that's what she wanted. She wanted him to love her.

Reeve drew her close and she responded to the good wishes from those crowded around her.

Jamie watched her all during the meal. Her gaze gravitated to his empty chair as if commanding he move next to her. He should commend himself for fooling her so completely. But his heart ached when she scanned the room, for her rival he suspected.

He gave her what support he could when Reeve

made the announcement, but he couldn't stay and watch the rest. Instead, he put Rhona and Mara in their cart for the short ride to the village.

While the celebrations continued in the great hall, Jamie went up to Herbert's solar. He lit the candle and removed a volume of papers from Herbert's leather case. He carefully copied the map and indicated the position of the armies. How ironic that he played the traitor, the thing he found most vile. There was a lesson to be learned. One man's traitor is another man's hero. Much like one man's love was soon to be another man's wife.

He folded the paper and stuffed it into his shirt. Best to get this deed over with. He hoped this map would be the last. More than anything, he wanted to capture the traitor and return to Cumgour, where he belonged. He wanted to be far away from Laura.

He left the solar and headed toward his room. He didn't need a candle. He had an uncanny ability in the dark, learned after years of exploring tunnels with Richard. He stopped when a slow glowing light move up the stairs.

"Laura?" He waited at the top of the staircase.

She jumped, letting out a small yelp and dropped the candle. "Jamie, you scared me half to death."

Jamie retrieved her light and walked her to her door.

"You didn't answer your door earlier. Were you hiding from me?" He teased her, afraid if he were honest, he would tell her all.

"You knocked? I must not have been in my room. I've been... that doesn't matter."

"Laura, it's me. You know you were in your room and that it was me at the door."

"And why are you so sure?" She tilted up her chin in defiance. He loved that pose, so arrogant, so dramatic, and so not like her. One year, Laura practiced the technique for months, asking him to critique her stance.

"Because you were drenched in the courtyard and your skirts created a puddle down the hall to your door." He tried not to smirk. It made her crazy when he did.

"I didn't hear you knock. I must have been getting out of my wet clothes. Why are you here?"

"To extend my congratulations. I hope you and Reeve will be happy." He tried to be sincere, but even he heard the emptiness of his words.

"Thank you." She opened her door.

Before she shut him out, he moved inside the room, and closed the door behind them.

"What do you think—" she asked, surprised by his action.

"I thought I could be quiet and let it be, but you with Reeve makes my blood boil. You're only doing this because you thought I loved you." Rage seeped into his voice. He did love her, with all his heart.

"So, you're not congratulating me. And you think I'm marrying Reeve because you hurt my feelings. You think very highly of yourself." Her cool tone didn't put him off. He had no intention of speaking to her, let her be, he told himself. But he couldn't.

"You can't be serious. You're not some silly girl taken in by his soft words. Or has he done more than that on your daily rides together?"

A surprised expression washed over her face, followed by shock and anger. She fisted her hand and caught him on the jaw unaware.

"How dare you say such things to me? And if I did do something on my daily rides, what business is it of yours? You are nothing to me but a poor distant Scots cousin." Her voice was cruel.

He grabbed her by her shoulders and shook her. "You're a spoiled girl with no idea of the game she plays or with whom she's playing." He pushed her away, then went to her dressing table and took the black gem.

"Give that back to me. The pin is not yours." She reached for it and pulled him around, tearing his shirt open. Papers fell to the floor. She whisked them up and stared at the map.

He grabbed them out of her hand.

"What are you doing with Herbert's papers?"

He crowded her, intent on intimidating her as he stowed the map and pin away. "Stay away from this, Laura. Far away. This is none of your affair."

"And who I marry isn't any of yours." She glanced up at him, her eyes glowing with an inner fire.

He delighted in her warm breath against his cheek. He stared into her eyes, recognizing he was lost. Gently, he pulled her close. She didn't resist. He lowered his mouth and softly kissed her. She parted her lips and sighed. He took full advantage, slipped in his tongue. Her answer was to step closer to him. He rewarded them both by deepening the kiss. Her low soft moan made him stop. She was his. He closed his eyes and ached for her, for him, for them both.

He broke the kiss and held her head to his chest. He let the feeling linger. It wouldn't last long.

"You can't tell me that Reeve's kisses make you moan like that?"

Laura pulled away. A look of resolve colored her face as she pushed him to the door.

"How my fiancé makes me feel is not your concern. I'm not your concern. I assure you, I will marry Reeve." He knew her better than she knew herself. Her voice didn't match the expression on her face.

Laura opened the door. He walked out, waiting for the door to slam behind him. Instead, there was only a soft click of the lock.

He entered his room and put the brooch away. He was about to stashed the map, when someone tapped on his door. Laura.

He threw the door wide and immediately controlled his face. Rhona stood at his door.

"You appear surprised. Who were you expecting?" She slipped under his arm and entered. He glanced up and down the hall, then closed the door.

"I put you and Mara in a cart to the village."

"Yes, but I returned with a message for you." She walked around his room, touching things on his bureau, running her hand along the counterpane. She came up in front of him, then stepped closer.

"What's their message?" She was a breath away, but she held no appeal. He suspected he didn't appeal to her either. They were both caught in this drama, playing their roles. Her part was to keep him away from Laura, which had its advantages since all he wanted was to keep Laura safe from the traitor. But he didn't count on Laura having a part in the production. He left Reeve with an open opportunity.

"If you have the information, they're willing to meet you tomorrow."

"Tell them I have what they want."

Chapter Fifteen

Jamie hiked through the woods to the old castle. The lower floor was flooded by the recent rain. The place was picked clean by builders for the new site and villagers. He waited for his contact perched on a low stone outcrop that had once been the footing for one of the outside walls.

The muffled clinking of metal findings on a horse's bridle disturbed the silence. Slowly, three horses came into view. He waited and watched as the small party skirted behind a stand of small bushes. Their horses secured, three people approached him.

Disappointment drained him. These people weren't who he expected. Although they wore masks and were heavy clothed, Mara's bent posture and stiffened walk easily identified her. He suspected Rhona and one of the reivers were the other two. None of them were the leader. Jamie'd have to play more games until he found him.

Mara sat next to him and took off her mask. "There's no need for this. My disguise didn't fool you.

Your face is easy to read."

"You are wise, maybe even crafty, but you are not the leader."

"No, but the leader sent me to speak to you. The one who leads us would surprise you. Come, walk with me."

"I'm surprised you'd be against The Maxwell," he said as they moved toward the river.

"I could say the same for you, but I'm sure you have your reasons. Mine are not too complicated. Profit. Trading secrets and goods to both the Scots and English fill our sparse coffers. Lord Herbert has been good to me, but I must take the side of my family. That's where my allegiance lies. And yours?"

"I want to farm my land and let everyone else fight for their cause. I have no intention of declaring who I support. My family is on both sides. Being patriotic to one makes me a traitor to the other. I cannot win." He easily he saw that now. How different was he from Holger? That was a sobering question.

She stopped and turned to him.

"No one will win. You don't need magic to see that. Too many want to take for themselves and leave nothing for the others. But enough. What did you bring me?"

He took the map out of his shirt and handed her the package.

She inspected the map.

"Yes, this is what we thought. You prove yourself trustworthy." Her raspy laugh punctuated her choice of words. *Trustworthy*. The word hung in the air like a bird and settled around his neck like an albatross.

She tucked the package into his shirt.

"Replace the map before The Maxwell finds it missing. Rhona will tell you what to do next." She pulled open his jerkin. The black stone pinned in place.

"I thought the gem was a rumor. Where did you get the stone?"

She closed his jerkin, patted his chest and stared at him with her good eye. "Don't let anyone know you possess the gem. Keep it hidden. Defend it with your life."

"Why? This jewel doesn't appear to be special."

"Holger died for the gem because it wasn't meant for him. The stone in the center is ancient, from a legend lost over centuries. Lady Darla may be able to tell you more. She has knowledge of the ages. From the little I know, the stone is a herald from an ancient family's curse."

He touched the stone.

"The gem doesn't appear different than any other."

"Its magic is silent. When the time is right, the magic will summon its rightful owner. The markings are no longer visible on the center stone. Intentionally removed, I suspect. Without them, there is no way to know who the stone will draw, angels or devils. The gem chooses its champion. The new champion may be you."

"How did Holger come to own this?"

"I suspect he bartered for the jewel." Mara cackled. "We spoke about the stone. He wanted to learn about the legend. He never told me he had the brooch. If he had, I would have told him to sell the cursed piece to someone, or give it away. Ach, he wouldn't listen to me anyway."

"Why are you telling me all this? If the piece is so rare, I would think you'd want it for yourself."

"The cursed gem is of no value to me or mine. In the wrong hands, it leads to destruction. The gem didn't protect Holger, did it?"

"Is that what you wish for me? Destruction?"

"No, Jamie," she said softly. Something in her

tone made him ache. "Since you were a boy, I suspected you were marked for great things. Why do you think The Maxwell keeps you close?"

That made him think as they walked the rest of the way in silence.

"I'm ready," she called to the others. He helped Mara onto her horse. Without a word, the three left as silently as they came.

Jamie watched them disappear into the forest.

Laura drew her shawl close and crossed the chilled courtyard, heading for the jeweler's wagon. Her morning had been spent accepting everyone's good wishes on her coming marriage. Her female cousins congratulated her on marrying an earl from a fine house. She wasn't sure if they were envious or truly happy for her.

"Lady Laura. Congratulations," the jeweler said as she approached.

She smiled. "Many thanks."

"I have the chain you requested. I thought about the beads and designed a necklace that I'm sure you'll like. I'll string the beads so if the chain breaks again, only one bead is in jeopardy." He stretched a gold chain out. Laura took the leather pouch from her pocket and emptied the beads onto the black velvet mat.

"Notice how the eight links in the middle are larger. I'll secure a bead onto each one. This will take me a few minutes."

"I'll return when you're done." She was relieved she wouldn't return to Glen Kirk and give Lisbeth her necklace in pieces. The day had warmed, rare for the end of October. She wandered to a nearby stall filled with bolts of material. The stall backed up to a house and was busy with women looking for winter goods.

"M'lady, I'll be with you soon. My wife went to the village to visit her mother today. I brought velvet from Edinburgh. I put the bolt in the back. I'll—"

"I can look for myself. No need for you to be concerned." She stepped into the house and the small storage room to the side. Bolts of cloth were stack against a wall, but she was drawn to the rich rust-color velvet that was on a table near the window.

"They met with him as you predicted."

"Yes, I'm not surprised."

Her head popped up. Reeve. Set close to the ground, the small window only allowed her to see as far up as men's chests. She had no idea who was with Reeve.

"He brought the map. We gave it back as you instructed."

"Yes, won't Jamie be surprised when the map winds up in the traitor's hands and they point to his dead body and name him their accomplice."

"But they can't. They gave the map back as you instructed."

Reeve tapped his chest. "Collins isn't the only one with access to Herbert's solar. I've waited a long time for this. Now, come with me. We have more to do before I meet with my bride."

Laura leaned her back against the standing bolts. Reeve was going to expose Jamie as a traitor. She walked into the stall. Reeve spoke nearby with Mara and Rhona. Too close for her to move past without being seen.

"M'lady," said the merchant's wife. The woman drew her to one of the tables. "Did you find the velvet? I knew the color would suit you. The fabric and color would look lovely with this pale orange satin or this blue silk."

"We'll take the velvet, the silk, and the satin." Laura swung around. Reeve stood over her. "Consider the fabric a wedding present."

"That is very generous of you." She inclined her head. *Hold steady*, that little voice inside said. *Think before you do something you'll regret.*

"Not at all. I want my wife to be the envy of everyone. The material will make a beautiful wedding dress."

She started back to the gatehouse, Reeve by her side.

"You'll have to work quickly on your wedding dress. We only wait for the priest."

"But—" She stopped by the gatehouse door and glanced at him as he walked on.

He took her hand and tugged her along. Caught off guard, she stumbled. "We marry at once," he ordered in a voice of authority.

"That's impossible." It was his voice that disturbed her more than his statement. This was the Reeve she remembered. Her misgivings increased by the minute. She threw her head back and placed her hands on her hips.

"I'm quite aware the king wants us to marry. I don't think he wants to give the Scots any advantage, do you?" A tendon in his jaw tightened. One small victory.

"Of course not," he snapped. She met his accusing eyes without flinching.

"The king would have quite a temper if we married here, giving my Scottish relatives an advantage or a claim to Glen Kirk. He would much prefer we wed on English soil, at Glen Kirk."

There was something in her tone that made him pull up. Or was it her mention of Glen Kirk? It didn't matter. As long as he agreed to wait until they got to Glen Kirk.

He searched her face with feral eyes that turned soft, almost loving. "You are a surprise. There are brains on top of that beautiful body," he said and his gaze slid over her body. His mouth softened. "I can't wait to enjoy it."

A rush of heat raced up her neck to her cheeks. His leering smile said he thought she was aroused. Let him think that for now. He stroked her cheek with the back of his hand.

"Ah, you're eager as well, but I agree. We'll delay until we reach Glen Kirk. Waiting alters my plans considerably, but I will rearrange them for you. We'll leave tomorrow and be married by the week's end." He bent to her ear. "That will have to be soon enough."

Reeve was unaware of the anger that rippled up her spine as he marched off toward the barracks. As soon as he was out of sight, she rushed up the stairs.

"Jamie," she said and knocked on his door.

"Jamie," she said more urgently.

When he didn't respond, she rushed inside and came to a halt. His room was empty. She checked everywhere. Nothing. Her heart squeezed in anguish as she realized he left without a word.

Disheartened, she went to her room and found a scrap of paper in Jamie's handwriting on the floor. *Glen Kirk*. She turned the paper over. Nothing. Did she feel any better that he had taken time to leave her a message? She dropped into the chair and stared at the message. Jamie had left for home without her.

She idly touched her necklace and played with the beads. Her body stiffened in shock. The beads were cold. *Lose a bead, lose something dear*, repeated over and over in her head.

She would be home soon enough. Although she and Jamie had words he would... he would come to her, and Reeve would kill him. She touched the bead at her neck and felt its warmth.

Laura paced her room. Perhaps she could catch up

with Jamie. No, she had to get home and rally the Glen Kirk men. They would never let anything happen to Jamie. Neither would she.

"M'lady?"

"Come in."

The door opened. Mrs. Turner entered with two other women.

"We're here to pack your things."

Chapter Sixteen

"Laura?" Jamie banged on her door. The sky was dark except for a rim of light on the horizon. It would be an hour or so before the first rays of sunshine brightened. He pushed the door open and walked in. "Laura," he said, impatient. He didn't care if he woke her. He had to make sure she was there.

The room was dark, the hearth cold. All Laura's things were gone. He stood by the small table, half his note on the table, *Glen Kirk*. The rest of the note, *we leave today*, was conveniently missing. Had Laura removed it, or someone else?

He sat on the edge of her bed. The rumor was true. Reeve had left Caerlaverock yesterday afternoon and taken Laura.

He entered his room and stopped. His bed was stripped and his things gone. He stepped out into the hall.

"Lord Jamie." Mrs. Turner came down the corridor from the servant's quarters. "I thought you left us."

"Not at all. I was in the village working with the men to restore the granary. What made you think I had left?"

"I thought it odd. One of the soldiers told me to pack your things and bring them to the stable. He said you were leaving last night."

"Who told you?" A tingle rushed through him. He must be getting close. The leader wanted to keep him from speaking to Laura.

"The Earl's captain."

"Thank you, Mrs. Turner."

"Will that be all? I'm expected in the kitchen." The woman hurried down the stairs.

Jamie rushed to Herbert's solar. He lit the taper on the desk and pulled out the folio.

"Jamie?" He closed the leather cover with the maps and stared at Herbert. The Maxwell's hand rested on his dirk.

"Yes." Herbert stepped closer into the small circle of candlelight, relief etched on his face. "I wanted to see if the map was here."

"My stable is empty. Reeve is gone. It is a relief." Herbert brushed dirt off his coat, put his case on the floor, and sat at his desk.

"He's taken Laura with him." Jamie dropped in the chair by the desk.

"Yes, Oliver gave me a report. How dare he take her from my house without my consent? Although, she went quite willingly, or so she thinks." Herbert appeared tired and worn, but the expression on his face indicated anger simmered beneath the surface.

Jamie didn't like the sound of that. "She thinks?"

"I can't believe Edward would decree the match without Wesley involved. This entire story is too preposterous. And why demand a quick wedding?"

"To be married before the king stops it," Jamie

said. "Beg for forgiveness. He's in love with Laura and can't live without her." The idea made him sick. "So while we sit and wait, Laura is married to Reeve."

"Laura convinced him to postpone the wedding until they returned to Glen Kirk. She's in for a surprise when she finds Reeve's men manning the castle."

"What do you mean Reeve's men manning Glen Kirk?" Jamie sat at the edge of his seat.

Herbert clasped his hands on the desk. "It's the reason I rode most of the night. Donald sent word. Glen Kirk has fallen." His voice was rough and low.

"While Reeve visited Caerlaverock, his troops marched against Glen Kirk. Donald moved quickly once he discovered the plan, but by the time he arrived, Reeve's colors flew over Glen Kirk."

Jamie slammed his hand on the desk. His anger became a scalding fury.

Worst of all, Laura was with the traitor.

"What of Wesley and Darla?" Jamie's chest heaved as he listened. He got to his feet. "When do we leave?"

"Not so fast. When Donald came to me, he had chased after them, but Reeve had already crossed into England. He went no farther. And there's more."

"More?" He paced.

"Donald's sources confirm that Laura is a pawn. Reeve wants to marry her for access to Glen Kirk. She was clever to convince Reeve to wed her on English soil. I assume her motive is not for her father's blessing, but for his support to stop the marriage."

"If he hurts her—"

"Donald told me Laura was not restrained or being guarded. We assume she is not aware Glen Kirk has fallen. With her an Englishwoman and now on English soil, I cannot move against them. We stay here for now. Wesley and Darla are in London. Ned should be back with news from Howard. It's up to them and the king to act. My hands are tied, as are yours. I think we'll find that Edward never ordered this marriage. Reeve created the story to obtain what he wants: Glen Kirk."

Taking no action only let Reeve move further toward his goal. Jamie didn't care for that strategy.

"We can't sit here and wait. The message could take weeks, Faith, it could take that long for Howard to be granted an audience with Edward. You can't take action, and I can't sit here doing nothing while Laura is at Reeve's mercy. She thinks I abandoned her."

"Why do you say that?"

Jamie gave Herbert the note.

"There was more to the note. The full note read, Glen Kirk. We leave tonight." Jamie walked to the door.

"Hold," Herbert said. Jamie turned.

"I will not wait. I'll leave immediately. You cannot convince me otherwise. If I had returned her to Glen Kirk when I wanted, none of this would have happened," Jamie said.

Herbert let out a scratchy laugh. "You think so? I will overlook your arrogance and attribute it to you being distraught. Reeve would have found another way. But I ask you to hold not to stop you. Take what you need. Many of our men have families in England. They will ride with you."

Jamie took a calming breath and let it out slowly. "I'm grateful for the offer, but I don't want to deplete your ranks. Reeve may have planned something here once he is gone. I will not put the clan in jeopardy."

"Your farmers are a fighting force, an elite one at that. Be careful, Jamie. Reeve cannot be trusted. I have no idea how far he will go to acquire what he wants."

Jamie nodded and left for the barracks. The sun peeked over the horizon. His men were ready to start their day. He gathered them together in the empty armory.

"I have word Glen Kirk has fallen."

His men rumbled. "When do we leave? Do we help Donald?"

He was humbled by their willingness to fight for Glen Kirk.

"No. Donald went after them and got as far as he dared."

"They crossed into England," Sean said in disgust.

"Yes. Donald wasn't able to go any farther. I come from The Maxwell. His hands are tied. I'm leaving—"

"You mean, we're leaving. Together. You'll not go without us," Sean said. The men nodded their agreement. Jamie looked from one man to the next. Each stood with him. These men were farmers, like him. Herbert was right. They were a strong fighting force. He nodded.

"I don't know what we face. I can guarantee it won't be easy."

"Is there any news of the family?" someone asked.

"Gareth took Lord Wesley and the family away to London. They are speaking with their king."

"Who took Glen Kirk?" asked another.

"The Earl's flag flies over Glen Kirk," he said. Another rumbling went through the group.

"Jamie, Lady Laura is to marry... She's not involved..."

"The Maxwell and I don't think she's aware her family has been routed or that Reeve has taken the castle."

"Then we'll have to wrestle it back," a man shouted.

"Gather your things. We'll leave one or two at a time and meet by the cemetery when the sun is full up. There are people sympathetic to Lord Reeve and I don't want to alert anyone that we're leaving. They'll find out soon enough. By the time they do, we'll be close to home."

Laura's head snapped up. She glanced sideways, relieved no one had noticed her dose. Her rhythmic bouncing on the horse and the steady beat of the metal tack made her eyelids heavy and difficult to keep open. She straightened in her saddle and adjusted her seat. She wished she had cold water to splash on her face. Anything to stay awake.

This was not the same route she and Jamie had taken. Reeve had chosen an easier, more southern trail that took them up through England, rather than through Scotland. Reeve pushed the party hard yesterday. If he hadn't stopped to refresh and rest the horses, she was sure he would have driven them straight through. She had no illusions. This route was not for her convenience. He wanted to be off Scottish soil.

After stopping for a cold meal under a full moon that lit the trail, Reeve pushed further until they came to a coach house by the Northumberland Forest. She had slept soundly last night, but ached this morning. Another grueling ride was not what she wanted. She'd be sore for a week.

She couldn't reach Glen Kirk fast enough. Why had she listened to Herbert? She should have returned to Glen Kirk right after she and Jamie put Evan to rest. There was no need for her to stay in Scotland.

She glanced at Reeve riding next to her. The soft seductive tone of the last three weeks vanished yesterday. Other than seeing to her needs and comfort, now he ignored her.

How could she marry him, the king's decree or

not? As a child, there was little gentleness or understanding about him. He could be kind and considerate when he wanted, but his outbursts said much about him. Reeve and Bryce, Harmon when he was alive, were all of the same temperament—hurtful and mean. Not like Richard or Jamie who...

Jamie. Her thoughts always came back to him.

"You've been deep in thought since we started this morning," Reeve said.

She jumped at his voice. He'd been silent for hours. What would he say if she told him her thoughts? That she knew his plan to kill Jamie.

"My thoughts are of Glen Kirk." The caravan continued through the forest along a well-traveled trail.

"You set a good example for the men. Eager to return to Glen Kirk and claim your rightful place," Reeve said.

"My rightful place? I'm my father's daughter—"

"You're my wife."

Her snapped around toward him.

"I'm not your wife. At least, not yet. My dowry is not Glen Kirk."

"Your father may outwear the king's pleasure with his neutrality. Now that Edward is finished with Wales, he'll look to the north. Confrontation is coming between England and Scotland and the king needs leaders he can depend on, not ones who would sympathize with the enemy."

She faced forward. The air was mild, but his words sent a chill ran up her back.

"As my wife, you'll support my decisions. That is foreign to you, but you will learn. Your father may tolerate your mother's insubordination. I will not. Of course, you can voice your opinions to me in private."

Her mouth hung open.

Chapter Seventeen

Jamie and Sean had caught up with Reeve and his troop, but stayed away so they would not be detected. Crouched low, the two highlanders scaled the rise, then peered over the rim. In the small valley, Laura, Reeve, and his men rested.

"He's pushed them hard," Sean whispered. Jamie motioned for him to retreat. He didn't want to risk being seen. Jamie and Sean backed down off the rise and stood at the bottom.

"He must be anxious to get to Glen Kirk."

"Lady Laura seems calm. Do you think she knows the Reeve's flag flies above the castle?" Sean asked.

"No, I don't." Jamie let out a breath. "Take my horse. Go back to the men and get on the other side of Bells Burn. I don't want them in England."

"Where are you going?" They brushed themselves off and headed for the stand of trees where Jamie's men waited.

"Ravencroft isn't far from here. I want to observe

what Bryce and his men are doing. If I cut across the ridge, I can get to Glen Kirk before Laura and Reeve."

As they approached, he signaled the men to mount up.

"I don't like leaving you with no one at your back," Sean said.

Jamie handed him the reins to his horse.

"If anything happens, send Ned back to Caerlaverock to tell The Maxwell and Donald. I'll need you to protect Cumgour."

Jamie waited while his men moved quietly toward the border. He hiked up the trail, then angled off to the East.

He quickly gained the second hill and looked through the trees at Ravencroft in the distance.

The sun hung low in the sky. The wind had picked up and sent leaves scurrying into circles. He listened to the forest. He breathed in the woodsy fragrance of pine cones and wild flowers. All was as it should be.

He reached the familiar old tree and climbed almost to the top. From the perch, he had a clear view of the castle battlements. As boys, he and Richard had come often to spy on Bryce.

His heart thumped at the memory. He kept watch for a few more minutes. All was quiet. No one prepared for battle. No one cleaned weapons. He glanced toward the stable, but there wasn't much activity. The sun would soon be setting. If he wanted to be at Glen Kirk when Laura arrived, he better leave. He climbed down the tree, feeling better. He wouldn't be fighting on two fronts.

He rushed through the forest like a sure-footed deer and came to the meadow. He ran along the deer path moving from tree to tree. A column of riders led by Laura and Reeve came into view. He glanced at the castle, relieved to see the Reynold's flag flying.

Laura rose in her saddle when Glen Kirk came

into view. Her horse stamped, trying to break free of Laura's grip.

Reeve held the column back, but it appeared Laura would have none of that. She gave her horse the lead and it responded. She flew across the meadow and made for the gate, leaving Reeve and the others behind. Reeve slapped his horse's hind quarter and charged after her. Reeve didn't look pleased.

Laura came to an abrupt stop in front of the gatehouse. Her horse, eager for the stable, was a handful to control.

"Open the gate." Her voice carried on the wind.

Dark clouds streaked across the sky. Every so often, they blotted out the moon and made it easier for Jamie to move without being noticed. The village was quiet and tucked in. Not unusual for a late October night.

Torches on the battlements revealed men wearing Reeve's colors standing guard underneath the Reynold's flag. Best to keep hidden and not tempt fate. He stepped back into the forest and came face-to-face with a small charm hanging from a branch. He turned and squinted in the darkening light. The trees were filled with Lisbeth's polished stone charms that in the daylight caught the sunlight and twinkled like fallen stars. The charms were Lisbeth's doing. This one was for protecting the area. He kept to the edge of the forest.

He waited in the shadows of the cemetery wall. He snorted. He was sure Reeve's men had opened a barrel or two of Wesley's brew. The ale was Wesley's best weapon. Now, there was magic. The brew went down smooth and easy, but after a few tankards, one became incoherent. He'd wait until he was sure the ale had taken affect.

He opened the cemetery gate and made his way to the small building where the 9th century remains of William the Brave rested. In the building was a hidden passage that led inside the castle. A dangerous place for boys to play. He and Richard prided themselves on being the only people aware these tunnels existed. Forgotten over the centuries, it had taken them weeks to clean out the debris and shore it up to make it usable.

The hair on the back of his neck stood. Someone was with him inside the cemetery. He crouched behind a tombstone. In the distance, a dark shadow proceeded along the path.

Jamie took stock of the man as he made his way to the Reynolds' family graves. He thought at first Reeve came to pay his respect to Richard, but the form was all wrong. This shadow was bigger, more agile. The man stopped and waited. For whom? For what?

Jamie moved for a closer look. His brushed against a tombstone and knocked loose pebbles that rested on the top to the ground. In the complete silence, the cascade of stones sounded like boulders echoing in a valley.

In an easy, elegant move, the man drew his sword. No, this wasn't Reeve. Jamie did the same.

The darkening shadows made it impossible for Jamie to identify who he fought. That didn't stop either man. His attacker put him on the defense. Jamie retreated in a matter of seconds.

Jamie and the shadow parried and lunged. Evenly matched, neither gave signs of tiring. Several times he almost had the man, only to have him bound over an obstacle and come back for more.

Just like...

"For a moment I thought you fought like Lord Richard," Jamie said. The man answered with a barrage of strikes.

But Jamie held his ground. He fought stroke for stroke until they came into a close battle position, the hilts of their swords locked against their chests. Clouds moved and the man's face was revealed under the moonlight.

Jamie dropped his sword and froze. His heart pounded. The man threw his head back and laughed.

"Richard?"

The laughter subsided. Richard put his arm around Jamie and squeezed him close. "I wonder if Father has any ale? How I would love to taste it one more time."

He gazed into the eyes of his close friend and experienced the warmth of his friendship. How was this possible? No. He shook his head and searched the man's face again.

Eager to be close, and share his joy of seeing him, Jamie grabbed Richard's hand. Cold and as icy as the winter stream.

"You should see yourself." Richard took on a serious expression. He broke away from Jamie, picked up his friend's sword, and handed it to him. "Dropping your sword. I've never seen that maneuver before, unless of course it's the result of being killed. You're better than I remember. The farmer has turned into a warrior."

"Come sit with me," Richard said.

The two friends sat on a stone bench chiseled with the Reynolds name.

"I practiced. With Laura. She's quite good with a blade." A nervous laugh bubbled up as Jamie shook his head. "If I hadn't met Evan and Angel at Caerlaverock I wouldn't have thought it possible. How easily I accepted them. But, am I crazy? Are you... here?"

Richard's pale and drawn face stared at him with pain-filled eyes. "I'm here only—"

"Because you have something unfinished that needs

to be done." Jamie closed his eyes. It was painful losing Richard before. He'd have to lose him all over again.

"Yes, something important." Richard glanced toward the castle. "You are aware that this is a trap." He turned back to Jamie. "Reeve went to great lengths to capture you, and is using the one person for whom you would sacrifice your life. Laura is his bait."

"Edward ordered their marriage." Jamie stared at the ground.

"I fear my king is going to be very angry that someone is making statements attributed to him that he never made."

Jamie sprang off the bench. "What? He would lie about the king?"

"Reeve wants Glen Kirk. It will give him the prestige he seeks for his empty title. He'll drain the Glen Kirk coffers dry before the end of next year. With me gone and no other heir, Reeve could marry into the family and have property and a vast fortune." Richard made sense, of course. If Edward didn't order this marriage, then he had to tell Laura before it was too late. But—

"Why Laura, when Lisbeth is the oldest? No, I have no ghostly powers." Richard raised his hands and wiggled his fingers. "Your question is easily readable from the expression on your face. Reeve holds a grudge for a long time."

"Reeve has known from the start that I caused Harmon's death."

"He can't prove you killed Harmon," Richard said, one corner of his mouth pulled into a smirk.

"I went mad when Harmon attacked Laura. You and Herbert were there. If you didn't stop me... Well, that doesn't matter. The next day he was dead. I did the deed and you took the blame." The image of that night haunted him. Thinking about it made him angry enough to pummel the man all over again. Richard touched his arm.

"I let them believe I fought Harmon because they would declare it an unfortunate accident."

"What do you mean, at the time?" Jamie asked. Richard smirked again.

"Things aren't always as they appear. Harmon didn't fall asleep never to wake up. He was suffocated. Unless you held the pillow over his face, you didn't cause his death."

"Wait. You make my head hurt. In this last hour, I've encountered your ghost, found that Reeve is tricking Laura into marriage, and now I'm not responsible for Harmon's death." Jamie turned to him. "I can believe the first two, as odd as that sounds, but I know I killed Harmon."

"Who had the most to gain when Harmon died? Certainly not you."

"Gain?" Pensively Jamie stared out into the darkness. "Reeve. He became the heir."

"Correct. If Harmon still lived when his father died, Reeve would get nothing. Harmon was already spending through his allowance. Once he got hold of all the assets, there would be nothing left. His father was too sick to stop him, so Reeve did."

"You think Reeve killed Harmon?"

"I don't think, I know. He didn't risk having someone else do it. Too much was at stake and time was of the essence." Richard slapped him on the back. "All you did was fight with Harmon. You beat him badly. He had it coming for what he did to Laura."

"How are you so certain?" Jamie asked.

"Nothing so unworldly I assure you. The tent walls on the Welsh battle grounds were thin. Reeve and Bryce had been drinking heavily. Reeve complained about being short on funds. He spent a great deal on trying to impress Edward. He mentioned he should have seen to his brother sooner."

All these years, he carried this guilt. Jamie stared at Glen Kirk.

"She loves you," Richard said, matter-of-fact.

"Aye. I love her, too. I will until the day I die." He closed his eyes. His words burned deep.

"Then why do you hesitate? And don't tell me because she is my sister. There is no better man for her than you. I had Evan tell you."

Jamie let Richard's words soak in. Finally, he let out a long breath.

"These are difficult times. A Scots in residence at Glen Kirk would never be tolerated. One English lord or another would be at the gate with their demand."

"Laura loves Cumgour. For some reason, which I cannot understand, you want to be a farmer. Make her a farmer's wife."

Jamie was too startled by his suggestion to offer an objection.

"Don't look so surprised."

"But—"

"If you love her, and the family, you mustn't let her marry Reeve. If she does, the family will fall. Reeve will not only bring the family to ruin, he will bring it to extinction. You're their last hope."

"You give me a heavy burden."

"I give it to the one person who can handle it. By the by, I would think with Reeve you'll need the direct approach. He isn't a clever thinker."

Richard stood.

"Must you go? The family would..." The pain of Richard leaving tore at him.

"They lost me once. I couldn't make them go through that again. No one must know I am here. My destiny has always been Glen Kirk. My last deed is to secure Glen Kirk for the future. For that, I need your help. No one else will do."

Slowly, Jamie got to his feet. "You put much trust in me."

Richard put his hands on either shoulder. "Your shoulders are broad enough to carry the burden. Until my parents and Gareth return, you need to keep Laura safe and away from Reeve."

"I will," Jamie said.

"Next time you come, bring me a tankard of Father's ale. I would like to taste it one more time." Richard turned.

"Richard, what happened in Wales?"

Richard stopped walking, and looked over his shoulder.

"I didn't watch my back."

Chapter Eighteen

For the last few miles, glimpses of Glen Kirk's spires teased in the distance. To navigate the dense woods, Reeve slowed their pace. It made these last miles seem endless. She could walk faster than the column traveled. Several times she stopped herself from giving her horse his lead and letting him gallop ahead.

A tiny glint of light pulsed from a tree ahead, and she broke into a broad smile. She scanned the area, pleased to identify Lisbeth's charms swinging from branches. Giddy with anticipation, she reined in her excitement and continued on next to Reeve.

Minutes later, they came out of the woods into the meadow. She halted and stared at Glen Kirk bathed in the rich colors of the setting sun. The castle wasn't as impressive as Caerlaverock. That didn't matter. She was home.

It was torture to wait any longer. She kicked her horse into a gallop and raced across the meadow, eager to be with her family. She was almost upon the door when she pulled her horse to an abrupt halt. The gate, which was always open, was locked up tight.

"Open the gate," she shouted. Her horse danced, eager for the barn. With an expert hand, she kept the animal under control.

"Open the gate." Finally, the small wooden peep hole in the solid door slid open.

"Who goes there?" the gatekeeper asked.

"Who goes there? Lady Laura. Open the gate," she demanded. The man stared at her and didn't move.

"Who are you? You're not one of Father's men."

The man said nothing, closed the small door, and took no action.

Reeve pulled up beside her. "Open the gate, you imbecile, before I have your head," he bellowed.

Her head snapped to the right as the chains clanged into action and the large gate lifted.

Together, the column moved into the bailey. She was born and raised at Glen Kirk. Every stone was familiar, yet she moved along as if she'd never been here before. The bailey was empty. The merchant's stalls and farmer's carts that lined the wall were gone.

She rode in a daze as the column moved into the courtyard. Where was the organized chaos of activity that marked the marketplace? There were no villagers rushing about or buzz of conversations. As Laura rode on, she peered at the few people she passed. None were familiar faces.

They came to a halt in front of the barn. Reeve helped her down. She ignored him. Instead, she headed up the front steps and pushed open the keep doors.

Empty. Reeve stepped in behind her. The castle had been in mourning when she left, but this was worse. The atmosphere was foreign, painful, and frightening.

She hurried up the stairs and burst into the solar.

"Father, Mother, I'm home." She stood in the center of the room, bewildered. The hearth was cold and the room deserted.

"Should the guard put the Huntingdon standard back on the battlements?"

Laura spun around at the soldier's words.

"He should not," she answered quickly over the choking beat of her heart.

"Leave the Reynolds flag," Reeve ordered. The soldier nodded and left. Reeve took Laura's hand, moved her into her father's study, and closed the door.

"I'll forgive you this time, but I won't be so lenient the next. As your husband, I will answer all questions." He threw the words at her as if they were stones. She glared at him, her eyes burning with contempt. She didn't know what angered her more: his words or her missing family.

"This is Glen Kirk, not Huntingdon Manor. Your flag has no place on the battlements here. I will remind you, you're not my husband." She wouldn't let him intimidate her. Instead, she put on her armor and prepared for battle. Yes, that's what this was. She had to be up to the challenge.

His mouth spread into a thin-lipped smile.

"I was so taken with you at Caerlaverock," Reeve said. "I overlooked your faults." Faults. She met his accusing eyes without flinching. His arrogance, evident as he swaggered across the room to her father's desk, irritated her even more.

"My men arrived—"

"Why are they here?" She found perverse pleasure in her challenge.

"My men arrived to find the place abandoned." He showed no signs of responding to her question. "They secured the castle for me until I arrived. In their eagerness to please me, they raised my flag. It was all innocent enough. As you heard, I told them the Reynolds flag stays."

"Abandoned. That is ridiculous." Until she knew her family was safe, she had to be careful. She had to try to keep ahead of Reeve. That hadn't been hard in the past.

"Neither your father nor your mother was in residence. Lisbeth is nowhere to be found. I suspect she went with them." He tossed the words away as if her family's whereabouts was unimportant.

"Surely Gareth told you—"

"Perhaps he would have, but he wasn't here either. One of the old soldiers left behind said he escorted your family to London. You're upset over nothing." He went to the sideboard and smelled the contents of each decanter. When he found one he wanted, he poured two glasses of wine, then handed one to her.

"This should settle your nerves."

Laura put the glass down, untouched. "It's not my nerves that should concern you."

"Ah, then I suppose I should be concerned about your lover. Do you expect him to come and save you?" His curt voice lashed out at her.

"My what?" Laura placed her hands on her hips. She wanted to wipe the cynical smile off his face.

"You didn't think I was aware of your liaison with the Scot? I've known his feelings for you for some time. I wasn't sure how strongly you felt for him until now. I've watched your drama these last weeks. It's obvious his intentions do not include you. And you still defend him. You're fortunate I'm willing to overlook your indiscretion."

"This is ridiculous." She threw her hands in the air. "What does Jamie have to do with anything?"

In two steps, he had her in his arms. "I'll wipe him out of your brain once and for all. You always took his side, followed him around. You even played his squire. Not anymore. You're mine now. His life is in your hands."

She couldn't prevent her quick gasp of breath. She peered closely into his eyes. Hate, stark and vivid, glittered in them. How had she forgotten?

"Yes, I see you understand me." He lowered his face to hers until they were a breath apart. "Don't try to stop or hinder my plans, wife. You won't like the consequences."

He grabbed her hands and squeezed until she thought every bone would break.

"I know your tricks. Use them, just try and it is his life you forfeit."

Laura freed herself and pushed him away, rubbing the sting out of her hands.

Reeve strutted to her father's desk and slowly lowered himself in the chair as if he was already the master of Glen Kirk Castle. Her mind raced as she looked on motionless from the middle of the room. Her parents. That's why Herbert didn't want her to leave. She was sick at the thought. Without realizing it, she was at the brink of helping Reeve achieve his goal at the cost of her family losing everything.

"You will be a grand lady as my wife. Not only will I take Glen Kirk, but you'll bring me Caerlaverock as well. Herbert and his family will not survive there much longer. I've seen to that. I will wield enough power to make the King of England take notice. In his indebtedness, he'll make me his adviser to Scotland. I can just imagine Herbert's face. He and his puny parliament have kept me out. Watch them grovel, if they survive at all."

Blind. That's what she was. Now she saw the spoiled boy she'd disliked all those years ago. He hid it well, but he was still the same hurtful, self-centered person.

"You should be proud of yourself, my dear. Without you, none of this would have been possible. I owe you a great debt. The House of Huntingdon will rise and once again prosper." He got out of the chair. Laura schooled herself not to step away. He gave her his arm and escorted her back to the solar.

"I don't want to alarm you, but there have been threats made against you and your family. Reliable ones. We can only hope that your family made it safely to London. The reivers are a brash group."

She shivered at his threat.

"My men are diligent. They will capture any intruder. You're to stay inside the castle. I won't jeopardize your life."

"Reeve, this is my home—"

He put his finger on her lips. "Yes, yes, I know this is upsetting, but I'll keep Glen Kirk and you safe. Tom," he said and snapped his fingers, "will be nearby to protect you. You look tired. It's time for you to retire for the night. I'll have your meal brought to your room. Things will look better in the morning. For all you know, your family may return tomorrow." He stepped close and kissed her gently on her forehead.

Laura hurried down the hall and entered her room. Tom stepped inside. She paused to catch her breath. Her fears were stronger than ever.

The soldier checked her room thoroughly. He closed the door when he left without a word and with the turn of a key.

She ran to the door, and pulled on the handle. It wouldn't open.

"Let me out." She slammed her hand on the door. How dare he lock her in her room.

"Let me out." Her voice pitched high with fear. Over and over she pounded and screamed until her voice was hoarse and her hands bruised.

Laura slid to the floor with her back against the wood. "Let me out," she pleaded, as tears rolled down her cheeks.

Jamie needed a place to stay, and time to think. He made his way from the cemetery to Wesley's hunting lodge in the woods. The smell of a warm fire quickened his footsteps. He came up the lodge's path and was greeted with a small wisp of smoke rising from the chimney.

A broad smile burst on his face. Lisbeth. He didn't think she'd go far from the castle.

He barged through the door. "Good evening." His smile fell. Sean and his men sat, drinking Wesley's ale.

"Welcome and bring up a chair," Sean said. "Give Jamie an ale."

Dumbfounded, Jamie fell into a chair and held a tankard someone put in his hand.

"Let me introduce you to the Friars. This is Brother Steven, a former royal guard who has seen the light. Here are Brothers Dan and Asher. Both have taken vows of silence. Ah, but not abstinence," Sean said, motioning to three friars sitting with his men over several tankards of ale.

Jamie looked at Sean in interested amazement.

"I see you're a bit surprised. You didn't think you could leave us in Scotland and have all the fun?" The captain raised his ale and took a gulp. "Or all the ale?"

Jamie laughed. He should have realized when they didn't fuss that they intended to follow him. Jamie drank half his tankard.

"Nice to meet you," Jamie said to the friars. "You usually don't come to Glen Kirk at Samhain. What brings you here?" Jamie asked.

"Lord Wesley has summoned us. His daughter is to marry." The friar handed Jamie a message.

His chest heaved as he looked at Wesley's distinctive handwriting. The document requested the friars perform his daughter's marriage. He rolled the message and handed it back.

Wesley must have been forced to write the request. There were no plans for Lisbeth or Laura to marry when he was here last month.

"What did you find at Glen Kirk?" Sean asked, taking a seat next to him.

"Yes, Glen Kirk." Jamie would speak to Wesley. If the day went his way. He couldn't think about that now. "Reeve's men stand guard. I didn't see anyone with Wesley colors, even though his flag flies."

"That's not a comforting thought. When do you plan to go inside?" Sean sipped his ale.

Jamie turned in Sean's direction.

"Don't look so surprised. I know you, and how you think."

"Yes, you do know how I think." Jamie looked at Sean. "So does Reeve. He knows I would walk up to the gate and demand entry."

"You'd be dead before you got to the gate." Sean took a drink.

"Yes, you're right." He looked at the friars. Brother Steven's eyes were closed as he savored Wesley's ale. "No, we're going to send in the friars."

Sean spit out the ale in a fine spray.

"Careful, that's a waste of good ale." Jamie finished his tankard. "Come with me, and bring three bottles of ale."

"Where are we going?" Sean asked as they came to the cemetery.

"To pay our respects." They went through the gate

and walked to Richard's grave. Jamie put two bottles of ale on Richard's tombstone.

"Now what?" Sean asked.

"I'm not sure." Jamie looked around. "I think we wait." He and Sean sat on the stone bench.

"You've gone deep into the traitor's circle. Too deep. I can't imagine they will let you walk away."

Jamie put his elbows on his knees. "No. I suspect they have great plans for me. The only person that suspects I'm the traitor is Laura. I think they intend to have her speak against me. That's why I'm so sure Reeve is behind this."

"What did you do to make him hate you that he'd wait all these years for his revenge?"

"He could never control or frighten me, and to him, I'm from the wrong side of the border. Now he has the one weapon that can wound me."

"Laura. Turn her against you and marry her."

"Yes. I played into his hand by infiltrating the traitors. I had to make her hate me. I pushed her right into his arms."

"Exactly what he wanted. Now he'll force you to watch as he marries her." Sean's face lit with understanding. "That's why you want the friars. Give Reeve what he wants, for the moment. Is there a reason you brought me here to tell me all this?"

"He thinks I'll show myself." Jamie and Sean spun around. A wide smile spread across Jamie's face . Sean jumped up, all color drained from his face.

"Richard? Is... Is that you?" Sean asked. "I thought you were..." Sean looked at Jamie, then fell back on the stone bench.

Jamie gave Sean the third bottle of ale. "Like Evan at Caerlaverock, Richard has unfinished business. His is to secure Glen Kirk for the future."

Sean's mouth hung open.

"If you're not going to drink the ale, perhaps you wouldn't mind giving it to me," Richard said.

"You two are not playing a trick on me."

Jamie sat next to him. "I wish I were, but no. This isn't a trick." Jamie turned to Richard. "I have an idea. It requires getting me and the men into Glen Kirk unnoticed."

"Go on," Richard said.

"And three friars." Jamie paced in front of Richard's grave. "I want to use the old tunnels under the castle. I'm taking a chance. All the passage doors are bolted from the inside."

"You get me into the castle, I'll open the doors," Richard said.

"You can do that?" Sean asked. Jamie didn't think Sean's face could get any paler.

Richard chuckled. "Not the way you think. One of the passages is in the chapel. If we go there, I can open it. The others are in the dungeon, nursery, and great hall."

"You two and one of the friar's will make up the ecclesiastical team. The other two can remain behind at the lodge," Jamie said. The plan had its flaws, but he saw no other way. "I'll let Reeve capture me. What better justice than him forcing me to witness Laura marrying him? My men will take over the castle during the ceremony."

Richard nodded. "The plan sounds good."

"If the plan fails," Jamie said, "there is one responsibility, protect Laura and get her away to Cumgour. If Cumgour falls, then to Herbert at Caerlaverock."

Sean nodded his head.

Richard paced and rubbed his neck. "I can't think of anything better other than the king's troops saving the day. Your plan is bold. We'll make it succeed."

Jamie rose and rubbed his hands together. "Sean and I will get the friar and some robes and meet you at the forest edge."

Chapter Nineteen

The late morning was crisp and clear. The winds had died down and the sun was especially bright. A fine day for a long walk. Three friars, their cowls pulled over their heads emerged out of the forest and approached the Glen Kirk gate.

"Who goes there?" The guard eyed the three holy men, up one side and down the other. He blocked the gate with no obvious intention of moving. Sean, who wore Brother Dan's robes, folded his hands inside the wide sleeves and held his dagger in case he misunderstood the situation. Richard, who wore Brother Asher's robes, did the same.

The brightness of the day did not influence the atmosphere of the castle. That alone made him suspicious and kept him on high alert. He traveled with Jamie to Glen Kirk often enough to recognize familiar faces. The usually busy entrance had only a handful of people. He didn't spot anyone he recognized. Sean remained attentive and scanned the area for any sign they had been discovered. They were vulnerable waiting to enter the castle grounds. Sean gripped his dagger tighter and calculated his alternatives. There were few and none had promising conclusions.

"I'm Brother Steven and this is Brother Dan and Brother Asher." The guard didn't move at the introduction. "We're here for our monthly visit to see the sick and your elderly."

The guard glanced up the wall. Sean kept his head down but managed to glimpse the man on the battlement. Reeve nodded his approval.

Their heads bowed, Brother Steven led the trio in a single line through the bailey toward the small chapel.

"Hold." The short line stopped. Brother Steven tilted his head in the direction of the soldier.

"Keep your heads down and whatever you do, do not move or say a word," Brother Steven remained calm and whispered.

"Where are you going?" The soldier advanced toward them, his weapon ready.

"To the chapel, my son." Brother Steven slipped his dagger into the sheath attached to his arm, removed his cowl and gazed at the man.

"Brother Steven. I didn't recognize you." The soldier lowered his sword and looked at all three friars. "You all look alike."

"We are all the same in the eyes of God. Will you come and pray with us?" Brother Steven plastered an angelic smile on his face.

"You best move on. We're keeping the bailey clear." Brother Steven tilted his head, stepped back into line and without a word led his small group into the chapel. Once inside, Sean closed the doors behind them.

"I'm—"

Steven put his hand over Sean's mouth. "Not a word, you have taken a vow of silence," Steven whispered in his ear.

Sean nodded. Richard, his cowl still on, closed all the shutters and made sure the door to the tunnel was open while Steven searched the room and retrieved three prayer books from a cabinet. Their tasks done, the three sat on a remote bench, their prayer books in hand.

What now? Sean mouthed.

Steven and Richard opened his prayer books and began to read. Sean shrugged and did the same. They waited.

His cowl around his neck, Sean dozed slouched on the bench with the prayer book open in his lap. Steven and Richard, their cowls drawn over their heads, sat erect reading.

Sean's eyes sprang open. Richard's icy hand covered his mouth. He motioned toward the chapel door.

Righting himself on the bench, Sean picked up the prayer book. Richard leaned over and turned it around.

"Your hand is cold," Sean leaned and whispered in Richard's ear. A soft chuckle escaped his lips at the private joke.

Steven tapped Sean on the back of his head, much like a mother silently scolding a wayward child, on his way to the door. Sean grabbed the back of his head and stared at Steven with innocent eyes.

"Brother...?" Darren walked into the chapel.

"Steven and Brothers Dan and Asher. How can we help you, my son?"

"Do you marry people?" Darren stood at the doorway, the tendon in his jaw clenched.

"Yes, my son. You must be new here. I know most of the people in this village. Who is to be your wife?"

Richard covered up his laugh with a loud cough.

"There, there Brother Dan. I told you to be careful of the damp," said Sean. "It will be the death of you." Richard nodded his thanks and coughed some more.

"Not me." Darren surveyed the chapel and stepped closer to the door. "Lord Reeve and Lady Laura are to be married."

"Will Lord Reeve come to speak to us or Lady Laura?" Steven asked, his head tilted and his voice innocent.

"Neither. You speak to me." The irritation in Darren's voice was clear. "The wedding is this afternoon."

"Have the bans been posted—" Beneath his cowl, Richard had all he could do not to laugh.

"Yes. Make a list of what is needed." His irritation moved to impatience.

"We don't need much, the bride and the groom will do," Steven said.

Laura's bedroom door opened. Startled, she pricked her finger with her sewing needle and jumped from her chair. The rust velvet and silk material in her lap tumbled to the floor in a heap. Reeve sauntered in. Would she ever have any privacy?

"Three friars have arrived for their monthly visit." He picked up the material at her feet.

"Why did you lock me in my room last night?"

He gave her a questioning look. "I didn't lock you in our room. The door must have jammed."

He gave the impression of being so sincere. She wanted to scream. This is what she had to face. Lies and denials.

He picked up her hand and brushed his lips across her knuckles, then kissed her palm. Last week his kisses thrilled her to the point of making her knees weak. Now, she wanted to pull her hand away and scrub it clean.

"Come with me. We'll plan our wedding. It won't be a grand event. Unfortunately, Wesley and Darla won't be in attendance." He tucked her arm through his and walked out the door. "We'll marry this afternoon."

She turned and faced him. "This afternoon?"

Jamie pried open the door to the small cemetery building. Built on top of a barrow, it held the bones of previous generations. He covered his nose at the dusty, dank odor and decaying debris. Taking a fortifying breath, he pushed his way past cobwebs and other things he didn't want to think about. He crossed to the other side of the room to the marble wall that hid the doorway to the tunnels beneath the castle.

Jamie turned toward the graveyard and glanced at Richard's tombstone. He and Richard had found the underground maze by accident. They had locked themselves in the dungeon ante room and searched for a way out. Neither of them wanted to admit how scared they were. Countless times they had been told to stay away from the underground prison. No one came down here. No one would find them.

Their candle burnt down to almost nothing, Richard put it on the shelf. To their amazement, the flame flickered. They followed the shift in air current to its source, the hidden door. They quickly exchanged their terror for the thrill of adventure. For weeks they explored and cleaned the tunnels of debris and created their secret place. They bonded like true brothers and stayed that way no matter where life took them.

"On my honor as a Maxwell." Jamie set back to his task. He put down the torch he brought and ran his hand along the marble wall until his finger found and pushed the latch. The marble gave way with a whisper. Gripping the edge, he pulled it back until the space was wide enough for him to squeeze through.

Jamie lit the torch with his flint and steel then climbed through the opening. He shot a look beyond the cobwebs and musty earth to the stone staircase that led to the tunnel below.

Once down the stairs, he stepped with care around fallen stones and piles of earth until he came into a modest size chamber. He was under the castle wall.

They made this their secret place. It's where they hid from Bryce, Reeve, and Harmon and on occasion from Garth, Lisbeth, and Laura. Richard filled the time with tossing his knife, a skill that Gareth didn't encourage. Not interested in weapons, he kept score and commandeered ale from Wesley's brewer.

From here four tunnels branched off.

Of all the tunnels, he and Richard used the one to the nursery the most. It was the easiest to maneuver, with an added advantage, the nursery was empty. Now, he climbed up the stone steps, his shoulders rubbing against the walls. He was almost to the second level. The nursery was up ahead. He set his torch in a wall bracket and went on to the small landing in front of the door.

"We'll marry this afternoon."

He leaned closer to the wall. Jamie opened the peep hole, an addition he and Richard made, and peeked in. Gone were the furnishings of a child's room. In their place were the trappings of woman's rooms.

"This afternoon?" Laura said.

A hint of misery crossed Laura's face before she stuck on a serene expression. He didn't doubt he would save her from Reeve, but he didn't know if their relationship would survive. Friendship at least, but after how badly he treated her even that was questionable.

Laura took the shawl from the chair and draped it around her shoulder. He gaped at the shadow she became. She moved like a beautiful puppet, under someone else's control. This wasn't the defiant feisty Laura he knew. She and Reeve went out the door.

Jamie waited for the click of the door shutting then a few more heartbeats. His fingers ran over the edge of the tunnel door and found the hidden latch. Ready to pull the small lever, the click of the door latch made him freeze. Someone entered the bedroom. He peeked in again.

Rhona hurried in and glanced around. One by one, she opened the bureau drawers and rummaged through them. She slammed the last one shut and scanned the room.

What was she looking for?

Rhona went to Laura's chair and rummaged through the sewing basket. She hesitated, her hand on her chest. A few heartbeats passed. She pulled a piece of paper out of her bodice and stuffed it into the basket accidentally tossing the scissors on the floor.

Rhona grabbed the scissors, her fingertips touching the velvet material. Her face turned scarlet. She yanked the material off the floor and cut one strip after another until nothing was left. Her deed done, she replaced the scissors and slipped out of the room.

He had no false illusions about Rhona and the attention she gave him. Her interests didn't lie with him. He witnessed the seductive stares she gave another man and his silent answers. Reeve was her man. If it wasn't clear before it was now. Rhona led the reivers at Reeve's instruction. Everything pointed to Reeve being the traitor. Everything.

He waited for several minutes to make sure she didn't return, then pulled the latch. The door opened. He had no idea how Richard managed to unlock the door and at the moment he didn't care. In three strides he stood at the table. He dug deep into the basket until he found the folded note.

The map of the Scottish defense position. This was not the map he showed Mara. This was the real map of Scottish defenses. So they knew about him all along. That didn't bother him half as much as Laura's involvement. He stuffed the map in his shirt.

Ready to leave, he hesitated. Should he let Laura know he was close? No, she may not welcome him now. He retraced his steps to the central chamber and moved to the tunnel that led to the dungeon. If Richard had opened the nursery door, perhaps he'd opened the dungeon, too. He hurried on, propelled by the image of his men overrunning Glen Kirk from two directions.

This tunnel plunged lower than the others. It had always been a muddy place with a small stream trickling down the middle. Old crates he and Richard stored here were still stacked along the side. If he took a close look, he would probably find the muddy handprints they put on the walls.

He kept moving until the tunnel leveled out and pulled up. The steps were a crumbled mess of stones. He lowered his torch and touched the stone. Did someone dismantle the steps? The stones were polished and smooth. No signs of hammers or chisels. He stood and glanced up the staircase. Water dripped in a rutted channel down the side. Yes, water damage, but could he still get up the stairs?

He stretched to see what was ahead. Yes, there was a way over the debris to where the steps continued. Would climbing up the rest of the steps disturb the stones and bring them down? Cause a cave in?

Getting to the dungeon was a necessity. It would give his men two ways into the castle, twice the chance of success. He'd have to chance it. Jamie climbed over the debris and tested his footing until he gained the small landing at the dungeon door.

"How long do you think they'll keep us here?" Surprised to hear voices he put his ear to the door. "Settle down. You'll be fine." Jamie's head shot up. Gareth. Wesley's soldiers? If Gareth is here, where is the family? "The guards should be back soon."

Jamie peeked into the room. It was as dark as night. He wasted no time, found the lock and pushed the door open.

"Who's there?"

Jamie stepped into the dungeon. With his lit torch he made his way toward the cells. If the guards were coming back he needed to be quick.

"Jamie?" said Gareth.

"Aye." He spun toward the guard's table and grabbed the keys.

"Hurry, the guards will be here soon," a soldier said.

Jamie unlocked the cells.

"Stay in the cells. We don't want the guards to sound an alarm. We'll overpower them when they come in and lock them in the cell. We can leave the way I came in, through the tunnel and from there to the hunting lodge."

The men mumbled their agreement. Jamie took Gareth aside.

"Where are Wesley, Darla and Lisbeth?"

"They are safe in London. I sent them one way with the majority of men and took a small group in another direction. The ploy worked."

"Lord Jamie." He took stock of the man who approached him. "We're Reynold's men. We'll take back what's ours, Glen Kirk. Tell us what to do."

He searched the men's faces, each filled with determination, loyalty, honor.

"They're yours to command," Gareth said. Jamie stared at the man, surprised at his suggestion. For years he strove to pattern himself after his mentor, a man who leads by example and who is loyal to his duty, to his men, and to Glen Kirk. Gareth gave him an encouraging smile.

"I know you think you're a farmer, but there are times even a farmer is a warrior. Give them their orders."

Jamie searched Gareth's eyes. They were filled with trust and encouragement. He turned his attention to the men.

"Here is our plan."

Keys jangled and four guards entered the dungeon and locked the door behind them. One of the men put their torch in a wall bracket. The guards moved in front of the cell. Before they could torment the men, Jamie doused the torch and the room plunged into darkness.

"What happened?"

Jamie, holding the lifeless torch, listened to the grunts and groans as Wesley's men knocked out their guards.

"They're all... asleep," Gareth said.

In moments the torch flared into life. The guards lay unconscious inside the locked cell.

Wesley's men filed out of the dungeon into the tunnel. Jamie closed the door behind him.

"Careful at the bottom. The last four steps have crumbled," Gareth said.

"Gareth, you're familiar with the tunnels?" Jamie asked.

"Don't look so surprised. Wesley and I agreed the tunnels should be put into working order years ago. You and Richard were doing a fine job of cleaning them. We waited until you were done."

"Richard and the men trained here from time to time. Before Reeve took the castle, the men made sure the doors were unlocked."

Jamie shook his head. They continued down the tunnel. That's why Richard said he'd take care of the doors.

As he passed, men opened the crates and handed out weapon.

"I never thought I'd be happy we stored weapons here. It was Richard's idea." Gareth pulled out a sword and shield. "I'll get the men into all the tunnels. We'll replace as many of Reeve's men as we can."

The men were already moving into the tunnels.

"Gareth, I need a man to take me to Reeve."

"I'll do that myself," said Gareth. "Come, we'll use the tunnel to the Great Hall."

"The friars are here. Darren will call us soon." Reeve sat near the hearth in the Great Hall while his staff arranged the room for their wedding meal.

"Thank you," Laura said. Her voice was soft and quiet. Her tears were spent, not only for her brother, but for herself and Jamie. She stood at the window and fixed her gaze on the bailey. A brisk wind whipped through the sky. Ominous black clouds flew overhead. The place looked deserted. It was Samhain. She and Lisbeth enjoyed the bonfires on the hill and the festival in the courtyard. She closed her eyes and ached for her sister, her parents, Jamie.

The tramp of feet echoed in the silence. She scanned the battlements. Groups of soldiers were everywhere. The Portcullis was down. She clenched her fists until her nails bit into the palms. The soldiers waited for him. Over and over she repeated to herself, *stay away*. Was this how Celia felt? She sent Jamie to his death.

"Lord Reeve, the friars are ready," Darren said.

"Come, Laura. I'm eager to get this done." He held out his arm to her. There was no use hesitating. He would marry her no matter. Her hand intertwined with Reeve's, for a moment she speculated if he held her to keep her from running away.

She walked into the Chapel. There was a beauty in its simplicity. The room was special, quiet and holy. Today it was a room like any other. He led her down the aisle. Three friars, Darren, Rhona and six guards joined them. She hesitated.

"Why is she here?" He pinched the back of her hand and pulled her down the aisle.

"Rhona's my... guest." Reeve laughed at his joke.

She stood with Reeve in front of the friars. Two had their cowls pulled over their heads, their hands tucked into their sleeves. Vows of Silence she remembered. Brother Steven smiled at her.

"You can begin." Reeve waved his hand in a haphazard gesture.

"Is there any reason why these two people should not be joined in holy matrimony?" Steven asked.

"I'm sorry, am I late?" Everyone turned at the intrusion. A guard in full battle gear brought in Jamie.

"Jamie." Laura lunged for him but Reeve pulled her back.

"He mingled with the merchants and walked in with them." The guard said from underneath his helmet.

"I'm not surprised you joined us. Bring him up here to the front, for a better view. I want him to see me kiss my wife." Reeve glowed with excitement. She was numb with defeat.

Jamie gave her a sweet smile. Reeve stepped between them and blocked his view.

"I don't know what game your lover plays," Reeve

said. The soldier delivered him to the front of the chapel. Reeve spun and shoved Jamie to the floor, then turned to her. "You understand he's a traitor."

"He is not." She pushed past Reeve and rushed to Jamie's side.

"How touching. The Parliament will think otherwise once I bring them Jamie's body. Once The Maxwell falls, I will lay claim to Caerlaverock as your husband. The only way you two will be together is in the hereafter."

"The Maxwell will not fall," Laura said her hands fisted at her side, her voice firm and final. Jamie stood up.

"He plans to call us all traitors."

She gaped at Jamie.

"He's gone to great pains to marry you. Without a male heir, Wesley's title and the lands associated with Glen Kirk are in question. Marrying you is his perfect answer."

"How does that bring down The Maxwell? Nothing could bring down Herbert. His position is secure," she said.

"He's made Herbert appear to be a traitor who gave important defense information about Scottish positions to England. The Parliament will hang him for treason and strip the family of all their lands and titles. Married to you, he has a claim to Caerlaverock."

"Very clever, Collins, and very brave of you to come here."

"I'm family and always welcome. You, I'm not sure. It did take me a while to figure out why you had Rhona put the map in Laura's things."

"You think you know." He straightened himself, eased his shoulders and lit his face with the whisper of a defiant smile.

"The only person who stands in your way is... me.

Should anything happen to The Maxwell and his sons I'm the next in line by written decree. However, you capture me with Laura and the map, and kill us both in the name of Scotland you become a National hero. There you have it. When were you going to tell Rhona that once you had Caerlaverock you planned to expose her scheme and name her the traitor and leader of the reivers?"

Rhona jumped to her feet. She met Jamie's accusing eyes without flinching.

"Reeve?" Jamie was almost sorry for her, looking to Reeve for support she wasn't going to get.

The muscles on Reeve's neck corded in anger.

"You said... What we did—" Rhona wrung her hands and stammered. Did she see her prize vanish? No, he didn't feel sorry for her. The woman understood what she was doing.

"We did? You did. And it was all for the coin I gave you and the warmth of my bed. Did you really think I would marry you? Make you a lady?" He waved his hand dismissing her.

"You told me you would—"

"Be quiet." He shot her a hostile glare.

Wild with anger, murder was in her eyes. Her heaving chest calmed. She hurried out the door into the arms of Gareth's waiting guards.

"Take him away." Reeve pointed to Jamie.

Darren rushed toward Jamie, but stopped. The tip of Gareth's sword pointed at his heart. Sean took off his friar's robe. One-by-one the guards pulled off their tunics and exposed their Reynold colors.

Jamie, his hands fisted at his side, was on his feet and ready.

Reeve glanced from one person to the next. He boldly met Jamie's glare.

Wesley's men started to move. Richard put out his arm and blocked their way.

"Let them fight. This has been a long time coming," the friar said.

"Give this to the Friar and stay with him." Jamie gave Laura the map and nudged her toward Richard. The Friar tucked her behind him and provided a solid wall of protection. She peeked around at Jamie.

Jamie and Reeve squared off. They circled each other looking for their opportunity, a few steps to the right, a few steps to the left. Jamie eyes never left Reeve's. He kept his eyes open for the telling signal, a flare of the nostrils or widening of the eyes that said, here I come.

Reeve stepped forward and swung a right cross. Jamie blocked the punch and hit Reeve with four jabs to the face in rapid succession.

Stunned and bloody, Reeve shook his head and came at him again.

"Gareth warned you to keep your left fist up," Jamie said. Anger flared in Reeve's eyes.

Reeve let loose a barrage of body punches. Jamie held his arms up for protection. The people around them moved to the edges of the room to give the men space.

Reeve pressed forward taking aim at Jamie's head. Jamie stumbled into the benches sending them everywhere.

Jamie untangled himself from the debris. One by one he threw the benches out of his way and made his way toward Reeve.

Reeve rushed at Jamie, attacking him with close body punches.

Jamie tightened his mid-section to deflect Reeve's punches.

Breathing hard, rage and hate distorted Reeve's face.

Jamie's lips curved in a half smile. It enraged

Reeve more. At the moment, Jamie didn't care about Scotland or England. It was Laura he wanted. She was all he ever wanted.

Reeve advanced, with a burst of energy. Jamie was ready. He ducked and stepped away, his back inches from Richard.

"Sometimes a farmer must be a warrior," Richard said for only him to hear.

Jamie gave a curt nod and exploded with rapid left jabs that connected with Reeve's jaw. Reeve's head snapped back at each punch.

"That's for Ned." Jamie said. He didn't give Reeve time to recover. He advanced, letting loose with a punishing right hook that caught Reeve in the side of his head and sent him to the floor. Reeve's face was bloody and bruised.

"That's for Laura." Jamie's knuckles were red and swollen.

Stunned, Reeve staggered to his feet. He struggled to lift his fists for protection. They didn't come close to his face.

Jamie threw a series of punches, left jab and right cross in quick succession. He shifted from one foot to the other and put his full weight behind each blow.

Reeve's arms dropped to his side. Dazed, he stared at Jamie. A right cross exploded from Jamie's shoulder and sent Reeve to the floor.

"That's for Harmon," Jamie said standing over him. The man paled at the reference.

Reeve pulled on the benches, but the teetering pile gave way. He collapsed sprawled on the ground. It was over.

"Jamie." Laura made her way to his side through the tangle of seats. He held her in his arms and reveled in holding her close.

"I knew he set a trap. I had no way to warn you," Laura said, her tone apologetic.

"Hush, it's over." Jamie smoothed her hair and cradled her head against his chest. He glanced over his shoulder at Richard standing with his head bowed and his hands tucked inside his sleeves

"What should we do with him?"

Reeve stood between two of Wesley's guards.

"Put him in the dungeon along with Darren and Rhona. Wesley will decide what to do with them."

Jamie and Laura made their way through the overturned benches toward the door.

Reeve tore the sword out of the guard's hand and rushed at Jamie.

In a swift move, Richard pulled a dagger from his sleeve and threw it with precision.

The dagger found its mark and dug in deep. Reeve stiffened and arched his back then crumpled to the floor.

Richard moved to Reeve's side. The mortally wounded man turned his head to see who was near.

"But Bryce..." His face turned into a mask of fear.

"Next time watch your back," Richard said. Reeve's mouth opened but nothing came out.

"Hell has a special place for traitors." Richard stuffed the stolen map in Reeve's shirt. He twisted the knife then pulled it out.

Reeve let out his last breath before his eyes fluttered and closed.

"Jamie, Wesley is here, with the king's soldiers," one of Jamie's men announced.

"Laura, go with Gareth. I'll be right with you." Jamie made his way through the chaos to where Richard last stood, but all he found was the friar's robe in a heap on the floor. He picked up the robe and glanced at the tunnel entrance as Richard disappeared. The door closed behind him without a sound.

Chapter Twenty

The tumult and uproar in the family's private solar reached Jamie's ears.

"Jamie," Sean met him at the door. "I searched the cemetery. I couldn't find him. I left a small keg of ale." Jamie put his arm around Sean's shoulder and entered the room.

"I'm glad the others didn't know he was here. I think it would tear them apart to say good-bye to him again."

The room was controlled chaos. People were everywhere. The three friars stood to one side. Brother Steven was having a spirited conversation with Brothers Dan and Asher. Brother Steven did all the talking.

Wesley's soldiers, some still in Reeve's colors, were mingled with Jamie's men.

Darla, Lisbeth, and Laura were in a tight knot by the fireplace.

Laura found him as soon as he walked in. She had some magical way of knowing he was near. That made him snicker. Magic. She'd turned him into a believer.

"Jamie." Wesley signaled to him.

"I'll see to our men." Sean moved into the group.

Jamie crossed to the fireplace. Wesley welcomed him with a strong embrace. Gareth stood next to him like a proud father.

"Laura told us what happened in Caerlaverock. You two had quite an adventure. I'll send a report to Herbert."

"Reeve is dead."

"Yes, Gareth told me. The guards took his body out of the chapel. The King demanded Reeve be brought to Scone Parliament, no matter his condition. With Herbert's paper tucked into his shirt he will make them a pretty prize. The king was irate. He didn't take kindly to Reeve invoking his name on a non-existent royal decree."

"What about Rhona?"

"Gareth will bring her to the Marsh Warden for him to deal with."

"I'm glad this is over," Gareth said. "Wesley, I'll finish gathering Reeve's men and securing Glen Kirk."

"With your leave, it's time for me to see to Cumgour."

"You can't leave now." Wesley glanced at Laura. "I thought..." Laura, Darla, and Lisbeth came to Wesley's side. "Let me get to the point. Do you two love each other?"

Startled, Jamie didn't have any idea what to say.

"This is a simple yes or no answer. Do you love her?" Wesley cocked his head to the side. His voice rang with command.

"Yes, I do love her." Jamie gazed at her, a strange sensuous light passed between them.

"Laura—" Wesley's patience frayed at the edges.

"Yes, Father. I love him with all my heart." She hadn't taken her eyes off him.

Jamie turned away, pulled out a paper and put it in Wesley's hand.

"What's this?" Darla took the document from Wesley and read it.

"Wesley, when did you send a request to Brother Steven?" Darla held out the document and shook it at him.

"I wrote the request after you asked me to write Herbert."

Darla flushed and turned away from everyone.

"What did you say in the message to Herbert?" Laura stepped toward her mother. Darla stood motionless then swiveled toward them and shrugged.

"Only that you two are stubborn and in love and he was to... help it along."

Everyone started talking at once. "I can't hear myself think with all this noise." Lisbeth grabbed Jamie and Laura and led them down the corridor into the nursery.

"I don't understand the problem. Look at you, holding on to each other. Anyone can see the two of you love each other."

"With Richard gone..." Jamie didn't know how to continue. Suddenly all the excuses were just that, excuses. Like a sailor in a sinking ship looking for safety, he gazed into Laura's eyes. He filled his lungs and pushed on.

"With Richard gone, Glen Kirk needs a strong defender. An English defender."

"I agree, but what has that to do with Laura and you?" She glanced over her shoulder at her sister. "I thought you loved Cumgour."

Jamie stood tongue-tied. Richard had said the same thing.

"This is for you to discuss, no one else. Remember, together you can face anything." Lisbeth turned to Laura. "As for Glen Kirk, I'm Father's heir by right of succession and legal writ. Father and the King drafted a document so there would never be any dispute. You're free to do what's in your heart."

Jamie and Laura stood holding on to each other. Only the soft click of the door closing indicated they were alone.

"What are you thinking," he asked not sure he wanted her answer.

To his relief, she smiled and drew her delicate long fingers down his shoulder, over his arm and intertwined them with his. He tucked her head against his chest and breathed in the scent of her.

"I'm sorry you suffered. I hated myself, but I thought it was the best way to protect you. Reeve was crazy, but he skillfully managed us to achieve his ends. It was me he targeted all along." Jamie pushed the hair out of her eyes.

"He focused on you, but he wanted revenge for all the injustices he imagined against him."

Mentally and physically spent, he led her to the edge of the bed. "I kept watch over you. Even when you were with him." He sat and drew her onto his lap, needing her to be close.

"Yes, I always sensed you with me. When you left Caerlaverock without telling me, I panicked."

"Reeve managed that, too, from emptying my room to leaving you only part of the note I wrote you."

Curled up in his lap, he gazed into her eyes and stopped talking. He didn't want to talk about Reeve or Glen Kirk. He wanted her, in his heart and in his arms.

"Hold me. Don't let me go," Laura said. She nuzzled his neck and sank into his strong embrace. "Love me," she whispered in his ear. His muscles tensed in response. She wanted his arms around her, his lips touching hers.

They sank on the bed and held each other close. She was afraid to let him go, afraid the emptiness would find her, afraid of losing him, again. With an unending thirst, she focused on his mouth, the shape of his lips, the kisses that they promised.

His hand stroked the side of her body from her breast to her thigh, claiming them. One stroke of her breast and she tugged on his shirt. He didn't hesitate. He obliged her and pulled it off. Her hand played down the hard planes of his chest. Her eyes widened at the sight of the scars on his chest.

"These weren't here." She traced them with her finger.

He stopped her hand and brought it to his lips. "Fighting for The Maxwell comes with a price. I don't want to think of the Maxwell." He kissed her fingertips. "I thought I lost you forever."

She closed her eyes and reveled in the tingling sensation racing through her body and put her head on his shoulder.

He opened her bodice and stroked the top of her chest then, with trembling hands, touched her breasts. A low moan escaped her lips.

Jamie bent and kissed each breast.

He ignited a flame inside her that set her on fire. Delicious shudders pulsed through her. She pulled his head away and kissed him.

Her fingers traced the scars and the muscles of his chest danced at the light touch. "Where did you get this one?"

"In a fight with the English." His rapt gaze focused on her face.

Her lips brushed against his skin. His skin deckled in gooseflesh. Her finger moved on. "And this one?"

"A reiver attack," his voice was husky and seductive.

The hooded passion in his eyes encouraged her. She kissed the scar and moved on. The tips of her fingers traced down his chest. "Here is another." The scar snaked below his navel. Another kiss. Her fingers trailed down further.

He pulled her up and rolled on top of her. Her body instinctively arched against his. "You are mine." His warm breath brushed against her face. Two heartbeats passed. "Do you hear me? You're mine," he said more urgently.

"Yes." Her voice an intimate whisper. His lips tugged into a sideways grin.

His smile that made her bones go limp. It was his magic.

"Mine," was all he said and settled between her legs. Every inch of him was hard and ready. She focused on his lips while her hands ran over his body. The insistent need to touch him consumed her.

"Love me, Jamie. Now." She wanted to taste him, smell him, feel him.

He bent down and let his lips brush gently across hers. Jamie soothed and calmed her with his touches and kisses only to build her heat and her passion. Tiny licks of pleasure shot through her while his manhood pressed against her.

He slipped inside her and she let out a sigh of relief. "I please you," he said, his voice rough with passion.

She wrapped her legs around his hips and pulled him closer. Heat rippled through her body fed with combustible desire that ran through her with every stroke. The last wave peaked, they both found their release.

She picked up her head. "I want you. I'll go where ever you are, Caerlaverock, Cumgour."

He took her head in his hands and brought his forehead to hers. "I love you. I've loved you forever."

He cradled her in his arms. "Marry me," he commanded.

"Yes," was all she said.

"Kneel sir," the friar, sword in hand, demanded of Jamie. "Kneel and prepare for the sword of courage. Take your rightful place and humble yourself before your maker. As you bravely and solemnly come here today, you have shown to all present that you are worthy and ready to care for this woman, Laura, you have chosen from this day forward. To take thy woman's hand is an act of bravery only supplanted by the call to arms. Do you understand and accept this, sir?" He glanced at the restored chapel with the benches in place past the small alter to the hidden tunnel door.

"Yes, I understand."

Brother Steven easily handled the sword. "Three times I tap thee, once in the name of our king..."

A shout rang up from the attending audience.

"...once in the name of our bishop, and once in the name of our holy protector. Now that you have knelt and been christened and tapped, I declare thee ready to receive your bride. Now this is the day and time appointed for betrothal, Lord Jamie and Lady Laura are here with family, friends, and neighbors, standing together.

"We are gathered here to join this man and this woman in a binding of life. At this day of binding, if any man declares any reason why they may not be coupled together, speak now."

"It is all well with us—let them marry," responded the crowd in unison.

Brother Steven turned to Jamie. "Lord James Maxwell Collins, do you take this woman, Lady Laura Reynolds, daughter of Lord and Lady Reynolds to wife?"

Jamie gave the obligatory response but he didn't hear the rest of the ceremony. He made a pact with the Lord. He vowed to honor her, care for her, but more than anything he vowed to love her and gave thanks she was his.

"Lord Jamie, I said you can kiss the bride," Brother Seven said.

Jamie took his wife in his arms and kissed her to the shouts and screams of their family and friends.

"We have guests," Lisbeth said. Wesley, Darla, and the bride and groom glanced at the entrance. Bryce and his captain walked through the crowd.

"The information I was given must be wrong. I was told Glen Kirk had fallen. Reeve's flag is not flying the Reynold's flag is still there." Bryce took stock of the room. "I thought I was coming to your defense."

"Not at all," Wesley said. "To Laura's wedding."

The muscle along Bryce's jaw tightened.

"You knew Glen Kirk had fallen? Where have you been?" Wesley asked.

"On a fool's errand for my father. I came across a merchant who told me Reeve's flag few on top the castle. I didn't think you would hand over Glen Kirk willingly. I came as soon as I could. "I didn't think Reeve had the nerve. Where is he?" Bryce scanned the room.

"The king ordered him to London. Unfortunately, he's in a box."

Surprise siphoned blood from Bryce's face. "He always thought too highly of himself," Bryce said in a biting tone. "Do you think it wise for a Scot to control Glen Kirk?"

Wesley was a superb statesman. He kept things to himself. But Jamie noticed the brief flash of anger that lit his eyes.

"As my son-in-law Jamie will provide support, but he has Cumgour. Surely you know the rules of succession. Lisbeth is my heir."

Bryce boldly met Lisbeth's benign stare. He slapped his gloves against his thigh.

"All is in good order here. I'll leave you to your family." Bryce gave Wesley a curt nod.

"You're not staying to celebrate with us?" Jamie asked. Bryce stiffened at the question.

"No, Collins. I know my place." Bryce, his captain at his side, turned on his heel and left the hall.

"I'm not sure Bryce gave us a full story. Reeve could have fooled Bryce to remove him from the area. Enough. This is a celebration." Wesley moved on.

"Lady Laura Reynolds Maxwell Collins," Jamie said his arms around her.

"I like the way it sounds. I used to say it over and over when I was younger."

He crushed her close and kissed the top of her head.

Laura tipped her chin up at him. "I'd like to go to the cemetery."

He took two bottle of ale from a passing steward. "I'll lead the way."

They left the castle and walked to the cemetery. The afternoon waned and a chill penetrated the late October air. He helped her through the gate and led her to Richard's grave site.

He set the two ales on the tombstone and put his

arm around her while she silently said her words to Richard. Her soft sobs tore at him.

In the darkening shadows Jamie found Richard and his heart sank. He had done the calculations over and over. It had been nearly sixty days from the time Richard passed. His friend was doomed.

Laura searched Jamie's face and followed his stare. She gasped and took a step toward her brother.

"Richard," she cried and ran to him. He didn't deny her, but rather took her in his arms and held her close.

"If my heart still beat it would burst. You've shed enough tears. You'll have the flowers growing on my grave if you don't stop."

Her head popped up at the ridiculous image and she laughed.

"That's better." Richard glanced at Jamie. "Take good care of her."

"Always." He handed Richard the two ales.

Laura twirled around to Jamie. "You knew Richard was..."

"Don't be angry. I don't let everyone see me."

"Richard, it's been more than thirty days. What will happen how?" Jamie stood helpless.

"I can't stay here," Richard let out a heavy sigh. "Tormented souls have a way of fouling the area, but it was worth it."

"Richard," Darla and Lisbeth ran up the path. Wesley wasn't far behind.

"I didn't want a family gathering." He moved Laura away. "It will only make my leaving harder for you all." Something in Richard's tone overwhelmed Jamie and made him ache.

"No, one more time to tell you I love you. To hold my boy and tell him how proud I am of all he did," Darla rushed into her son's arms. His father's arms embraced them both.

Lisbeth held back and waited. "I spoke to Richard earlier."

Everyone stared at her. "We spoke at the hunting lodge. But all is not lost. Today is Samhain when the veil between the underworld and ours is thinnest. We can help Richard, but we must hurry and complete the ritual at midnight. I've brought the candles and spices we need."

"Laura and I will help." Darla grabbed Laura's hand and followed Lisbeth.

Wesley, Richard, and Jamie sat on the stone bench. Richard fidgeted.

"I'm glad for the ale," Richard said. Wesley let out a strained laugh. "I have so much inside me..." Richard touched his hand to his chest. "But I don't know what to—"

"The silence doesn't have to be filled. I know what's in your heart." Wesley took his hand. It was a small action and one both men appreciated. "We'll sit here and enjoy the time we have together."

In the distance, the bonfire burned. The villagers danced and celebrated their last harvest and the beginning of winter.

The quiet unnerved Jamie. It was unreal sitting here waiting for the women to finish their preparations and the hour to be just right. How do you tell someone you love them and value their friendship? He glanced over at Wesley and Richard. Both sat silently next to each other and stared at the ground. The minutes dragged on. The silence was deafening until he couldn't stand it another minute. He pulled on his tunic and Holger's brooch flashed from inside.

Richard touched the gem. "Where did you get this?"

"I found the brooch. I'm looking for its owner."

Richard rubbed the gem between his fingers, then handed it back. "Owner? The brooch is yours."

Jamie's mouth dropped open.

"The brooch chose you for its champion. The brooch may be silent now, but when the time comes, the magic will tell you what to do. Keep it safe."

"Magic? You never believed in magic," Jamie said.

"It's amazing what you learn." A slow secret smile spread across Richard's face. He put his hand on Jamie's shoulder. "I have a favor to ask."

Jamie gave him his full attention.

"One other person is aware I'm here, Tom, Donald's spy. He was one of Reeve's soldiers. You can trust him. I had him lock Laura's door last night to make sure Reeve didn't disturb her. Take him to Cumgour. He will serve you well."

"Consider it done." The words stuck in Jamie's mouth and came out in a whisper.

"It's almost midnight," Richard said and got to his feet. He and Wesley followed him to his grave. "Jamie, will you stand guard for me?"

He nodded, the hot knot in his throat made it difficult to speak.

Five lit candles formed a pentagram around Richard's grave.

"Richard, stand in the center." Lisbeth gestured toward the pentagram her soft voice sounded is if it came from a long away.

In silence, Richard hugged each one of them then stepped into the middle of the pentagram.

Jamie took his place and stood guard to ensure Richard safe passing. The others made their petition.

"Hail, Guardians of the East. I summon the power of the air." Lisbeth said in a clear voice, faced east and began to set the wards.

"Be with us now," Laura and Darla replied. Lisbeth turned to the south.

"Hail, Guardians of the South. I summon the power of fire."

"Be with us now," the women refrained. Lisbeth turned to the west.

"Hail, Guardians of the West. I summon the power of water."

"Be with us now," filled the air. Lisbeth turned to the north.

"Hail, Guardians of the North. I summon the power of the earth."

"Be with us now." Darla placed oak branches in the middle.

"To renew your soul and heal all wounds. From your mother's heart. So mote it be." Darla placed bay laurel on top of the branches.

"To protect you on your journey. From your sister with devotion. So mote it be." Lisbeth sprinkled the branches and leaves with rosemary.

"To help you find your way. From you sister with love. So mote it be." Lisbeth stood back and raised her arms to the heavens.

"As above, so below. As within, so without. Four stars in this place be to open the door to eternity." She lowered her arms and gazed at Richard. "So mote it be." He could hardly hear her voice.

Richard let out a deep breath. He gazed at each person with a silent farewell then closed his eyes. His deep baritone filled the air.

"Watch over those I leave behind. Keep me close to their heart. Take me now. Take me now. I am ready to depart."

The evening mist gathered over the ground shrouding their offerings and candles. "Watch over those I leave behind. Keep me close to their heart. Take me now. Take me now. I am ready to depart." The mist grew thicker. The tombstone was almost all consumed.

"Watch over those I leave behind. Keep me close to their heart. Take me now. Take me now. I am ready to depart. So mote it be." Richard opened his eyes, stared at Jamie, and raised his ale in a farewell salute.

Jamie blinked the tears from his eyes. When he opened his eyes the candles were out. Richard was gone.

"Thank you Great Mother for easing his passing," Lisbeth said.

"Come, we'll go to the bonfire," Wesley said. "We have much to celebrate."

Lisbeth, Darla, and Wesley covered the spices on the ground with dirt, gathered the candles and moved toward the bonfire.

Laura stood next to Jamie. "You stood sentinel. He left us happy."

"He left us with a tankard of ale in his hand."

Laura gazed at him in disbelief then laughed. Jamie put the second tankard on Richard's tombstone.

"Come wife. I want to go home." He put his arm around her.

"To Cumgour?" she asked.

"To Cumgour."

If you enjoyed **The Highlander's English Woman,** please spread the word by leaving a review on the site where you purchased your copy, or a reader site such as Goodreads or Shelfari.

Thank you!

Want to know more about Laura's sister, Lisbeth and
The Stelton Legacy?
Find out in **The Guardian's Witch**.

England, 1290

Lord Alex Stelton can't resist a challenge, especially one
with a prize like this: protect a castle on the Scottish
border for a year, and it's his. Desperate for land of his
own, he'll do anything to win the estate—even enter a
proxy marriage to Lady Lisbeth Reynolds, the rumored
witch who lives there.

Feared and scorned for her second sight, Lisbeth swore
she'd never marry, but she is drawn to the handsome,
confident Alex. She sees great love with him but fears
what he would think of her gift and her visions of a
traitor in their midst.

Despite his own vow never to fall in love, Alex can't
get the alluring Lisbeth out of his mind and is driven to
protect her when attacks begin on the border. But as
her visions of danger intensify, Lisbeth knows it is she
who must protect him. Realizing they'll secure their
future only by facing the threat together, she must
choose between keeping her magic a secret and losing
the man she loves.

Chapter One

Northumberland, England, 1290

"You won the wager with His Majesty," said Lord Bryce Mitchell astride his Arabian. He cantered down the forest trail with Alex Stelton, the newly minted Lord of Glen Kirk Castle.

"The entire court placed odds on whether I would succeed." The two men slowed their horses to a walk. Alex glanced at Bryce. "Did you lose much?" He refocused his attention on the trail ahead. "You should have put your coin on me. I only wager when I'm certain of the results."

"After one year of holding the old stones against the Scots, he actually gifted the castle and his ward to you." Bryce shook his head.

The ring of surprise in Bryce's voice and evident disbelief on his face amused Alex. "His Majesty is a man of his word. Did you have any doubt?" asked Alex, his head cocked to the side with one eyebrow raised. His face split into a wide grin.

"About the king being a man of his word or of you holding off the Scots?" Bryce colored his smooth retort with a smirk.

The two friends looked at each other, exploded into laughter, and continued on until they reached the crossroads where they brought their horses to a halt. The tower of Glen Kirk Castle, bathed in the setting sun, peeked through the trees still some three miles to the north. Alex surveyed his new holding. His chest swelled with pride. *Mine.*

"Though Edward did make you pay."

Alex was peeved by Bryce's patronizing tone. He masked his emotions until they were as unreadable as stone.

"Yes, you could say that." Alex tried his best dismissive tone. Best he forget the king's retribution for now. There would be time enough to deal with it later.

"Could? Surely you knew if he lost the wager he would find some way to make you pay. He doesn't lose gracefully at anything, but to actually marry you to his ward by proxy. I can still see the apoplectic look on your face."

"Yes, Bryce— what about the look on my face?" demanded Alex. His voice sounded strident even to him.

Bryce turned all shades of purple trying to conceal his mirth but he said not one word more. Instead he diverted his attention and polished the gold clasp, embossed with the Mitchell coat of arms, on his cloak.

Alex bristled at being the center of anyone's jest. He didn't take it well from his brothers, although the six of them only teased to vex him. Even though he was the youngest, his brothers deferred to him. They knew his worth and, it appeared, so did the king.

His teeth clenched at the thought of his proxy wedding and his humiliation. He knew he had to take a wife. He had to make his own way in the world. The Stelton holdings were extensive but not enough to provide him with an income. He'd have done anything to prove himself worthy of a holding of his own. Maybe even marry. Perhaps even Lisbeth. He never thought he would marry on the whim of the king. He had tried to argue, but there was no arguing with Edward. Faith, the king all but patted him on his head and sent him off like a new page. A page. He raked his hand through his hair.

With a nod of his head, Bryce motioned toward Glen Kirk in the distance. "Marrying Lisbeth does secure your claim to Glen Kirk."

Lisbeth. He had lived at Glen Kirk for a year and hardly saw her. The only way he knew she was near was the little charms she left or the serenity that surrounded them. She kept herself in the forsaken hunting lodge and managed to elude him at almost every turn.

On odd twinge of disappointment hung round him. She hadn't been like that years ago when they encountered each other at court. She had laughed and didn't have a care in the world. Four years later he wouldn't have known it was her if she hadn't presented herself at the castle. The impish girl had grown into a poised beauty. Dark hair fell in long waves down her back. Her slender body was punctuated with soft curves that couldn't remain hidden by the black mourning gown. Large green eyes stared at him from under a fan of long dark lashes. Even with her dour expression her full lips tempted him. He moved uncomfortably in his saddle. How things change. How people change.

"You do know you're the envy of everyone. Not because the king gave you Wesley's treasured Glen Kirk or daughter." Bryce turned serious. "You inherited Wesley's brewer and ale recipe. That should give you some compensation. I understand it's a long-held family secret. Wesley was all about family."

Family. He let his mind wonder. It landed on memories of his early days at court with his parents and siblings. He enjoyed the candor and tumult around the table in their assigned apartment. How he would appreciate that safety and security today in the midst of a court filled with politics and intrigue.

"I intend to leverage our close friendship," said Bryce, "I'll sample each batch and make certain it retains its high standards."

Alex grinned at his friend's declaration. Lord Wesley and Lady Darla Reynolds had been close friends of his parents. They didn't bring their daughters to court often but Richard, their son, was always with them and became close to the tight-knit band of Stelton boys. Richard's death on the Welsh battlefields had been a shock to them all. He and Wesley had spent a good deal of time together consoling each other over a good many tankards of ale.

It was only a short time after Alex left for the Welsh Wars himself that he heard of Wesley and Darla's fatal accident. He felt their loss deeply. Now in a twist of fate their beloved Glen Kirk and daughter were his.

"Have you sent word to her?" Bryce's question hung heavy in the air.

Alex broke away from his musings. "No, I will tell her when the time comes." Alex suppressed the annoyance in his voice. What if she didn't want to be married to him? He had expected a warm welcome from her a year ago. She had made it obvious she wanted nothing to do with him. He'd have to find a way to approach the subject, see how agreeable she was to the idea. A seventh son, he never thought the king would care who he married. The last thing he wanted was a political wife. He relaxed his death grip on his horse's reins, let out a deep breath, and changed the subject. "I've heard your border farms were raided. How bad were the attacks?"

Bryce took a bannock out of his saddlebag, broke off a piece and offered it to Alex. He leaned forward in his saddle, a conspiratorial tone in his voice. "And your Glen Kirk farmers?"

Relieved to get Bryce off the subject of his new wife, Alex's brows knit together at the mention of his farms. He took a bite of the cake and washed it down with some ale from the skin he carried. He passed the ale to Bryce. "No attacks on my farms." He wiped the crumbs from his lips with the back of his hand. "I set up patrols before we left for London. Since our lands are adjacent I'm certain it's only a matter of time before the Glen Kirk farms become targets."

"Yes, a good strategy. I'll have my men patrol my border farms as well. That should give us a better chance of catching these men before they strike your farms."

Alex's chest tightened at the insinuation that he

couldn't protect his people, although Bryce's offer did make good military sense. The tactician in him knew the benefit of working both sides of the border. He moved back in his saddle. Yes, Bryce's men would be helpful.

"You still believe your Scots are blameless." Bryce passed back the skin.

"Bryce, this is more than a border raid and a few cows being taken—much more. And they are not 'my' Scots. Everyone at Glen Kirk has told me they have never had an incident with the border clans, so why now? You live here. Surely you know that to be true. But, if not the Scots, who? That is the question."

"You do know most everyone at court suspects the Scots." Bryce straightened in his saddle.

"I too heard the rumblings."

"You were quite outspoken. The debate you sparked was lively to say the least."

"You know where I stand on this issue. I clearly do not agree. The Scots are not involved in these raids."

"How can you be so certain, Alex?"

"I've been dealing with them this last year and they're just as concerned about these raids as we are. They're worried the raids will move to their land. I know they are truthful. I can't explain it more than that. You'll not convince me otherwise, Bryce. We're on different sides of this argument. Let's leave this discussion for another time."

It was good to see his friend talking again. Bryce had been preoccupied for a good part of the journey. He wasn't certain what attributed to Bryce's attitude. Perhaps it was the delay caused by his unexpected nuptials or Bryce's private audience with the king, which apparently did not go well. Bryce didn't offer to share what had happened, and Alex wouldn't pry. He supposed the man was entitled to his mood. Over the last year Alex had grown to know Bryce and his father,

Ramon, well. Bryce would seek him out to talk when the time was right. For now it was good to see the heaviness lifted.

"Well Lord Alex, this is where I leave you."

Alex didn't need to peer over his shoulder but rather knew Bryce's small retinue approached.

"How long do you plan to stay at Glen Kirk before you return to Wales?"

Alex looked at the knight. "I've decided not to accept the king's invitation. I'm certain he will understand." He glanced at the castles towers in the distance. "Glen Kirk will do."

Bryce followed his gaze. "Yes, I'm not surprised." His men emerged from the forest and entered the small clearing. Bryce's horse danced, eager to get under way. "We'll wait here with you for your men and wagons," said Bryce, easily bringing the horse under control. "They can't be too far behind."

"No need. The sun is mostly gone and you've another hour's ride before you reach Ravencroft. We're on Glen Kirk land. There won't be any trouble."

"As you wish. Then I will leave you to continue to gaze at your gift, m'lord, and contemplate your evening." Bryce affected a mock bow. "Well done, Alex. You made me a pretty penny." He wheeled his horse to the west.

"If I had known you had wagered I would have claimed half," Alex shouted out after him. "Safe travels."

Bryce raised his hand in salute and set off at a comfortable pace. His men fell in behind him.

Alex's gaze slid back to the castle's crenellated tower. Glen Kirk was anything but a gift. He had worked long and hard to make the castle prosper and to keep the people safe. He dealt well with the Scots through mutual respect and clear understanding. His eyes soaked in the view. He would never tire of staring at her graceful lines and majestic bearing. He never doubted his success. Something deep down told him Glen Kirk was his rightful place. He urged Prime, his destrier, forward.

Prime's ears flattened. Alex, instantly alert, detected a change in the surroundings. The stillness was deafening. He heard not a sound. He glimpsed the west trail. Bryce and his men were out of sight. Relief his friend was out of harm's way was only momentary. The rustling of the underbrush gave away the raider's positions. Whoever it was had started to move. He knew his men and wagons were not far behind but they wouldn't reach him in time. He would have to fend for himself. The crack of dried wood to his right drew his attention. A stout branch snapped back and struck him a hard glancing blow from the left. The combination of surprise and brute force unseated him and threw him to the ground.

His warhorse kicked and nipped at the raiders who broke through the trees. Prime stood defiantly by Alex and kept the attackers at bay.

Alex jumped to his feet with his sword drawn. He slapped the horse's rump, a signal he was ready. The horse turned south, bolted and stampeded through the knot of men. The well-trained horse raced down the trail toward Alex's advancing soldiers.

Alex quickly evaluated the field of attack. Prime had done a good job of thinning out the men. Many lay broken and bleeding on the ground. The advantage shifted to his favor. The few survivors who remained were dazed. He had to strike before they reorganized.

He swung his blade shoulder high in a wide arc. The men backed away. One slipped off to the right to circle behind him. Alex used the momentum of his swing to turn completely around and faced the lone attacker. He let his swing continue and drew his blade across the man's throat. Blood spurted from the fatal wound creating large blotches on Alex's tunic. The raider fell to his knees blood pulsing from his severed throat. His mouth opened and closed like a beached fish but he made no sound. He crumpled forward into the red mud.

Alex pressed forward. He bellowed his war cry and the seasoned warrior exploded into action. He slashed, sliced and skewered the less-proficient fighters with efficient and fluid swordplay. He progressed from one stroke to the next. His brown riding tunic and white shirt were splattered crimson. He continued his attack, now focused on the more senior men. His blade whipped through the air and whistled with a deadly cadence. The blows, in rapid succession, were marked by the ring of steel against steel a mere second or two apart.

The warm August air was thick with the pungent smell of battle. The coppery taste of blood permeated the rising mist in the small clearing. Alex advanced and pushed his attackers back toward the forest path. He would catch his enemy between him and his advancing men.

Someone approached from behind him, someone he knew and trusted. Alex didn't stop. He was too busy with the attack in front of him. The sound of his men advancing up the trail reached him. One man after another fell until someone with a well-placed knife broke through his rear defense. With a single stroke white heat seared his side. He tried to turn and defend against the attacker but all went black.

***

"Lord Mitchell, he's lain here for two days. I've sent John to fetch Lady Lisbeth."

Through the pain, Alex overheard Ann, his housekeeper. She stood vigil at his bedside.

"John? Why did you send him and not one of the messengers?" asked Bryce.

Ah, Bryce was with him too. Someone, he suspected Ann, straightened the bed linen with a gentle touch.

"There aren't many left in service. The king's protectors scared them away." Ann gave the linen a final tug.

"You mean the rumors of the curse." Bryce's voice held a bitter edge of cynicism.

"No, not because of the rumors, which are ridiculous, but because over the last two years no one in this castle has cared about the village or the people," she dipped her head toward Alex. "Except for him."

"Bryce?" Alex's whispered words went unheard. Exhausted and in pain, he fought to open his eyes, to no avail. He would not surrender control. Instead he struggled to take in bits and pieces of the conversation.

Barely able to stay awake, Alex glimpsed Bryce turn a curious eye to him. Bryce shook his head and gave Ann his attention. "He'll not be happy having her minister to him."

"Lord Mitchell, she may be his last hope."

Alex caught the worry in her voice. He gritted his teeth and remained motionless. He could feel it building. He braced for another wave of pain that would sweep over him.

"Why, Ann, you're fond of the man and still you bring in the witch? She's exiled herself to the old hunting lodge. Best she stays there." The words hung in the room. "But I suppose she won't be there much longer."

Alex knew from experience the hostile glare that accompanied the sound in Bryce's voice.

"M'lord, I know your feelings about the girl. I don't understand. I remember the way you followed each other around when you were children. We both know she's no witch."

"Then explain her unusual power with herbs and tonics."

"She's no different than her mother, rest her soul. She too was a gifted healer. That doesn't make either of them witches. Didn't Lady Darla help you when you broke your arm so badly everyone thought it had to be cut off?"

Alex could feel the anger rolling off Bryce but he couldn't dwell on it. He knew more than saw his close friend flex the fist of his sword arm. A sudden pinch of pain and he stiffened himself for another surge of agony.

Ann hovered over him. "His fever worsens. He'll not last the night."

The worry in Ann's voice compelled Alex to fight through the cobwebs and remain alert.

"I'm surprised he's lasted this long." Bryce whispered. "What will I tell the king?"

The slap of riding gloves against Bryce's thigh startled Alex.

"I told Alex the thieving Scots couldn't be trusted. I'd lead the English against them myself if the king would bring up his men from Wales."

Suffering the incessant pain was useless. He had to take command. Concentrate. He needed to concentrate. Little by little he fought to control his body. His eyes fluttered opened. He was unprepared for the assault of light streaming in from the window. He raised his hand to shield them and gathered his wits amidst his aching head.

Ann rushed, pulled the shutters closed to darken the room and returned to his side.

A cool cloth touched his feverish forehead. He silently thanked the angel. With his eyes closed, he relaxed and let the soothing cloth take him to a tranquil place. A few more minutes and he would try again.

A gentle knock brought him back to the present. The hinge creaked and a cool breeze danced across his damp face. Thankfully, the pain subsided enough for him to pry open his eyes again. Lisbeth glided silently into the room. Her long brown cloak billowed out around her and gave the eerie appearance she floated on air. Through narrow slits he detected her shadow approach. A fresh scent seeped into the stale room. He sniffed the familiar light evergreen mixed with mint, rosemary and spicy floral scent. Lavender. She handed Ann her small healing kit and cloak. In his dazed state he could still make out the outline of her black mourning dress next to him.

Something primal and compelling kept Alex conscious. He was always aware when she was near. Her soft lilting murmur drove the buzzing from his head. The ache eased into a dull roar. Everything was a struggle, staying awake, keeping his eyes open. Faith, breathing was an effort. He squinted and worked hard to take in the scene. There were a few minutes left before the light once again would be unbearable. He needed to rest his eyes, but not right now. He forced himself to stay in command of his senses.

"Good day, Lisbeth. I'll leave you to your patient." Bryce's voice was courteous yet arrogant.

Mine. The whispered thought rang in his head. The very idea startled him.

Lisbeth looked at Bryce. "Good day, Bryce." Alex heard the touch of sadness in her voice. Then all was quiet.

The flexing fist at Bryce's side was not lost on Alex. Neither was Bryce's discomfort at Lisbeth's silence and steady stare.

"Ann, send word when … I will need to tell the king," Bryce mumbled. The door closed behind him.

"You can wash up here."

Lisbeth stepped quietly to the porcelain basin placed on the battle chest between the window and hearth. She cracked open the shutter.

Alex heard the clatter of the basin and splatter of water hitting the cobbled stones on the ground outside his window.

"John told me about the ambush in the forest." Lisbeth spoke softly to Ann as she returned the basin to the campaign chest.

He closed his eyes and willed his sluggish body to respond. He grabbed on to anything that would kept him in the moment, the splash of water refilling the basin, the crackle of the fire and snap of clean linen.

"The attack came within sight of the tower," said Ann. "His big blade caught the last of the sun. The flash alerted the tower guard and he sent the men out. Prime, bless the beast's heart, raised the alarm with Lord Alex's soldiers who followed on the trail."

***

Lisbeth took the linen Ann offered.

"He was dazed but awake when the men brought him in. John helped get him out of his clothes, examined every inch of him, cleaned and dressed his wounds. His lordship was troubled and restless. He kept mumbling about someone behind him. He couldn't understand who attacked him or why. He wanted no meal but had an awful thirst. He drank several tankards of ale and fell asleep."

Her hands dry, Lisbeth gave the linen back to Ann and stepped to Alex's bedside.

"In the morning he didn't break the fast nor attend practice. He never misses practice. His captain attempted to rouse him but he found Lord Alex with a fever. No one could wake him. That was two days ago."

"You should have called me sooner." Lisbeth's eyes remained on Alex. "John told me none of his injuries were serious enough to make him this ill." His dark wavy hair was plastered to his head except for a stray lock that fell over his forehead giving him a boyish appearance. Lisbeth reached under the blanket and threaded her fingers through the soft hair on his torso to rest her hand on his bare chest. A sense of unease gnawed at her. She pushed her doubts aside for the moment and concentrated on the man. His breathing was shallow and slow but his heartbeat was strong. With her other hand she reached to lift his eyelid.

Alex's eyes flew open. He captured her hand in midair. His gripe was like a vise. Eyes like silver lightning pinned her in place.

She tilted her head and looked at his hand grasping hers. A tingling sensation sent a dizzying current from his grasp all the way up her arm. The room took on a golden haze. Her earlier unrest morphed into a shiver that raced up her spine. A fleeting image of him crushing her in his embrace skittered across her mind.

His soft breath heated something deep inside her when he brought his face closer to hers. Her heart thundered with anticipation. His firm lips kissed her eyelids and advanced to her ear. Mine, he whispered. A delicious shudder pulsed through her body. He marched on to her lips and coaxed them open. His spicy scent swept over her. He captured his prize and swept in with his tongue in victory. Forever echoed in her head.

She blinked and the haze vanished. A jumble of confused thoughts and feelings assaulted her. Once again she stared into his magnetic eyes. Her lips throbbed with hunger for his. She dropped her lashes to hide her confusion. A dream? A wish? She'd never had such visions. She gave herself a shake to rid herself of the final images.

Under her palm, still on his chest, she felt his swift intake of breath and quickened heartbeat. A disturbing thought swept over her. Had he seen it too?

She lifted her hand from his chest and attempted to retrieve the other from his grasp. He would not give it up. After a few silent moments he released her. His hand fell to the bed like a deadweight. His eyes darkened in agony.

"Where's the pain?" she asked with authority. Already the loss of his touch left her cold. She didn't wait for him to answer. She carefully slipped the blanket down to expose his well-defined chest and trim hips laced with recent bandages. In her work as a healer she'd seen many shirtless men.

Dark curly hair dusted his wide chest. The manly patch narrowed down his torso until a thin line disappeared beneath the blanket. She glimpsed at his face and noticed the devilish gleam in his eye amidst his pain. He pulled one corner of his mouth into a tight smile. Of all the naked chests she'd seen, his was perfect.

Ancient words filled her head and cleared her mind. His body was a field of scars. She touched the scar at his neck. He lifted his chin to give her a better view. She worked down his torso concentrating on the new wounds. Her fingers fleetingly traced each one. Satisfied they were clean and on the mend she moved on to the next one.

A swelling and redness peaking over the edge of the blanket quickly had her attention. She lowered the cover further to evaluate it. The hint of foul odor filled the space around him.

She continued to lower the blanket. Once again he caught her hand.

"You'll not want to look. I expect the wound isn't a pretty sight, surely not one for you to see," he whispered. She looked into his eyes and knew at once the grim reality he had accepted. He was going to die. He let his head fall back against the pillow. His eyes were fixed on the ceiling.

She placed a steady hand on his arm and looked at his enlarged pupils with concern. "I must examine the wound if I'm to help you." Finally, she felt his muscles relax.

He turned his head to stare deeply into her eyes. "You've avoided me at every turn. Why come now?"

"I'm here to see to your wounds."

"Aye, my death more likely." He released her hand. He scanned her face while she exposed the bandage.

Silently, she ticked off a catalog of plants. Ancient words and melodies swirled in her head and crept out her lips while her skillful hands worked. She carefully cut away the bandage and exposed the wound. The overpowering pungent odor assaulted her nostrils. She looked again at his eyes. His pupils were enlarged and confirmed her suspicion—poison.

A disturbing thought persisted. He'd been like this for two days. She pushed the thought aside and bent to saving him—if she wasn't already too late. The edges of the wound screamed an angry red. The infection was well past the edges of the lesion. The swollen area was crusted in some areas and drained ugly yellow pus in others.

"The wound must be cleaned." She said this more to herself to confirm her decision. She glanced around and took stock of what was at hand. "Ann, some linen strips please, lots of them and three large men." She looked at Alex's powerful body. "No, four men please." Lisbeth continued her preparations. Ann scurried out of the room. "Ann," she called after the woman. "Hot water. Lots of hot water. I'll need more than the hearth kettle can hold."

She looked at the man who became more awake and alert by the minute. Usually a good sign, but now she'd rather he was neither. She'd brought many a warrior to his knees saving their lives. He would be no exception.

He raised his head and looked at her squarely. "What do you plan to do?" His voice was ragged and tired.

She hid her concern around her matter-of-fact tone. "The wound's infected and must be cleaned."

"How? You think to hold me down?" The hard

lines on his face held no expression. He became more awake every minute.

"Yes, staying still may be difficult." She noticed his hand begin to shake—a result of the poison. She must act quickly. What was taking Ann so long? She took a deep breath and remained calm on the outside. She rummaged through her kit and found what she needed, then busily prepared a tincture.

"You'll not need to hold me down. I'll not struggle." His head fell back on the pillow.

She looked at him and noticed the shadow of a grimace pass over his face. "I don't think you'll be able…"

"I'll make you a wager. If I lay still and leave you to your ministration, you will let me kiss you." The teasing brought color to his gray cheeks.

Too surprised by his proposal to do more than stare at him, flashes of her vision raced through her mind.

"Do we have a wager?"

"And if you don't stay still?" She bent back to preparing the tincture.

The amused gleam left his eyes. "Then you can call my men to hold me. But I will not die fighting my own men." His teasing returned. "The thought of your kiss will keep me still. Do you agree to the wager?"

She brewed some dark tea with the water from the kettle and added the tincture. "I'm usually paid with chickens and vegetables. I've never been paid with a kiss." No one could remain still. Not even him. She turned and faced him with the cup in her hand. She hesitated and reached in her kit and drew out an engraved stone. She put the cup aside and took the thin purple leather strip from her hair and threaded it through the amulet.

"If you wear this I will agree to your wager."

He took a quick breath as a flash of pain caught him. He looked at the trinket then back to her. He nodded and let her put the amulet around his neck.

She knew he humored her but she didn't care as long as he wore it. She retrieved the cup.

"And what's this concoction you give me?" He sniffed at the cup.

"It's to activate the spell in the amulet."

His eyebrows flew up in surprise.

She let loose a mischievous laugh. "No, it's only to take the edge off the pain."

He relaxed and took the cup from her hand. "I'd rather drink your father's ale."

She lifted his head and helped him drink the tincture.

He downed the contents. His mouth puckered. "Let me live long enough to collect my wager. I'd rather die with the taste of your sweet lips on mine." He chuckled but was caught once more with a spasm of pain.

He rested his head back on the pillow and turned to watch her. "Alas. My kiss will leave you wanting more I'm afraid. It's a good thing you've called for my men. They may have to restrain you."

She couldn't keep the smile from her lips. Did he always face death with such boldness? She reached for the basin. "We shall see, m'lord."

"Call me Alex. If we're going to be intimate, we're past polite."

She froze at his suggestion the basin still in her hand. She took a calming breath. "We shall see... Alex." She put the basin on the table near his bed. She was ready.

Ann arrived with four of Alex's men close behind. She handed Lisbeth the linens and went off to refill the kettle.

"Have the men wait outside the door. I will call out if we need them," said Lisbeth.

Alex gave her a grateful nod.

"*Zhure nas sheer naf durzh.*" The ancient healing song filled her head. "Ancient one give him strength to endure." She submerged the linen strip in the basin of steaming water. "*Zhure nas sheem naf sarzh.*" She wrung out the cloth. "Ancient one give me knowledge to succeed." She turned and noted him look at her hands, which were bright red from the scalding water.

He took up the soft soothing sound of her whispered words. "*Zhure nas sheer naf durzh,*" he said softly.

"*Zhure nas sheer naf durzh,*" she repeated under her breath.

She placed the compress on the festering wound. He barely stirred. She pressed the cloth lightly into place to draw the infection onto the linen. She removed the cloth when it cooled. The crusted pus loosened and clung to the rag. Over and over, she plunged her hands into the scalding water and wrung out the fresh hot linen. Before long the wound wept profusely. Little by little, it ran clearer, the linen eventually tinged with red. "The blood needs to run rich and red before you'll be out of danger."

"You're doing fine." His voice was rough with pain.

Startled by his encouragement, she stopped her hand poised to soak the next linen. She felt his eyes on her but resisted meeting his gaze for fear she would give her inner thoughts away. She doused the cloth and wrung out the water. She continued to save his life.

When the wound bled freely, a signal the infection was gone, she stepped back. Tired, relief flooded through her. She noticed his hand lying along his side and watched his fist open. She wiped the sweat from his face. She studied his eyes, pleased to see them clear and bright. Ready to apply the preparation to the wound, she hesitated. Something niggled at her. She learned long ago not to deny the feeling. She placed one more hot linen on the wound.

"Faith," he swore. "The burning's from the inside."

"From the inside?" She removed the linen and carefully searched the wound. He squirmed from her touch. "Patience, I'm almost done."

He let out a chuckle. "You'll need to do more than that for me to lose the bet."

She peered at him. Through all her ministrations he only voiced words of encouragement. As he had pledged, he remained still and did not complain. "You've found me out." She continued her search. "I may have to concede."

"Of course you will." He shifted his hip toward her.

He may have moved to ease his pain but it provided her with a better view. Something caught her eye. "There's something lodged in the wound." A quick glance confirmed her suspicion. The pale color on his face told her the pain once again gripped him.

He nodded his acknowledgement.

She rummaged through her kit and took out small pinchers. With a gentle touch she parted the swollen flesh. His muscles tensed "It must come out." She knew the pain grew worse.

He held the bed linen in fisted hands and said nothing. His body glistened with sweat. His chest labored in short shallow breaths. He moved not a muscle.

How he lay there without screaming was a testament to his endurance and control. She probed a bit deeper. Her instrument touched something hard. It was not bone.

He drew in a deep breath.

She took only a brief notice and remained set to her work. Carefully she snagged the smooth corner of the object and began to withdraw a piece of slender steel. The metal slipped from her grip and the fragment slithered back into the wound. Alex stiffened. She froze.

"Go on, don't stop now," he said through clenched teeth.

Beads of perspiration danced on her forehead. She hesitated with the pinchers over the wound, ready to proceed. No, she needed the other corner of the metal. She looked at Alex. His gray face told her she must act quickly.

"Go ahead."

She held his eyes for a moment then continued. She attacked from the other side of the wound. The pincher latched on to an engraved edge. With a steady hand and a tight hold of the steel she plucked out what was left of a blade.

Alex let out a sigh of relief.

She brought the steel to her nose. An acrid smell caught her attention. She dropped the fragment into the basin. Poison. She suspected it was nightshade. No, there was something different about this poison. The preparation she usually administered would not be adequate. She searched through her things until she found the vial she needed. A few drops worked into the preparation would be enough. She applied the poultice with great care and bound up the wound. "You've won the wager," she said while she finished applying the dressing.

"Did you have any doubt? Thank you, Lisbeth. You have my gratitude." His eyelids slowly slid down and he settled into an exhausted sleep.

She turned to the basin to retrieve the fragment and watched tendrils of blood swirl in graceful patterns. The water clouded while she stared mesmerized at the shapes. When the liquid cleared, she removed the metal, dried and slipped the fragment into her pouch. Relieved, she took a deep breath and emptied the basin. He wouldn't die. He would live to fight another day, not because of her care but because the vision in the basin told her so.

Also by Ruth A. Casie

MEDIEVAL ROMANCES

The Druid Knight Series
Knight of Runes
Knight of Rapture
Knight of Redemption – Coming Soon
The Druid Knight Tale: A Short Story Expanded

The Stelton Legacy
The Guardian's Witch
The Highlander's English Woman
The Maxwell Ghost featured in Once Upon a
Haunted Castle

TIMELESS TALES – SHORT STORIES

Medieval Romances
Mistletoe and Magick featured in Timeless Keepsakes
Whispers on the Wind featured in Timeless Treasures
Contemporary Romances
Second Chance by the Sea featured in Timeless Escapes
Forsaking All Others featured in Timeless Vows

HAVENPORT – CONTEMPORARY NOVELLAS

I'll Be Home for Christmas featured in Christmas in
Havenport
The Game's AFoot featured in Welcome to Havenport
The Witching Hour featured in Haunted Havenport
Snowbound in Havenport – Fall, 2017